Haunting Echoes

Mai Griffin

U P Publications
2010, 2017

In Life and Death there is no Black and White,
No core construct that always must be right,
No path or light that clearly shows the way
But filters through a Deadly Shade of Grey.

When some can hear and others single sight
How can they find a soul to lead them to the light?
Ghostly Echoes make confusion and tend to disarray,
So pander to the madness of what the seers say

In Death's dark realm, where none of us may stray,
The light glints through a Poisonous Shade of Grey.
A Glimmer glimpsed, beyond a heart's endeavour,
Where lost souls wander in their dark forever.

A soul that's lost in Death's last cunning sway
Can still fright the living from the depths of their decay.
A Poisonous Echo sent by the unforgiving,
Reaches out, with hate, to scar and maim the living.

Now mourners gather to share a lasting glance
Where grief full memories perform a final dance
and movement stills as with departing breath
the music plays the last Grey Masque of Death

As each note rises to reach its audience
The spirits strain to meet each consequence
When souls conspire to circumvent the truth
Their Dangerous Echoes ululate sans ruth.

Ghostly movements flicker through the night
Where mortals peer and seek to soothe their fright,
The living lost far from the light of day
Where shadows play their Haunting Shades of Grey.

The Haunting Echoes of lives long lost
Resonate without a single thought to cost
Revenging wraiths seek living dreams to claim
And guilty souls who need to take their blame

Anon

In memory of my friend **Mary Llewellyn Jones, Jávea,
Spain**, Mai Griffin

Haunting Echoes

Clarrie's familiarity with the "Other Side" is about to become far more intimate than she has ever wanted. Her mother, Sarah is too distraught to care what else is happening, so it is left to their friend Polly to work out whether Amy's fall from the car park was suicidal, or something more sinister. Then there is the mystery of the hitchhiker and why he is haunting the village.

In whatever order you read her books, Mai Griffin's series of supernatural thrillers, Ghostly Echoes, will grip you.

~~Haunting Shades of Grey~~

Originally published as 'Haunting Shades of Grey', the fourth of the ORIGINAL Shades of Grey series – long before any of a number of other Shades of Grey were published by other people, this book is a Ghost Story – with little or no sadomasochism in its content! Well, to be precise, it hasn't any! We, the publishers and the Author, give up. Our series came first and we are fed-up with the assumption that this series is in some way a spinoff from any other when, in fact – we repeat – this series was written and published FIRST!

Published in Great Britain in 2017 by
U P Publications, St George's House, George Street, Huntingdon, Cambridgeshire, PE29 3GH. UK

Cover design copyright © G. M. G. Peers 2010, 2017, 2020

A CIP Catalogue record of this book is available from the British Library

Originally released as Haunting Shades of Grey under

ISBN 978-0-9557447-6-1 and 978-1-9081352-8-5

This is the Third Edition (the First as Haunting Echoes)

ISBN 978-1-908135-54-4

eBook ISBN 978-1-908135-86-5

7 4 8 5 6 3 9

Published by U P Publications

www.uppbooks.com
www.maiwriting.com

1 – Clarrie

Clarinda Hunter did not normally mind being watched as she worked, but the two small boys were beginning to get on her nerves. She had chosen to set up her easel where it was hidden from the road by the rising ground behind her. As there was woodland on each side it was just bad luck that they saw her painting. The boys had suddenly burst out from the trees, in hot pursuit of an excitedly yapping dog… goodness only knew what the terrier was chasing, but they both forgot it completely when they almost knocked Clarrie off her stool.

"Wow – are you a real artist?" asked the older boy

"What are you painting, please miss?" queried the other, quite politely.

They seemed, on first impressions, to be harmless enough so Clarrie answered both questions and a stream of others. Surely, she thought, they'll soon be bored and move on. Optimistically, she reminded them about the dog, but they were totally disinterested in it. She was a far more promising substitute. Before their intrusion, Clarrie had been at work for only an hour, so there was very little on her canvas for them to criticise, but they were following every brushstroke and competing with each other, guessing what was coming. Clarrie could not remember ever before being so disconcerted by casual onlookers and was at a loss to understand why their comments bothered her.

Clarrie's gaze returned to the view. On this side of

the hill cattle grazed on the uncultivated fields and, in the distance, a few horses stood in a paddock. Just below was a smallholding ...the farmhouse was beyond a vegetable garden and chicken runs. The outbuildings looked old, not in good repair and consequently made an interesting group for a painting. The road leading into the village would appear on the right of her canvas and she was surprised that she had not noticed the lane leading to the farm when she drove in the day before; where it met the main road, the junction looked quite wide from above. Before tackling the background, Clarrie was intent on placing the roads, barns and house but every time she made a stroke, one or other of the boys interrupted.

"What is that square thing?"

"Why are you painting that roof?"

"What is that yellow blob going to be?

"Aren't you going to paint any big buildings?"

At last, she could stand it no longer and asked them if they would be kind enough to leave and allow her to paint quietly. "Why don't you go away now and come back in a couple of days? You'll be able to see what the finished painting will be like then." Although aggrieved at being dismissed, they went with a fairly good grace, but as the day wore on, it was obvious that they must have told everyone they met, *'There's a woman up there, painting a picture'*. At first a few and then a constant stream of people appeared, trying to look casual as they strolled past. By the time Clarrie realised what was happening, the painting was too far advanced to abandon so she worked on regardless.

Fortunately, very few tried to engage her in conversation. Clarrie was surprised, but thankful that her audience was content to view and mutter amongst themselves. When the sun lost its strength and began to sink, Clarrie covered her palette in plastic film and started to pack her brushes away. Having been alone for only the last hour, she had not achieved as much as she'd hoped but wasn't unduly worried. A stranger, in a village that did not boast even one hotel, would have been an object of interest anyway, but when the stranger sat alone on a hill, painting, the novelty was obviously too much to ignore! Surely, it would wear off by tomorrow and her room at the guesthouse was booked for the whole of next week, so there might still be time to paint two canvases.

Although all Clarrie's painting gear, including her easel and stool, packed neatly into a manageable carrying case, it was always tricky carrying a wet painting. Walking up the hill was no problem but there was no protection from the blustery wind as she walked down the other side to the roadway. Keeping a tight grip on the stretcher of a wildly swinging picture was not easy, so it was with considerable relief that she suddenly heard the screech of bicycle brakes and a friendly offer of help.

"You must be the artist I've been hearing about ...staying with Mrs Lynch, next door to my shop!" The man climbed off his bike and laid it on the grass verge. I'll come back for this in a minute. Shall I take the case? I wouldn't dare take responsibility for the painting."

Immensely glad to accept the offer, Clarrie introduced herself and discovered that her benefactor was known as 'Postie'. "When I took over the post office I inherited the title," he said, "and as I was probably one of the lads who nicknamed the old postmaster, I have only myself to blame." As they strolled the few hundred yards to the village, she discovered that he and his wife Betty took over the Post Office a few years after they married and eventually bought it. "Coming up to our Ruby wedding soon and we wouldn't live anywhere else," he laughed. "It isn't as quiet as it used to be but folk can still let their kids out to play without too much worry."

Clarrie was aware that he had been trying to catch a glimpse of the painting as she continually tried to hold it away from her flapping coat, so when they turned the corner into the terraced street, where it was much calmer, she wasn't surprised when he asked if he could please see it. What did surprise her was his look of astonishment and his words… "Well, I can see why everyone is talking about it," he said. "I don't think there has been anyone in the shop today, over the age of fifty who hasn't described it to us. I see what they mean. It's amazing. I thought it was your first visit to the village. What made you decide on this view?"

"Well," she replied, not quite sure how to take his remark, "I was actually planning to drive on to Greater Peasey – I didn't know there was a Lesser Peasey and was intrigued when I saw it signposted so decided to stop for coffee. It seemed such a pretty place that I couldn't resist walking around, always being on the lookout for interesting subjects." A gust of wind almost took the canvas from her grip and she was relieved to find her lodgings were within sight. By the time she was safely inside, there was no necessity for further conversation and her neighbour departed with the hope that he would see her later in the Wench's Arms.

Clarrie recalled her impressions of the Pub on her first drive through the village – a picturesque old building with a thatched roof. She had stopped to ask if she could stay there but there was no accommodation for visitors because it was a family home where the publican employed his three married sons. Presumably they and their families all lived-in.

Never mind, she was happy with the place they recommended. Mrs Lynch was anxious to ensure that her new guest wanted for nothing. Visitors were expected next month apparently but, for now, she had only Clarrie to fuss over and she started the minute Clarrie shut the front door.

"My brother-in-law will be back soon – he'll carry everything up to your room, don't struggle with the case now, it looks heavy. Come and have a cup of tea to warm yourself up. I've baked too, so there's chocolate cake."

It was easier to accept than argue, so Clarrie just took the painting upstairs and propped it where it could lean safely, before joining her hostess in the kitchen. Mrs Lynch resumed her conversational flow from where she left off and waved her hand towards the table, where a plate of sandwiches had joined the promised cake. "He does like his chocolate," she said, "just like my late husband, God rest his soul." A pot of tea waited under a flowery tea cosy and as she placed teacups on the table, she wound up at last by saying please call me Doris and then asking how Clarrie had fared outside all day.

It was over an hour before Clarrie managed to impart enough of her personal details to satisfy Doris's curiosity and escape upstairs. The chocolate-lover must have returned because her workbox was in her room, so she was pleased to be able to set about cleaning brushes. While swishing them in white spirit and adding water to her soap-jar, Clarrie was careful not to let any paint come into contact with the sparklingly white vanity unit and it was almost therapeutic rolling the brushes clean in the palm of her hand. Later, she would wander round to the Wench's Arms; now, all she needed was to lie down and rest.

Doris Lynch must be one of the few people in the village who were indifferent to her picture, not even glancing at it when it was carried in, which was a shame really, as Clarrie might then have discovered why it was causing such a stir. Half asleep, gazing at the canvas as her eyelids drooped, she imagined she saw the figures moving; the boy with the spade stopped digging to stand and gaze around him and the young man with the bright yellow backpack walked purposefully down the path to the house. When the boy flung aside the spade and moved furtively to the back door of the building, a wave of apprehension swept over Clarrie. When the walker entered the open front door, a sharp pang of terror jerked her back to reality. She still felt sick with fear although fully awake, but why? What caused the sense of panic that swept over her?

It took her several minutes to calm down, whereupon she felt more able to dismiss her weird experience and put it down to tiredness after an exhausting day. Pulling herself together, she prepared to go out, resisting with determination the urge to glance again at the unfinished painting.

Feeling better after the short walk, Clarrie settled in a quiet corner of the saloon with what she considered was a well-earned drink. Apart from the wind, which made it difficult to return with everything intact, things were going well. The opportune arrival of Postie proved heaven sent – she surely would have lost her grip of something without help, and as the thought crossed her mind, he walked into the bar with several other men who all seemed to be together. Laughing and joking, they went straight to the end of the room and took over the dartboard while Postie stayed at the bar; presumably, he was buying the first round! She really could not keep calling him that; she must ask for his name later. In the quarter hour since her arrival the room had become more than half full and another brother joined the barman on duty – there was no doubt they were twins. The clientele chattered noisily to them and each other and to add to the noise, someone put a coin in the jukebox.

While waiting to be served, Clive Parker eyed Clarrie's reflection in the mirror. How long would it take her to get around to telling him exactly what was she after, he wondered nervously. He scarcely believed his eyes when he saw the picture she was painting, so he did not doubt that she meant trouble for him. He would lose everything he had worked for and achieved over the past forty years. What led her to come here – turning up on his doorstep? It certainly could not have been by accident. How could she have found him, when his traces were so well covered… more to the point, who was she and what possible connection could such a young woman have with his own distant past? It was difficult to believe that they had a mutual link to those old times because in those days he hardly ever left the house and villagers had no reason to call. No local had recognised him, he was quite sure, but she must be in league with someone old and the reason they had kept silent for so long was a poser. Now they were using this young woman to make outrageous demands… probably too frightened to make contact personally, knowing what he was capable of.

Parker continued to fantasise; someone much older must have told her the sordid details, and now she wants to cash in. Is she seeking revenge, or money? Of course, it was possible that others were already in the know, but hardly likely; divulging such information would render it unusable for blackmail! He could see only one option open to him… and he needed to act soon.

Clarrie felt many eyes upon her as she sat alone, sipping her gin and tonic. It was faintly disturbing as she was more used to fending off potential company than looking for it. Any hope of discovering what it was about her painting that caused comment was fading fast; everyone seemed wary of her. Although it was not late, she decided to leave, get some sleep and have an early start in the morning; the valley might look quite romantic with a faint mist rising from the fields. At that moment, the Postmaster returned to the bar, and nodded as she walked past the counter. He smiled, and offered her a drink. "Thanks," said Clarrie, thinking it was a shame he had not made the gesture earlier, "but I'm on my way now."

"Oh, shame, maybe another night then. You won't be leaving the village for a while, will you?"

Assuring him that she would indeed be around until next weekend, Clarrie made her way out and walked back to her lodgings. It occurred to her that she still didn't know his name but he said everyone called him Postie, so it hardly mattered really – at least she'd made one friend.

Clive Parker stared after her as she left the bar and for a mad moment contemplated following her, but dealing with her now would have been risky. He needed to act quickly but not precipitately… no sense in removing one threat and creating another! How to remove her without bringing suspicion on himself needed careful planning, but what he had done once he was confident he could do again. He smiled as he sipped his last drink of the evening. Yes, he was quite confident.

2 – Sarah

As Sarah drew the curtains across the windows of Clarrie's studio bedroom, she wondered why she went through the ritual of opening them every morning and then shutting them again as she went to bed. It was no use trying to kid herself – she missed her daughter and doing something for her was just an excuse to feel a little closer. Clarinda's commissions often took her away for the odd day or two, but it was not often that she took off for a few weeks to paint for her own pleasure – able to stop when she felt like it: not planning far ahead. It worried Sarah, but Clarinda was quite good about keeping in touch and rang up whenever she changed location.

A few hours earlier when the sky darkened, Sarah reflected that her daughter must have finished work for the day and, almost immediately, she was plunged into a mood as black as the night. The sensation was only momentary and with her usual optimism, she decided that there was no reason to connect it to Clarinda. Her psychic sense was so finely tuned that she was always susceptible to attempts at contact from the spirit world. Constantly wary, in spite of being an experienced medium, Sarah started and finished every day with a prayer for guidance and sought protection from evil. Her faith had to be kept strong; if it were not, how could she offer comfort to others. For a few minutes, before leaving the studio and going to bed, Sarah concentrated hard on her daughter and sensed nothing untoward, so she dismissed her wave of depression. Eventually, whatever caused it would be revealed and there was no point in worrying until it was.

During the night, Sarah's sleep was disturbed several times, and always, as she emerged from her dreams, they seemed very real. It was like watching a film, which took up where it left off as sleep claimed her again. At six-o-clock, giving up any hope of relaxing, Sarah went down to the kitchen – a cup of hot chocolate might help. To her surprise, the lights were on and Polly had already boiled the kettle.

"I was going to bring you a drink. I knew you were awake," Polly said as she poured scalding water into the two waiting mugs." In answer to Sarah's immediate query as to how she had known, Polly sounded surprised... "Why, the banging, of course – and I was wondering what you could possibly be hammering in the middle of the night. Has something broken or were you hanging pictures?"

Sarah's dream came vividly back to mind. She actually had been watching someone else wielding a hammer as they put up posters along a country lane. She wondered when she woke up if a message lay in the strong imagery but she was always cautious about attributing meanings to dreams and tended to look elsewhere for corroboration before taking them seriously. The fact that Polly also heard the ghostly noise was a good reason for accepting that it was definitely an attempt to gain her attention, so Sarah decided to divulge every detail of her vision.

When Polly realised that she had actually heard sounds that emanated from the 'other world' (for what other explanation could there be?) she sat heavily and almost fainted with shock. In all the years she'd known

Sarah and even living with her as companion housekeeper, she rarely witnessed anything at first hand.

There had been ample proof of life after death – both Sarah and Clarrie were psychic, although in different ways and even the police sought their help sometimes but, knowing that the sounds in the night were not of this world, thrilled her to the core.

When sufficiently recovered, Polly listened with mounting excitement as Sarah recounted her dream.

"I was standing on the grass verge of a busy road when the dream began. The nearness and speed of the traffic woke me within what seemed like minutes. Then I fell asleep again and gradually realised that I was in the same place. Even in my dream I was surprised and thought it odd to be back there, but I walked to a crossroad where there was a signpost."

"What did the sign say?" Polly asked breathlessly.

Sarah frowned in concentration and obviously could not remember. Then she explained how the hammering noise distracted her and she saw someone nailing something to a nearby tree. Looking back along the road, Sarah saw two people putting posters up on each side of the road, to face oncoming traffic. They were on the outskirts of a town about half a mile away, beyond them. Answering Polly's stream of questions helped Sarah to squeeze the most out of her memory. The people were middle-aged. They were neatly, but not expensively dressed. The cars were not modern but most did not look old. Sarah distinguished a Hillman Minx exactly like one her mother drove in the early 50's… "It looked brand new," she added, realising that whatever someone was trying to tell her, it was something that had been troubling them for nearly half a century.

There was no point in going back to bed. By the time they talked themselves out, it was almost time for Polly's niece to arrive. Pat had taken over her aunt's daily chores a year or so ago, when Sarah and Clarrie insisted that at Polly's age her duties should be light. Although indignant initially, Polly settled well into her new routine, making sure the household ran smoothly and doing most of the cooking.

Keeping Sarah company, freeing Clarrie to come and go as she pleased, was no hardship – Polly would not have changed places with anyone else on earth.

Sarah was regretting now, that she succumbed to the urge to leave her bed for a drink...

If only she had laid her head on the pillow again, she might have seen more. The half-glimpsed poster carried a photograph – a young man perhaps – and a name, but her memory failed her; she could recall nothing of the lettering or the signpost ...if only she had stared at it long enough to see any of the places on it! She sighed heavily, but was sure that if she relaxed and allowed the troubled spirit to come through again more would be shown to her soon.

As she walked back upstairs to wash and get ready to face the day, she heard the bustle of Pat's arrival downstairs.

Although Pat sensed an air of excitement about her aunt and commented, Polly was far too discreet to gossip about Sarah or anything to do with her psychic abilities.

In isolation, the dream was not important, but who knew what would follow?

Having several times witnessed the way the other world worked she felt certain that the dream was just a prelude to another amazing episode in their lives, but she tried to curb her enthusiasm.

After all, she nearly died last time she became involved – not through anybody else's fault but entirely due to her own big-headedness, thinking she was clever enough to cope alone. Luckily, she was rescued when Sarah tracked down her whereabouts.

Polly wallowed in the frisson of pure pleasure that consumed her as she remembered the hammering …the ghostly hammering. Who would have thought that she was what Sarah called clairaudient? A thought struck her suddenly. How could she be sure that she had never heard ghostly sounds before? After all, the noise seemed very real. Sarah says that many of the spirit people she sees look as solid as people in real life, so how many of the folk we see walking about are not living? Some might be long dead! The train of thought led her to consider the mediæval garb of ghosts reported to be haunting old castles. Their clothing suggests that they lived in another era but the recent dead would be in modern garb. Some of the tourists wandering around the grounds might actually be ghosts of the recently dead!

With a start, Polly uttered a cry of alarm – the milk, which she thought she was watching so carefully, surged up the sides of the pan and hissed over onto the glowing electric ring. She was still muttering with annoyance at her own carelessness when Pat breezed back into the kitchen. "Come on now auntie, sit down and enjoy a cup of coffee. I'll clear that up for you. It does me good to see that you're not perfect after all!"

"That's enough cheek from you, young lady," Polly laughed, taking advantage of the offer and pulling a kitchen chair away from the table. From one of the drawers she lifted what she called her Day Book. It was more than a diary; as well as reminders of things to be done, it was where she recorded happenings that she didn't want to forget. One single phrase, alongside the date, now read 'Hammering at night'. Whatever lay ahead, Polly was sure this was a significant beginning and, as she closed the book and replaced it in the drawer, she wondered how long it would be before there would be more strange things to add.

3 – Clarrie

Mrs Lynch had obviously been waiting to pounce on Clarrie when she returned last night, but with the kindest intentions. She wanted to know what time to make breakfast. "We're always up at seven, even on Sundays, but we never mind what time we eat, so you just choose when you would like it... No, No," Doris insisted when Clarrie said she didn't need anything cooked but would be glad of a packed sandwich to take out, "You need to start the day with a good meal, but cooking for all three of us together will save me time." Before saying goodnight, she nodded towards the end of the landing. "His room is along there next to yours so you might hear him come up, although he does try to tread lightly. He's out most nights, either with his son or baby-sitting for his daughter, but you'll meet him in the morning. Lovely, lovely man, don't know what I'd have done without him after my Sam died." The last thing Clarrie wanted was a rundown on the family history, so with a smile of thanks, she escaped quickly into her own room.

The painting drew her eye as soon as she switched on the light and for a second or two she thought there was movement within it... The clouds were drifting – the figures walking. The moment passed and she attributed it to being so tired. After enjoying a hot shower it wasn't long before Clarrie was drifting to sleep... until an image formed in her mind's eye, something else she'd glimpsed in the picture that she certainly didn't draw, or even see. The house was on fire. Splashes of flaming orange vibrated in the windows and licked around the frame of the open door.

In alarm, Clarrie hurriedly threw off the duvet and rushed to inspect the wet canvas again; perhaps the paint had run: no way! It wasn't that wet. To her relief, the unfinished picture looked no different from when she packed up for the day. Only after checking it, was she able to get to sleep, but it was a restless night disturbed by dream snatches that melted from her memory as she awoke. When she heard heavy footsteps passing her bedroom door she guessed that the lovely Mr Lynch was on his way down to eat and, although she would have welcomed a few more minutes rest, Clarrie hastened to get up, to join her hosts for breakfast.

Afterwards, they both helped to load her gear into the car. The weather seemed good but because the wind blew up so unexpectedly yesterday, Clarrie had decided not to walk to the hill. There, the road was wide with no parking restrictions, so there was no point in risking being caught in another gale. With her head in the open boot, through the windscreen, she saw Postie emerge from next door carrying a newspaper stand and she heard someone call, "Morning Mr Parker, nicer today than yesterday, thank goodness." Well, that's something, she thought, I needn't call him 'Postie' when I next meet him in the pub!

Standing on the pavement, watching her drive away, Clive gave a friendly wave... His thoughts churned. As soon as he could get away, he would follow. From the far side of the hill he would be able to approach her through the woods without being observed and be in a good position to see if anyone else was around. He didn't allow himself to plan beyond that point. Since leaving the so-called home of his childhood his life had been blameless. On that terrible day, looking down at the smouldering shell, he'd vowed to lead a normal life and never regretted it but, if he must revert to old ways to protect himself, then so be it; it wasn't his fault.

There were few passing cars and no one on foot on the outskirts of the village as Clarrie parked and unloaded her paint box and easel. She decided to carry them up the hill, leaving the picture in the boot while she set up, rather than risk smudging it. It was only nine-o-clock, the day promised to be bright and the air was still; it was sure to be a fruitful session.

4 – Bobby

Any other mother would believe her son when he declared his homework done, but no, not his! She was always inspecting his school exercise books and remembered exactly what state they were in last time she looked. He needed to add at least half a page to his composition to satisfy her, but instead of working, Bobby Goswell was gazing from his bedroom window. The house was an end of terrace property on the edge of the village and Bobby was lucky that his room, at the back, had a side window as well. His friend Joe, next door, could only see boring allotments where old people sat smoking outside little sheds when they were supposed be digging.

Because of the bend in the road, Bobby had a perfect view of the grassy hillock where Clarrie was unloading her car. He thought grown-ups never worked on Sundays but he saw her carry her case up the slope and disappear over the brow. He watched, knowing that the picture must still be in the car and sure enough, a few minutes later, she reappeared to fetch it. It was too far away to see how much more was painted on it since he and Joe saw it yesterday morning and he was suddenly gripped with curiosity; perhaps she was painting from the ground up – it sort of made sense in a way. He really needed to look at it again to see if he was right. What kind of artist was she anyway – probably what his art teacher called impressionable or something. It certainly looked nothing like the view of the valley. Bobby went back to his homework bursting with enthusiasm. The sooner he finished it the sooner he could drag Joe out to watch the artist again... Even though Joe was a year older than Bobby, he always did as he was told.

5 – Clive

Clive Parker glanced at his watch as he finished the last of his morning chores. It was almost eleven-o-clock. His plan was working so far – he had a perfect excuse to be away until early evening and he had already stashed a suitable weapon in the boot of his car; what could look more innocent than an empty champagne bottle? From the hallway, he shouted upstairs, "I'll be seeing Dave while I'm in Oxford – any messages for his wife?" Having the answer he expected – he knew the two women were chatting on the 'phone less than an hour earlier – he quickly left and was soon driving off towards the city. After a few miles, he would swing back round the hill to the motorway and enter the new housing estate from the heavily wooded far side. There was no way she would see him approach through the trees on foot. Ten minutes later, he left the car alongside several others in a chapel car park, entered the front of the building, exited from the side door to escape observation, and then went round the back into the municipal gardens.

He usually avoided crossing the park … it was inevitable that his brain would engage top gear as, like a lone sailor on a lake, he could fix accurately where the house used to be. He had often stood outside the old tool shed gazing longingly up the hill, wishing he lived beyond it, in the heart of the village or, in the other direction, watched smoke rising from the Greater Peasey rail station where trains carried people away to exciting new worlds. As he walked, images from the past flooded his mind. Just to his left was the site of the hen house and he felt almost sick as he realised he was walking over the old vegetable patch where the bodies lay. He clutched the carrier bag that held the water-filled bottle, heavy enough now to do the job, and regretted that he was being driven to kill again. He never wanted to harm anyone in the first place, but when you are only eleven years old, you do as you are told. His liberty to move around and mix with people was curtailed strictly from that moment on.

Initially he liked being kept home from school; in those early war years nobody took much notice whether kids attended or not. With bombs dropping and evacuees moving in from nearby towns, it was difficult for harassed teachers to keep track of all the kids. The staff was constantly changing anyway as some members were called up for active service and temporary workers came and went. Chores on the smallholding were soon done and anything was better than English and Arithmetic. Only in his mid-teens did he rebel against his isolation. He was then old enough to understand that, if he revealed to an outsider anything that happened at the farm, he was part of it and would hang or go to jail. He was so afraid that he willingly stayed away from the village and even hid when strangers occasionally approached.

He was at a loss now to understand why it had taken him so long to wonder why men who had been the most friendly to him often left without saying goodbye. He was horrified when he found out, but never felt responsible. In his escape, however, he committed the one act for which he was totally responsible and for which he carried the most guilt, but he did not doubt that disposing of this new threat was in a different category. The hapless boy had appeared at the wrong moment on that distant day – but this woman chose to threaten his future and was entirely to blame for what he was about to do. He felt justified and for her he would not shed a tear.

6 – Bobby

It was lunchtime before Bobby finished his homework to the satisfaction of his mother, and then she would not allow him to go out before eating. She was a real pain, he thought, as he sat down at the kitchen table. All his mates were allowed to eat on their laps in front of the telly – crisps and burgers too.

He eyed the heap of boiled potatoes gloomily and was only slightly mollified when it was joined by baked beans and several sausages.

As he was finishing his meal he saw Joe's face at the kitchen window. His leap from the table as he pushed his empty plate away brought his father's wrath down on his head. 'It's bad manners to push the plate away', as if there were servants to clear up... 'and it's rude to leave the table without asking to be excused'... What were they training him for, Buckingham Palace?

At last he managed to get away and found Joe kicking his heels against their dividing wall. "You'd better sit on your own side if you want to chip the cement out of the bricks," was Bobby's greeting. "You know what my Dad's like," he warned.

When he told Joe where they were heading he had to wait while Joe collected a painting of his own, to show off. Bobby sighed – as if a real artist would be interested in a kid's daub!

Sometimes Joe, who was more than a head taller, made him feel very old, but he was his best friend and hardly ever argued with him.

Without all the delays they might have reached Clarrie in time to save her – and, in doing so, would have avoided the horror of finding her...

7 – Polly

At home near Mapledurham, things were in turmoil. Within fifteen minutes of Polly's call the doctor arrived to tend to Sarah who had collapsed without warning just after lunch. Doctor Davis, the family physician for many years, was at a loss even to hazard a guess as to the cause but declared Sarah to be completely recovered from whatever it was. Polly looked cross. It was not in Sarah's nature to complain, but Polly felt that there must be a reason when someone fell into a faint in mid-sentence and lay there as white as a sheet, without moving and hardly breathing for almost two hours. She would have said more to the obviously incompetent, aging doctor who, she felt, should have retired years ago, had she not caught a warning glance from Sarah, who now seemed quite normal.

Doctor Davis continued fussing for over twenty minutes before accepting Sarah's assurances that she felt perfectly well again, then he accepted a brandy (it was, after all, Sunday and he was no longer really on call), which delayed his departure for another ten. At last Polly managed to edge him out of the front door and returned anxiously to the sitting room. When she saw Sarah resting with her hands loosely on her lap and her eyes closed in concentration, Polly sat down quietly and waited, filled with trepidation. Something must be seriously wrong and it must be connected with Clarrie; nothing less would have caused Sarah to react in such a manner. Polly was frightened. It seemed to her that Sarah might have gone into a trance and she knew enough about such things to understand that it was not wise for a medium to let it happen without the support, or presence of someone who would know what to do if things went wrong.

Pulling herself together, Polly tried to think clearly – in this instance she must be Sarah's support. The power of prayer was amazing, her own experience convinced her of that, so she sat quietly, praying as hard as she could that 'somebody up there' was helping Sarah and keeping her from harm. It seemed an age before Sarah opened her eyes and stared blankly around the room. "Clarinda …I know she's in trouble – I collapsed because I was stunned by a terrible blow across the back of my neck and of course I couldn't tell the doctor. There can't be anything to see because it wasn't a physical blow. It has to have been Clarinda's pain I felt… and I am unable to reach her! I feel so empty! Oh, Polly, what am I to do?" Sarah was shaking and nearly in tears.

The practical side of Polly asserted itself instantly. "Well," she replied firmly, "why don't you do what most people would do and telephone the last number she gave you?"

Even in face of her fears, Sarah managed the trace of a smile. "Bless you Polly; of course I should ring up. I have been dwelling so much on the sensations that filled me when I collapsed that I'm losing touch with reality! Your common sense is a blessing – I'd be lost without you." Glowing with pleasure at the unexpected praise, Polly told Sarah to stay where she was and went to retrieve the telephone book from the hall table. It was then that she discovered that in her earlier panic she failed to replace the receiver properly; anyone trying to reach them would have failed.

It was almost five-o-clock when the telephone rang at the Guest House. It rang and rang... Doris Lynch had been called away by the police.

8 - Clive

When Clive Parker turned his car into the high street and parked in front of the shop, the pavement was crowded with gossiping groups of people: some looking worried: all excited. The place was usually quiet at this time on a Sunday so it was evident that the woman's body had been found.

He wasn't surprised because he'd heard children shouting while he was with her and their closeness had stopped him from risking one more blow. Before escaping, he grabbed the painting from the easel. There was no way he wanted anyone else to see it; quite enough people were aware of it already. Later he would burn it but, for the moment, he was sure his job was done.

The blackmailing hussy was not going to destroy his or anyone else's life now.

The amount of blood was more and the whole thing messier than he remembered; had he not been prudent enough to strip to running shorts it would have been disastrous. Even though the stream water was uncomfortably cold, it was well worth the discomfort.

The few minutes submersion effectively washed away the worst stains and he was able to smash the bottle on rocks well away from the bank. He congratulated himself smugly that, knowing he would need a towel he'd wrapped one round the bottle to stop it rolling about in the boot and a brisk rub down before dressing again restored a little warmth to his body.

After walking briskly back to his car he began to feel more normal and as he drove away it was difficult for him to believe that the last forty minutes had been anything other than a dream.

He did as he used to in his youth; he put the episode behind him and let his thoughts dwell on the pleasures ahead. After several drinks Dave would forget that Clive was an hour late for their meeting; not that he would ever need an alibi – why should he be a suspect? It was, however, good to be prepared.

It was just after six-o-clock when he walked Dave back home. As usual, Dave's wife, Vera, greeted them with a wry smile and took her husband's arm to walk him to the lounge. "How few," she asked, "did it take this time? I keep telling him that anything over three pints is a waste of money, but at least he's not a nasty drunk. Would you like coffee Clive, or are you in a hurry?"

He declined coffee, adding that she was right; they ran out of intelligent conversation well before three – over three hours ago. Vera laughed heartily, and he left happily satisfied that she was sure to remember his witty remark. The only thing left to do was to put his shorts and towel in the laundry bin. They were spotless anyway after their submersion in the river, but would be through the laundry system within a day so he felt nothing but relief on the drive home.

After locking the vehicle, he walked to his front door, exchanging pleasantries. It seemed that everyone he knew was on the street, eager to tell him what had happened and he managed to convey that he'd been in Oxford most of the day. The shouted scraps of information he heard exchanged were contradictory; someone beat and robbed a girl; an old woman had been taken to hospital; a young woman was found stabbed.

Listening to the babble of raised voices he started to sweat as he assimilated the fact that nobody had actually said she was dead.

9 – Bobby

Joe and Bobby were questioned separately and gently enough but at some length, at home in the presence of their parents, and were now safe in their own beds. The policewoman who handled both interviews expected Joe who was over twelve years old to be the most coherent, but Bobby, barely eleven, was much clearer about what he'd heard and seen, although it actually amounted to very little. She commented to Bobby's parents that he had shown good sense and they could be proud of him because he stopped short of the crime scene and sent his friend to get help. It was obvious from the amount of blood splashed about that the woman was attacked viciously, but they didn't yet know whether or not it was murder. Her life was endangered and even if she recovered, it would be a long time before they could question her. Until then she would be under police protection in intensive care.

It proved easy to discover her probable identity, assuming it was her car parked nearby, but they were not yet able to contact her next of kin. It seems she was staying locally, booked in for a week according to the landlady, but all her personal information seemed to be with her and things were scattered everywhere. The assailant left valuable items behind but, strangely enough, took the picture she was painting with him.

Lying awake upstairs, Bobby heard the police officers saying goodnight to his parents and the front door closing. He was amazed that Joe was so upset and shaken by the experience, and yet perhaps even more surprised by his own reaction. It was a horrible thing to have happened, but he found the whole episode exhilarating. He glanced only briefly at the body – it was too yucky – but did try to take in all there was to see about the scene, just like his favourite TV detective, Jim Carver, in The Bill last week, looking for forensic evidence. He was not absolutely clear what forensic evidence looked like but knew it could be messed up if people trampled over it. He took in the scene carefully, already imagining himself giving evidence in court – but there was one thing he would never tell anyone – they wouldn't believe him anyway! After sending Joe away to get help, someone appeared out of nowhere, to stand looking down at the body.

He knew it was a ghost but was not the least bit scared because he'd seen them before but they never spoke to him. There was something familiar about the figure and when Bobby recognised what it was he gasped – his outline was like something the lady was painting in her picture and the yellow blob she put in was the bag on his back. The ghost's attention was drawn to Bobby and perceiving that the boy could see him, the young man pointed dramatically to the trees a few yards away. Bobby was sharp enough to know that the murderer must have gone that way and, for no reason he could have explained, felt that it was only seconds ago. The ghost faded away but Bobby stood still and listened. Among the usual sounds of waving trees and distant traffic he picked out a faint splashing and heard a sharp crack.

These were the details he gave to the police. He dressed his story up a little to convince them that someone ran that way, in the direction of the new housing estate, but he felt no guilt in relaying the information because it had come from a reliable source. He never felt the need to tell anyone else that he could see ghosts. He liked being able to see people who were dead and thought they might not let him see them ever again if he shared his secret. Added to which people would think he was insane and he definitely did not want to be locked up.

10 – Sarah

When the telephone was not answered, Sarah again looked anxious and sick. It was obvious that whatever she felt, saw or heard earlier shook her badly. Polly brought a blanket and wrapped it around Sarah as she repeatedly tried to reach the number of the guest house, which Clarinda gave her on Friday night. When there was still no reply, Sarah decided to ring her friend Alec Holmes. He was a Detective Chief Superintendent of Police who frequently sought her help when other avenues failed, so he would not regard her call as frivolous. Just as Polly pushed a laden tea trolley alongside her chair, Sarah ended the conversation and, turning to Polly, protested that she was in no mood to eat but having passed on her fears to Alec and knowing he would not rest until he located her daughter, Sarah seemed more composed. She sipped hot tea and ate a few sandwiches almost without realising that food was passing her lips.

Polly was worried too of course, and encouraged Sarah to describe her experience. It was not merely idle curiosity that made her keen. She genuinely believed that talking it over would have a calming effect, and be helpful. There was nothing more Sarah could do, and she couldn't shake off the feeling that there was a connection between the poster hangers and the plight of her daughter so she was now eager to talk over her experience, extracting from the re-telling anything she might previously have overlooked.

The heavy blow she felt on the back of her head was so agonizing that she collapsed but even as she fell she saw an easel holding a canvas and beyond it, blue sky. When she recovered, there was no doubt in her mind that she had experienced what happened to Clarinda. Only the fact that she could not sense her daughter's presence in the spirit world allowed Sarah to remain calm. Some troubled souls who pass on are not able to communicate immediately, for different reasons but, if there was reason to do so, many people on the other side would rush to comfort Sarah. She sensed strongly that her husband, Stephen, was close and tried to make him understand that she was now well again. He should look after Clarinda, wherever she was.

Polly listened as Sarah expressed her thoughts and her reasons for believing that in spite of indications to the contrary, Clarrie had survived the attack on her. It was difficult to understand why anyone would wish to harm her, but whoever it was would not escape retribution, of that Polly was absolutely sure.

11 - Doris

The house was empty when Doris returned home. The police had kept her hanging about for hours, first at the hospital, where they wanted her to confirm that the victim of the attack was her guest, then at the station where they asked her the same questions over and over. Where was the victim before coming to stay in the village? Did she arrive alone or with someone who was lodging somewhere else? Did she have any friends locally? Was there a Mr Hunter? If so, were they having marital problems? The questions were endless but she had few answers. How could she be expected to know who Mrs Hunter's enemies were – or friends for that matter? She could only say that her guest made no more than one telephone call, to her mother, and she thought the husband died years ago. Doris's house keys were borrowed by a policewoman who searched Clarrie's room but found no address book or diary with her mother's number in it and apparently no clue as to why anyone would want to kill her. They allowed Doris to go home but warned her not to break the police seal on the door to Mrs Hunter's room.

Now, all Doris wanted to do was sit in front of the TV with a cup of coffee. She had answered all the direct questions as well as she could but thinking about it quietly now, she remembered some of the things Clarrie told her at teatime yesterday. Her husband, Tom, died after a long illness several years ago, not long after her father died so she and her mother Sarah lived together. There was another man on the horizon but he was working in the Middle East; a writer or newshound of some kind, probably earning a bomb, Doris reflected. When she commented that 'Clarrie' was such a pretty, unusual name, the girl said that her mother always called her Clarinda, as she was named after both aunts, Clara and Linda. Very clever; neither could be upset. That was about it really. She would prepare another guest room in case the mother turned up; she would be bound to want to talk to her about Clarrie and might need to stay to be near the hospital.

Such a pleasant young woman and such a terrible thing to have happened, Doris reflected. She hoped they would soon catch the thug who beat the poor girl – nobody was safe these days she sighed, as she clicked over to her favourite programme and put her feet up.

12 - DCS Alec Holmes

The young police constable sitting outside Clarrie's room was nervous. Hospital staff members were going in and out all the time and he was beginning to recognise individuals, but he was well aware that any stranger could be the one who tried to kill the young woman and nearly succeeded. The villain must know he'd failed and might come back for another go. The responsibility weighed heavily on PC Penny's shoulders and he did not hesitate in barring access and asking for an ID when a well-built man in a civilian suit walked up to the door. By the time Penny established that the man was DCS Holmes another senior officer raced up to join them, breathlessly making apologies for the delay in his arrival. "We have her address now and were just about to send someone to the house when you contacted us. What would you like us to do, sir?"

Alec wanted to assess the situation personally, which was why he drove up from Reading immediately his initial enquiries connected Clarrie with the unfortunate victim of assault. By ordering the locals not to release names or details, or try to contact her family until he had seen the victim personally and spoken to the doctors, he extended Sarah's hours of anxiety but hoped to make amends by giving her a more truthful and accurate account of Clarrie's condition. The duty doctor joined them as the two police officers entered the room where Clarrie lay swathed in bandages, connected by tubes to bottles hanging from stands at her bedside and obviously not conscious. Alec was horrified and the more he questioned the doctor about her condition recovery prospects, the more worried he became.

On his way to telephone Sarah, he clung to the doctor's assurance that Clarrie was out of immediate danger. The bad news was that they could not predict when, if ever, she would recover consciousness.

13 – Betty

It was nearly ten-o-clock when Betty Parker arrived home to find her husband already asleep in bed. Usually on Sundays she spent most of the day with their daughter, Stella. He never went with her because he said you could have too much of grandkids no matter how much you loved them. He preferred to spend time with their son Dave. Anyway, it was his day for doing the books. If he finished early enough he went out for a drink, but he always got to bed before eleven, having to be up by six to sort the newspaper delivery sacks for the boys. Today, it was gone seven before she saw Stella because Stella's son Joe was one of the boys who found the woman who'd been attacked and the police were there for hours. As if little Joe could tell them anything! He was really badly shaken, poor lamb.

Betty was disappointed that she couldn't speak immediately to her husband; he must have heard about the young visitor next door being beaten up because everyone told him everything and she wondered if he knew any more details. She knew he'd met the woman; he said she was quite pleasant and confirmed what several of their customers had been rattling on about yesterday. The painting she was doing bore no resemblance at all to the view from the hill but looked just like it was thirty years ago, before the estate was built. As the artist could not be much older than that, everyone was intrigued. Exactly what was she up to?

Her husband brushed off the question with an indulgent smile, saying she might have seen an old picture postcard of the valley and liked it better without the buildings. Perhaps she was rallying support to have them demolished and restore the countryside. Betty shrugged; he never took anything seriously. Now, there was another thing she wanted to talk to him about: something really strange and puzzling that she discovered this afternoon. It was amazing that she never noticed it before but usually, when she went to the cemetery to put flowers on her parents' grave, Stella was with her and they talked all the time.

Today, alone, she wandered around looking at other graves and reading the epitaphs. When she saw the name 'Parker' she examined it with interest and realised that it marked the grave of the young family who died in a house fire, way back in 1937. She only remembered the little boy being called Andy but today she discovered his full name was Andrew Clive …now wasn't that strange, giving the same name to cousins born in the same year? So, until he died at three years old, that must have caused a lot of confusion. She had never heard of such a thing before. Downright silly, Betty called it!

Her mind still churned with all the events of the day and there was no way she would be able to sleep without a hot drink, so while the kettle boiled she retrieved the Parker family albums from the depths of the fireplace cupboard. The electric kettle boiled and switched off unnoticed as Betty became more and more puzzled about what she could not find among the old fading photographs.

14 – Alec

With trepidation, Alec picked up the phone and rang Sarah. They had been friends long enough for him to know that she would not react hysterically but Clarrie was the centre of her world and the fact that the girl might not recover from her terrible injuries was the dreadful message he must relay. He remembered the day he first met Sarah, when she called in at the station on a mission of mercy. His initial doubts about the veracity and worth of messages from the dead were soon banished and he'd lost count of the times Sarah guided him to the right solution. He naturally wondered if Sarah would have any insight into why Clarrie might have been targeted, but from what he understood, it seemed that communication became more difficult when she was personally involved; her ability to function could be disturbed by emotion but he had faith that Sarah's innate psychic ability would not fail her in this instance.

Sarah picked up the phone on the first ring.

Ten minutes later she was calmly relaying to Polly everything Alec had told her. Sarah was dry-eyed but Polly wept with frustration. She felt useless – there was nothing she could do or say to alleviate the situation. It resulted in Sarah being the one comforting Polly, pointing out how useful it was that she could drive – they would get a few hours sleep and then go to the hospital and who knew, perhaps Clarinda would be awake by then and be able to talk to them herself. It was nearly midnight when they said goodnight and made their way to their own rooms. Whoever woke first would make coffee and wake the other. In the meantime, Sarah said, trying to make light of the thought, they must pray for Clarinda's wounds to heal quickly allowing a complete recovery, and hope that somebody up there was listening.

15 - Bobby

Joe and Bobby both went to school on the New Peasey Estate. The old village school was now only for pre-school infants who, according to Joe, were looked after by a few child-minders while their mothers gossiped and drank coffee in the huge kitchen. They sometimes gave him a glass of milk when he took his little brother there. The Secondary School was on the far side of the common and perfectly visible from the top of the hill. They were excited when they thought it would be in the artist's painting and irritated when she drew just fields and cows in its place. She hadn't even been painting the houses! Now that the artist woman had been battered to death, it was the only topic as they walked across the common on Monday morning.

"Perhaps she was attacked by someone who lives on the estate," said Joe.

"Don't be stupid," Bobby sighed heavily. Sometimes he despaired of Joe. "Murdering somebody just because they missed your house out of a picture wouldn't be much of a motive, would it?" It wasn't what he meant, Joe protested, but Bobby's attention was gripped by the ghostly boy again: the one from the hill. He was standing near the drinking fountain, still carrying his yellow bag and pointing again but this time he wanted Bobby to look at the ground. How silly, thought Bobby, there was nothing there but grass. He knew about lip-reading and wished he could do it because he could see the ghostly mouth moving as it faded away; a bit like the grin on the Cheshire cat, he thought, although the boy looked anything but happy ...but then, he was bound to be unhappy. He was dead.

Shrugging off the incident, Bobby turned his attention back to Joe. After school, he informed his friend, they would try to remember everything in the artist's painting because the police lady said it was stolen. Joe was quite good at drawing so Bobby knew he would leap at the idea. The idea of trying to copy it came into his head as the image of the ghost disappeared. Perhaps that was what the ghost was telling him to do: perhaps not, but the idea appealed to him anyway and it might even help the police to find the stolen one. Joe too was excited by the plan and the boys ran the rest of the way as if, by hurrying, they could make the school day pass more quickly.

16 – Edna

Will Daniels and his wife Edna sat together in their modest semi-detached house in St Helens, which in common with all their friends and neighbours they still regarded as being in Lancashire, bitterly resenting its being known as Merseyside. Their town was nowhere near the Mersey and Liverpool was miles away! Warrington was next door to St Helens and was in Cheshire – it made no sense. Why things had to change was beyond them anyway; they felt as if their heritage and their roots were lost. William and Edna felt the loss more than most, because memories of their son Anthony revolved around the old terraced house in Creswell Street, which they were forced to leave under a compulsory purchase order soon after he disappeared.

In Church last Sunday, for the forty-seventh time, his name was mentioned in prayer as it was annually. They thought of him every day of every year but the Sunday nearest to their wedding anniversary, the last time they spoke with him, held special meaning. Together they looked through the box of oddments, which, although of no intrinsic value, seemed to link the good memories of old to the mystery of his last few weeks. The most treasured was the photograph his father took of him as he left on the fifth of May, at the door of their old home. It opened onto the street and several of their neighbours were smiling in the background.

It saddened Edna to realise how everyone had gone their separate ways after the terrace was demolished. Behind Anthony was Nora Finney. They were at her house in 1951 when he rang up on Mothers' Day. They didn't have a telephone themselves in those days but always spent Sunday afternoons at Nora's where Tony knew he could contact them, as he did on their wedding anniversary, the twenty-eighth of May, following up a beautiful bouquet of flowers already sent. In between, they received a postcard from him to say he was in Banbury on his way to Chipping Norton – exploring anything of interest, enjoying his holiday, before starting a new phase of his life.

He was keen on electronics and very good at repairing radios and even televisions: not that there were many about in those days. He was setting himself up in business with the small legacy left to him by his grandparents and signed the lease on the premises the day before leaving. He could not take the place over until mid-June, so he was going to enjoy touring the Cotswolds, mostly on foot. So for the first three weeks, they knew where he was and where he was heading; he had avoided Oxford but enjoyed visiting Blenhcim Palace on the outskirts, and intended to explore little villages.

There was a gap of nine days after the anniversary call, before another postcard arrived.

It was written four days earlier than the postmark, so he must have forgotten to post it, but they were relieved to hear that he was still well and happy. Another week went by before the next card came and William was examining it yet again. In shaky writing, it explained that Anthony had sprained his wrist in a fall, but was perfectly well and would write again soon. It gave no information about where he intended to go next. They only knew where it was posted because of the franking.

The next card was just as badly written and the last, which came during his fifth week away, was so sketchy that they started to worry. Tony was overdue back home, but made no mention of it, nor did he give any hint as to when he would return. They were frantic, sure that something must be terribly wrong. There was no way he would have run away from home, so on Friday of the sixth week, the day he should have been taking over his new shop, they could stand it no longer and went to the police. Days, weeks and months passed without any progress in the search until eventually the police advised them that although the case was not closed, it was unlikely that their son would ever be found. It was many years before William and Edna finally succumbed to the inevitable theory that by fair means or foul he had met his death.

About forty years after his disappearance, they went to a Spiritualist meeting with a friend who persuaded them that, if in the 'World of Spirit', Anthony would be able to make contact through the medium. Although not comfortable with the idea, they were willing to try anything. A tiny woman about Edna's age greeted them warmly and found places for them on the middle row of chairs, near the centre aisle. She didn't know them by name, but introduced them, to the people already seated, as newcomers to their group and hoped that if they asked questions someone would answer and make them feel at home. Their friend sat on a raised platform at the front of the room and soon stood to address the forty or so people attending.

He explained earlier, when driving them to the meeting, that he was like a chairman and would be conducting the Service. First, there would be a hymn (from Hymns Ancient & Modern) and following it would be, in his own words, "A prayer from the heart, delivered by one of our local gifted Clairvoyants." After a kind of sermon, from himself he said deprecatingly, he would introduce the visiting Medium. Apparently, a governing body ensured that these peripatetic conduits for messages from the departed never went anywhere they were likely to know the congregation, or to the same place twice. By the time another hymn was sung and the Medium, Esme, began to speak, William and Edna were less nervous.

There was to be a few minutes silent prayer, Esme said, and then she hoped she would be able to bring some comfort or guidance to any present who were troubled.

Waving her hand towards someone behind them she spoke about an elderly woman dressed in grey being present, whose name was Maria or Mary. William thought the odds were pretty high that most people in the back row could claim a dead relative called Maria or Mary, and he was suddenly overcome by a sense of despair. What were they doing here, with these strangers who really believed in life after death?

He really wanted to believe in an afterlife. If Anthony weren't alive, it would almost be a relief to imagine him being a happy spirit, free to roam. That was what he enjoyed most: walking for miles, seeking new horizons.

Time was passing and Edna began to worry that the meeting would soon end. After a dozen or more messages came through, from beyond the grave for other people, Edna felt like bursting into tears. She was extremely disappointed that nothing was coming through from her son. It was during an extra-long pause that Esme looked directly at her and as their eyes locked Edna saw the woman's features shimmer and change. She gripped William's hand fearfully and cried out in alarm, at which point, she later said, the Medium's face became normal again, but in those few seconds Edna had seen Anthony. He was gazing at her with a kind of eager intensity she remembered from his babyhood.

The medium gave her a few minutes to recover, and then confirmed, "You saw your son, didn't you?"

When Edna nodded, she said, "He wants you to enjoy life again and remember the good years. He promises that you will one day discover everything you wish to know with or without seeking for it. He knows you will never forget him and says he is often with you. God bless you both."

The service ended with the Lord's Prayer and an air of excitement – everyone was impatient to hear what Edna actually witnessed for herself and Esme said she obviously had the gift and if she wanted to develop it, there were classes.

Many times during the last ten years, Edna was often tempted to do as the medium suggested. By developing whatever ESP she possessed, she might have been able to see her son again, or even speak to him, but William would not hear of it. He didn't doubt her sincerity and that she'd had the vision of some sort, but the idea of her becoming more deeply involved in such a strange religion frightened him.

William and Edna often looked at the little things that Anthony had left behind: his school exercise books and scrap book pictures of his favourite things. They played records from his collection and had his attempts at painting framed. The only thing they tried not to do was mourn; they clung to the promise that one day, his disappearance would be explained.

l7 – Polly

Polly sat in the waiting room while Sarah discussed Clarrie's condition with the medical team. On arrival at the Hospital in Oxford Clarrie was almost dead. Only the efficiency of the ambulance crew saved her life. Polly took great consolation in the fact that they were in Oxfordshire's main accident and emergency unit; Clarrie could not be in better hands. After emergency treatment in the Trauma unit she was taken into Intensive Care and Sarah was informed that there was nothing anyone could do now but wait and hope that, when she regained consciousness, her brain would not be damaged; when and if, Sarah thought, trembling, unable to push away the fear. Clarinda had sustained heavy blows to the back of her head and until the swelling went down it was difficult to assess the long-term damage.

Whilst sitting at Clarrie's bedside for over half an hour before being invited to join the doctors in conference, Sarah concentrated all her thoughts on trying to reach her telepathically. They were not able really to converse in such a clever way, but intense thought usually resulted in a turn of the head in her direction if they were together, or a phone call within minutes. It was never a case of, "You were thinking of me, what did you want to talk about!" ... just a natural, albeit unplanned decision to ring up. Now, all she could sense was an emptiness; it was as if all the lines were cut, so Sarah tried to prepare herself for bad news.

Re-joining Polly, Sarah shook her head slightly, holding back the tears that threatened to spill down her over-pallid cheeks.

18 – Clive

Clive attempted to keep a low profile all day. He wanted to know what people were saying about the attack on the artist and, more particularly, what kind of rumours were going around about the picture she was painting but didn't want to be drawn into discussing either. He was not rid of it yet – it was still in his car boot and would have to stay there until he could burn it with the garden rubbish. With this in mind he was cutting a few branches off bushes and trimming the hedges. As he worked he worried ceaselessly about the condition of the girl he'd left for dead. Nobody held out much hope that she would recover fully – loss of memory was almost inevitable, even if she had much of a brain left.

It was a comforting thought, but he seriously considered getting into the hospital and making sure that she didn't come out alive. On the other hand, there was no way she could have seen his face, so he dismissed the idea. If she did recover enough to remember that she was planning to blackmail him, how could she accuse him without admitting her own guilt? Admittedly, his was the greater crime but having seen the lengths to which he would go to keep her quiet, she would surely keep her mouth shut. For now, he decided it was safer to do nothing.

19 – Bobby

When Bobby's mother first heard about his plan to produce a copy of the missing painting, she was amused.

On second thoughts, remembering how impressed the policewoman was by Bobby's powers of observation, she surprised her son by suggesting that they go immediately while the daylight was still good and he could do his homework later. Bobby's face lit up with delight when she told him to ring Joe to say that he was going straight away, then fell a little when she put on her coat, and announced that she would go with them. She said that, until the attacker was caught, nobody should wander alone in deserted spots, especially off-beaten tracks like the hilltop. At least, he was pleased to note that she picked up a magazine and her Walkman, which meant that she would have something to do and would not interfere with them.

Joe met them outside within five minutes of receiving Bobby's call. His arms were so full of drawing paper, chalks and pencils that his mother, Stella, came hurrying after him with a plastic shopping bag, stopping frequently to pick up bits that fell in his wake. "It is good of you, Pam, to go up there with them," she called to Bobby's mother, "Otherwise I wouldn't have let Joe go until I could get away myself. It seems really important to them to re-create the picture and I admit I'm looking forward to seeing what they come up with. I didn't see the original, did you?"

Pamela said she hadn't and declared that she was equally intrigued. "We'd better get on with the job then," she told the boys, adding to Stella that they would not be gone longer than an hour. As they walked along, Pam noticed that Bobby's 'twitch', as she and his father, Jake, used to call it, was back again. When about three-years-old he used to keep glancing suddenly left or right, so they consulted a doctor but nothing appeared to be wrong with him, thank goodness. As he grew older, it happened less often and those worrying months were almost forgotten. Now, Pam was alarmed when his head jerked sideways and he stared into the empty bus shelter.

Seeing that she was watching, Bobbie shrugged and said he thought he'd seen a rat running across the bench. He had learned very quickly to cover up his sightings after being dragged for examinations in hospital. Sensing his parents' anxiety, in spite of all the smiles, he did his best to please them by pretending to be normal. The whole episode convinced him that he was anything but normal and the longer he could hide the fact the better. Even Joe wasn't aware of his secret, which was a shame really, because he could see Joe's great-grandfather, sitting now where he used to sit so often in life – smoking his pipe, ready to chat with anyone getting on or off the bus. He wasn't smiling though, like he used to, he looked really worried as his eyes lingered on Joe.

20 – Edna

Edna Daniels was replacing their most treasured mementos of Anthony in the chest of drawers in the spare bedroom. She thought again that it would have been his room had he lived. She was not stupid – she knew, really, that by now he certainly would have had a place of his own, and probably a wife.

On the dressing table she propped the framed photograph of him: the one taken when he left: the last photo on the last day in the last few moments she had shared with her son on earth. It was strange, but recently there were changes in the way she thought of him. Since the beginning of the month, she had sensed her mood lightening. It was as if Anthony himself were with her, exuding optimism.

After seeing him in the features of a stranger all those years ago, Edna would have liked to learn more and go to a séance perhaps, but she would not act against William's wishes. Instead, she read every book she could find on the subject.

One aspect that fascinated her was Psychometry. Psychics receive impressions from things just by holding them. The whole history of any object is there to read if you have the gift. The aura of past owners clings to things somehow. She tried many times with her mother's old jewellery and possessions around the house, but felt nothing other than stupid, so soon gave up the idea. Certainly holding Tony's photograph could not work like that because he had not owned or touched it; he'd never even seen it!

Yet merely gazing at the old black and white photo soothed and encouraged Edna – as if it were actually doing its best to tell her something, but she was not clever enough to understand.

21 - Sarah

The booking for Sarah and Polly's hotel rooms was open-ended because there was no knowing how long they would be staying.

Until Clarrie's condition improved, neither of them could contemplate returning home. Polly's niece, Pat, was quite capable of taking care of the house and dealing with concerned enquirers.

They spent most of each day at Clarrie's bedside, taking it in turns to have a change of scene and refreshment.

Talking to each other and including her in the conversation was easier than speaking when alone, to the non-responsive, unfamiliar figure lying beside them.

After almost a week, the bruising was fading and reduced swelling enabled x-rays to confirm that the brain damage was not as extensive as had been feared.

There was nothing Sarah could achieve at the hospital and Polly knew how utterly frustrated she must feel. "We can't expect a sudden recovery so why don't you visit the village where Clarrie was staying? You say there are many questions you would like to ask, especially at the house where she was lodging. We can keep in touch by telephone," Polly added, when she saw a shadow of doubt cross Sarah's face.

It was true, Sarah thought. There was no getting through to Clarinda and the more she tried and failed the more frantic she felt. The thought that her beloved daughter would never be normal again made Sarah scream inwardly with fear and rage against the monster who attacked her. Polly was right. Today, according to Alec, the police were no nearer than they were on Saturday to finding out what happened on the hill.

There were no similar incidents reported in Greater Peasey, Lesser Peasey or New Peasey during the preceding week and nobody they questioned could remember any kind of conflict in connection to 'the lady artist'.

Not many people communicated with her at all because she arrived by car only a couple of days before the attack. There was some kind of mystery surrounding the picture though, which was deepening because the easel was empty and the painting was nowhere to be found.

The removal of the painting immediately grabbed Sarah's interest.

Being familiar with the way Clarinda worked she knew that there could have been very little on it, so she told Alec that they should look for a sketch, thinly painted with spirit rather than oils.

How could it have any value at such an early stage? It was the obvious place to start her own search for answers so she agreed to leave Polly at the hospital and do something positive to help the police. Alec was delighted and said he would arrive within the hour to pick up Sarah. After collecting anything necessary from her hotel, they could drive to Mrs Lynch's house, where he was sure there would be a room Sarah could rent.

His closing comment as he rang off was that he was expected at the village cop-shop anyway to see some kind of drawing two kids had done. "They say that they saw Clarrie's painting and it is a true copy".

Sarah's pulse raced. Alec sounded amused but she sensed that it was significant and was more eager than ever to start her quest.

22 – Sgt Harris

The desk sergeant who accepted the drawing from Joe and Bobby at the police station was impressed. He already knew that according to people who saw the picture being painted, it was nothing like the valley, but there was so much detail in the drawing that it was difficult to credit the youngsters with such good memories. After the boys left, somebody at the counter commented that she saw the original and there was nowhere near as much in it, causing the sergeant to wonder. Written on the bottom of the drawing (because although Joe could draw, his English wasn't up to much apparently) Bobby had written… 'This is what we remember about the picture the lady was painting on the hill. She was very nice to us and we hope you catch the crook that did it'. The critic pointed to the time and said, "I went by where she was painting too, hours later, on Saturday afternoon, and there was less to see then than there is in this, by a long chalk."

Having taken the woman's name as a potential witness, Sgt Harris wrote a note questioning its accuracy, to attach to it in the file. What would kids get up to next? He was annoyed; they should be taught that wasting police time is an offence.

23 – Bobby & Joe

Joe was even less happy when they left the police station, than he was before they handed in his drawing. Everything he remembered was in it before he asked Bobby to check it. He was quite sure that every part of it was right until Bobby kept jogging his memory. His protestations brought them closer to falling out than they had ever been before and he was so upset at the prospect that he gave in. He accepted that Bobby was cleverer and probably right, but he was better than Bobby at art and it puzzled him, how he could have missed so much that was in the real painting?

When Joe began to draw, Bobby turned away. He was jubilant but did not want to look at it until Joe said it was finished. There was nothing to occupy him other than watching people moving across the open parkland below. He stared at the housing estate wondering why the lady hadn't painted it properly; it wasn't that awful. Gradually, the buildings went fuzzy and seemed to melt away... It felt like a dream. Slowly, he realised that he was seeing what the artist had seen. There was plenty of time to take in the strange scene before Joe declared his drawing complete. It was therefore inevitable that Bobby's recent vision should obscure his memory of the painting.

Knowing he was right, he over-rode all Joe's objections to including things that he couldn't remember himself, until it came to the group of figures in the middle, close to where there was somebody digging. Joe protested that the only figure was the digger and flatly refused to add more until, eventually, Bobby convinced him that he must have run away just as the artist was scribbling the others in. Bobby prevaricated without a qualm, sure he was doing the right thing because the man with the yellow back-pack was standing nearby, nodding and smiling happily.

24 – Grace

A speck of colour swam in the depths.

Where? A mind, a brain, a head, a body: somewhere, from a swirl of foggy grey, emerged a dim light but before it could be grasped it was gone. Like a kaleidoscope, disconnected fragments lay in darkness until glimmers of light gave symmetry to each in turn, but the pattern was obscure. If the pieces could be separated – held – examined, they might have meaning but the desire to do so was absent and interest faded. The meaningless, shimmering flakes sank into oblivion as death hovered...

"She's gone, I know it. Why in Heaven's name don't they just switch these damn machines off?"

A nurse, catching the words as she entered the private ward, frowned and took it upon herself to answer. "I'm sure the doctor has explained that although the patient needs careful monitoring and is on a life support machine, she might start functioning on her own at any moment." Seeing the woman's pale, distraught face and the pain in her eyes, her tone softened. "Don't give up hope. Her body has healed and her brain could recover too. Talk to her. No-one can be sure whether she hears or not but, if she can, familiar voices speaking about everyday things will draw her back to life."

Polly, who was returning to Clarrie's bedside after a short break, heard the raised voices as she walked along the corridor.

"I've been coming for weeks – we all have – talking, talking, talking but she just lies there! I can't take it much longer. I want her back, God knows! If only we could be sure that it would work, I would move in with her and talk 'til I dropped, but it seems so hopeless." Grace Weston released her sister Amy's hand, placing it carefully as the nurse moved around the bed, getting on with her job, caring for her patient. "Sonja will be here soon, so I think I'll leave now," Grace added firmly as she stood and moved the chair away decisively, not wishing to be dissuaded.

"Ah! Miss Amy's friend: only just started coming hasn't she – has she been away? I thought I'd met all her family and friends over the last three months." Nurse Dawes seldom allowed herself to form opinions about visitors but Sonja Norris was so obviously devoted to the lifeless Amy that it puzzled her – why had she not been around until a week ago?

Grace buttoned up her coat, tucking a silk scarf in at the collar, not because it was cold outside but because it looked good; preserving her personal appearance was an important boost to her morale; if Amy opened her eyes Grace did not want to shame her by looking a wreck. "Sonja is an old school friend," she eventually replied. "She's been working in Spain for a year or two and didn't hear about poor Amy until she came over on holiday… Can't think what she has to talk to Amy about though, they've been out of touch for ages, but every little helps I suppose! She promised to be here at four-o-clock and surely she wouldn't dare be late after all her proclamations of concern…"

Wouldn't dare. DARE. You dare… Bright light, green gold, bodies bobbing, slipping sliding, burbling bubbling, soaring swaying…

Floating fragments like a frayed jigsaw came

together briefly... spinning slowly... rising falling, fading – almost matching, drifting away, always out of focus... Half-hearted attempts to understand the image, to comprehend and hold, failed and were abandoned.

Grace kissed Amy's forehead and whispered a few words of farewell. It was difficult to hold back her tears and her eyes were still moist when she almost bumped into Polly, who had just reached and opened the door to Clarrie's room. She composed herself enough to apologise and saw that there was a patient inside. Polly obviously wasn't a nurse so she said she hoped the person she was visiting was showing more response than her sister. Before long Polly heard the whole sad story of Amy's fall, from the top floor of a multi-storey car park.

Polly was warm-hearted and a good listener – never butting in or looking impatient – never fidgeting or letting her eyes wander. Her response was natural, not contrived, and people in trouble sensed that her sympathy was real. She was also sensitive to atmosphere and could tell that the woman, whose arrival broke up the conversation, was not high on Grace Weston's list of favourites.

Grace told the newcomer that there was no change in her sister and that their brother Gordon was coming with his wife later. She introduced Sonja Norris and then, turning to Sonja, said, "We mustn't hold you up. You'll no doubt be eager to go in and talk to Amy as you must have been delayed."

Leaving Polly, Grace said she was sure they'd meet again. Suddenly aware of how much she had told of her own troubles and how little interest she had shown in anyone else's woes, she added that she hoped Polly's young friend would respond to treatment more quickly than Amy, stressing, in order not to sound too depressing, that most people did. Sonja did not linger. After an apology for being late and a wry smile at Polly, she walked on to the next room with scarcely a pause in her stride.

A few minutes later Sonja was sitting near the bed patting Amy's arm and stroking her hand as she spoke of their shared childhood. As Nurse Dawes left she was reminiscing about infant school… "Do you remember the miniature house at Rose Street Kindergarten? We were allowed to dust and clean it if we came top of the class – and have tea in there before afternoon rest… The little beds were wretchedly hard and uncomfortable, but it was so exciting – much better than stretching on rubber floor mats in the gym!" Her laughter rang down the corridor as Jenny Dawes went on to her next patient. It struck Jenny that not many people could recall their infancy. Jenny certainly couldn't, in fact everything before she was nine was a total blackout. It might be a blank to Amy Weston too, but the sound of a human voice, whatever it said, was better than silence.

Amy interested her particularly. They shared the same birthday and this made Jenny more acutely aware of the sadness of the young woman's condition. It was bad enough to have met such a dreadful accident but initially the mystery surrounding it aroused the interest of the media. Nothing was solved, even if there had ever been a real investigation and speculation died down after a few weeks; other mysteries superseded Amy as objects of interest and gossip. Although Jenny got rid of the last reporter by promising to ring him if Amy emerged from her coma and was able to speak, it was a promise she feared she might never be in a position to keep or happily break!

25 – Polly

Polly was holding Clarrie's unresponsive hand and talking, almost shouting, about the time Clarrie nearly killed her sleeping mother with an axe, when Jenny walked in. It was difficult to say who looked the most shocked! Polly recovered first and quickly dismissed the incident as an accident when Clarrie was little, which they all regarded as funny now. It wasn't true of course, but it was preferable to saying that she'd been fully grown-up and possessed by an enraged ghost.

Jenny, reminded of her earlier thoughts, commented that perhaps that particular episode was too far back and it might be better to speak about more recent memories. "Stick with little, everyday things that she did often… Something that happened only once might not strike a chord, if you see what I mean. Of course," she added quickly, not wanting to sound discouraging, "just hearing your familiar voice might bring her back to us."

Polly had been with the Grey family for many years and known Clarrie's father, Stephen, before he met and married Sarah. She was with Sarah when Clarrie was born and looked after the child alongside her own daughter when Stephen and Sarah were absent. In spite of the ten-year age difference, the two girls were good friends.

Alone with Clarrie again, Polly took Jenny's advice and actually found it much easier to speak aloud about past events. "When you were little," she began, "you loved to hear over and over again, how I was named after a parrot... I was only nineteen when I went to work as a housemaid in your Grandparents house and every morning, when I took the cover off the parakeet's cage, I said 'Hello Polly'. It was a really lovely bird but it never spoke until it started saying the same to me, every time it saw me." Polly laughed aloud at the memory. "Of course, everyone started calling me Polly, and I really liked it. I'd never been happy being Gertrude anyway, and it made me feel accepted, and really at home."

Polly went on in this vein for well over an hour, wondering if any of what she said was penetrating the dreadful swathe of silence that clung closely around the still figure on the bed before her. Continuing seemed pointless but it was the only way she could help for now, so after clearing her throat and taking a sip of orange juice, she took up the tale from where she'd left off... "As soon as you were old enough to hold a brush, you used to love painting alongside your father. You were given your own little easel – but my goodness, what a mess you used to make!"

As her own memories rushed back, Polly almost broke down. Whoever had done this to Clarrie, and inflicted such pain on Sarah must be caught soon, and punished. Hanging should never have been abolished she fumed, but life on earth could be the worst hell if you crossed the wrong people and she smiled grimly, knowing that by injuring Clarrie, somebody had!

26 – Sarah

On the way to Lesser Peasey Alec assured Sarah that he was in contact with Del Delaney. He had succeeded in convincing him that there was absolutely no point in hurtling back to be with Clarrie; as soon as she showed the slightest sign of awareness, Alec promised to get word to Del immediately, through his news desk here in the UK. "I had to send a uniform in, to convince the editor that there was good reason why his 'Man on the Ground' should be contacted, not by him or any of his staff, but by me, personally. He eventually agreed as long as he didn't have to reveal which story was being covered." Alec sighed and commented further on the media; what a cutthroat business it is these days. Sarah was satisfied when she heard that Del would telephone the hospital directly every day, and speak to either herself or Polly. His editor also promised Del that a reporter would cover police progress and help in any way possible.

Sarah hoped that they were doing the right thing by advising Del to stay away. Clarinda was not at death's door now and although she and Del planned to marry when his present assignment ended, they knew each other for barely three months before he went away. The few memories they had in common were immensely important to share, but not likely to be deeply embedded, and Sarah could not bear the thought of time perhaps being wasted. In any case, Sarah felt instinctively that Clarinda, if she did not recover, would want Del's memories of her to be untainted by her deathlike appearance in a hospital bed.

Alec's deep resonant voice broke into Sarah's thoughts as he informed her that they were almost there. "In a few minutes," he said, "we'll be on the road into Lesser Peasey, with the hill where Clarrie was painting on our left. If you'd like to see where the attack took place, before it gets dark, I'll park where we found her car – in a little lay-by near the bus stop."

Sarah could not help a smile of satisfaction as she nodded. How well Alec knew her! He didn't need to confess that he was as anxious as she was herself to see if anything significant occurred to her while standing in the exact location where Clarinda had been painting. They could only hope. Alec was well aware that Sarah never asked for contact with the spirit world. She could subdue her inhibitions, be open-minded and willing to accept impressions but regarded herself as a tool, to be used. To this end, she always 'tuned in' by asking that only forces for good would be permitted to approach and prayed that they would keep evil at bay.

"It's a bit of a slope up the hill, but not far to the top," Alec told her as he parked. Hesitantly, when he helped her out of the car he asked, "Shall I come with you, or would you prefer to be alone? The area has been examined thoroughly and every trace of anything out of place in the immediate area had been removed for examination." When Sarah said that after recent events she would feel safer with him beside her and more able to relax, he followed up with another question; "Well, as a matter of fact, I just happen to have with me this pocket tape recorder. Would you mind if I switched it on?"

Sarah stared at the tiny black box. Alec could so easily have used it without telling her and the fact that he disdained to do so filled her with satisfaction. She knew she could always feel safe with him.

Taking his arm, Sarah walked purposefully up the stony track.

27 - Clive

At the village police station, they were discussing the merits of the boys' drawing. "Might as well tear it up," was the general opinion.

Clive was doing his best to see the drawing without being obvious, but it wasn't easy, as the sergeant was holding it below desk level and waving it about in his agitation. "We've got top brass coming in later tonight, just to see this. I'd better get hold of somebody to stop him – sheer waste of time and we'll look like gullible fools." He stopped ranting when he saw that there was a 'customer' waiting... "Evening, Mr Parker, what can we do for you?" After a short exchange, establishing that Clive wanted to report a lost briefcase, Sergeant Harris put the picture down next to his half-consumed coffee and moved away to check the report book, to see if one had been handed in. Although it was upside down, Clive could see that the coloured drawing was far more detailed than the painting, which was now a pile of ashes in his incinerator. He was shocked. Harris started to say that no case of any kind had been handed in, and turned to face Clive, whose face was white. "Oh, I'm sorry, sir, were the contents valuable?"

It wasn't easy to sound convincing when he said it wasn't leather and almost empty but was of great sentimental value. Idiot, he berated himself; who could get sentimental over a plastic bag!

He was a fool to have come in. It was only because the family was buzzing about young Joe and his mate helping the police that made him risk it. It was just his rotten luck that Joe was involved at all – but at least it should be easy to quiz him about where he'd seen the things he drew. He had to find out, because the only theory Clive could come up with was that it was copied from a plan the woman must have made. But where could they have found it? It wasn't with her, he knew, and it couldn't have been in her room either, otherwise the police would have found it and wouldn't need Joe's. Not that Joe's was quite so legible now, having had the dregs of a coffee cup spilled over it as it blew onto the muddy floor. Understandably upset over his non-existent case, Clive had knocked the drink over. "Never mind sir, I don't think we could have relied on its accuracy in a court of law!"

Once outside again, instead of walking home, Clive decided to pop into the Wench's Arms; a drink might calm him and there was always the chance of picking up more gossip. He needed to know that the woman was dead. While she lived, even in a coma, he would never feel safe. At any moment, she could come out of it and even though she hadn't seen him behind her, she might name him as the only person who might have wanted to kill her. Would she be able to tell them about his appalling past without admitting that she was holding it over his head, probably for money? As if he had any! That would definitely start rumours start flying; 'no smoke without fire' they would say. Once the older villagers started gossiping about the farm and his family there would be no stopping them, and no knowing what might come out. Family! That was a good one. His teenage mother abandoned him, leaving him with her own widowed mother and, when she died, Ben was taken into care.

He was only two years old when handed straight

over to foster parents. Soon after his third birthday, the local authority discovered that his grandmother had a younger sister, so the child's earliest memory was of being carried away from a tearful foster-mother. At first reluctant to take him in, the sister's husband eventually relented and accepted responsibility for him. For a while his life as Ben Gleasey was monitored by official visitors who always went away happy after he told them that he was 'very well thank you'. When he started school the visits stopped and the Gleaseys accepted that he was theirs and there to stay, but neither of them ever showed him a grain of affection. Glenda walked him across the fields on his first day, to join other Mixed Infants, as the sign over the Gate announced. She pointed to the door and told him that he must go in that way, every day.

After the first few weeks, Glenda gave him a glass of milk and a slice of home-made bread before waving him on his way from the kitchen door. When he proved to be reliable – always returning when expected, never being a nuisance, she usually carried on with her household chores while he made his own breakfast. She sometimes praised him for being such a clever boy, but never once hugged him. Clive could understand now how, from her point of view, she must have felt only relief that her husband had no reason to complain about taking in her sister's grandchild.

As he grew older, they both lost interest in whether he was educated or not. Even at seven-years-old, he was a strong lad and enjoyed doing anything around the smallholding so they encouraged him to feed the chickens, collect eggs and keep the hen house clean. They were glad of his help. He soon realised that they were not rich and was quite proud that he was helping to grow things to sell – making money was much better than school. When truant officers called as he grew older, the Gleaseys were more than willing to lie for him… even saying he was away, staying with relatives. Perhaps, if war had not broken out in 1939, his absence would have caused comment, but the staff changed constantly. Some were called up to serve in the armed forces and temporary teachers came and went.

The only drawback was that Ben hardly dared show his face outside the house and no friends came to play with him. He kept out of the way when people approached the house and if anyone did see him in the distance, Art and Glenda pretended he was a visiting nephew, "Doing a bit of land-work to help the war effort," Art would say: "Digging for Victory, as the posters tell us all to do!"

It began to dawn on Ben that he wasn't truly part of a real family. The radio was his constant companion and he looked forward every day to BBC Children's Hour. He never missed Toytown or Out with Romany and was fascinated to hear messages passing between kids his own age and their Dads who were away fighting Hitler. He knew nothing of that kind of love and began to feel deprived. Ben felt closer to Uncle Mac, who always came on at five-o-clock, than he did to Art, but in spite of everything, he never thought of running away. In comparison to what happened later, they were halcyon days.

Clive's mood mellowed as he reflected on those early years. After his fourth whisky he began to wonder; did it really matter if people were reminded what was in the valley before the buildings mushroomed? More than likely, the comatose woman would remain brain dead, even if the rest of her survived. Until he knew her fate, he would stop worrying about his own.

28 – Sarah

It was well after ten when Alec left Sarah at Doris Lynch's house. He had already made sure that there would be a room for her and after he carried her suitcase upstairs, Doris left them to talk privately together for a while, in what she called her parlour.

Sarah knew that Alec was sensible enough not to have expected a dramatic revelation but was sure he must have been disappointed. Standing where Clarinda was attacked so savagely, she saw and felt nothing other than a natural revulsion as her imagination took over. Sarah, in fact, was scared that she might experience again the agony that had stunned her, leading to her collapse from the terrible force of the blows. Her fear could well have created a barrier, or perhaps she needed Clarinda to be sentient in order to receive anything significant about those violent moments.

A knock on the door interrupted her thoughts and Sarah realised that the landlady must want her room back, so as she answered she stood and retrieved the few things she'd brought in with her from the car. Doris, realising that Sarah felt obligated to leave, immediately protested. "Please don't feel you have to stay in your bedroom – I do expect guests to use the whole house – not that the kitchen has much to fear in that respect, but I'm always willing to stop for a cup of tea or coffee if they stick their head round the door...

Oh dear, here's me rattling on and on when you must just want a bit of peace, being so worried about your daughter."

Thank goodness she needed to take a breath, Sarah thought, but she said politely that she appreciated Mrs Lynch's hospitality. In fact, Sarah had been hoping for a chance to learn everything she could about Clarinda's last day so she gladly accepted the offer of staying to enjoy a cup of hot cocoa.

They were soon on first name terms and once Doris heard that Sarah had already walked up to the place where her daughter was almost killed she was astonished, declaring that she could see no point in punishing herself; after all, she couldn't undo anything that happened. "And now it will be more difficult to put it behind you," she admonished, "You have to believe that she will get better."

It was not long before Sarah was hearing about the stir that the painting had caused, but Doris said she never saw it herself. She wished she'd taken more interest now, but she was never good at art when she was at school not like little Joe Biggs, grandson of the Parkers from next door, who is brilliant and has just done a drawing of it from memory...

Sarah found herself holding her breath as she waited for a break in the endless stream of words: the painting: that was what she wanted to ask about. What was there about it that caught people's attention? Had anyone in particular shown more interest than others? So many questions, so little time – and still Doris was in full flow. "...Joe's granddad is so proud of him, well, he and Betty both are, naturally, and he says, when the police have finished with it he wants to have it framed to hang on his wall. I told Clive I wouldn't be surprised if it was worth a good sum of money after being connected to a real crime..."

A strange feeling of foreboding swept over Sarah. She was tired and worried, and frustrated by her unusual inability to get to grips with any part of the mystery. Seeing the sudden change in Sarah's demeanour, Doris finally stopped, apologised, and helped Sarah to take the rest of her things upstairs. Tomorrow: Yes, tomorrow: the embryo of an idea seemed to be lurking in the dark recesses of Sarah's brain, only needing a spark of encouragement to grow. Tomorrow she must see the drawing, which Alec must have seen by now at the local police station. After ringing to tell them he was on his way, he had been quite dismissive of it, saying that it was obviously not possible for the boys to have seen even half of what was in it. In spite of his disappointment, Sarah was determined to examine it personally. Something was telling her that the drawing held the key.

29 – Edna

Edna and William did not celebrate their wedding anniversary on the twenty-eighth of May. They had never done so since Anthony disappeared. The greeting card, which accompanied the flowers he arranged to be delivered to them just after he left, was among their collection of memorabilia. Silly really, thought Edna: it was from a florist; Tony had not written it himself. Still, it was a reminder of his thoughtfulness and every little memory was worth saving. It was Friday the fourth of June today. Next Friday, the eleventh, would have been his birthday. They'd had a card ready to give him in 1951, because he'd planned to be back in time to celebrate it with them, and that too, they had kept. Every time she held it Edna felt sad and angry. If only there was a grave where they could put flowers and at least feel, in a way, that he was still close, perhaps they wouldn't need all the silly little things they clung to in lieu. She was sick and tired of the way years dragged by and nothing changed; this year was going to be different; she would make it different.

As soon as Will came in from the garden, Edna decided to lose no time in putting her idea forward and convincing him that it might bring a kind of closure and final acceptance that Anthony would never return home.

30 – Polly

Polly's mind kept wandering as she tried to keep up the continuous monologue at Clarrie's bedside. Instead of going over their shared past, she found herself speaking aloud about more recent things. "The hammering in the night, which I heard too, although it was happening in your mother's dream …gracious me, that really was amazing. It means that I am clairaudient. How about that? And your mother knew, the very second you were attacked. She felt everything you felt, and it must have been terrible, the pain you were in, because she passed out and I had to send for the doctor."

As the words came out, Polly felt that perhaps she should not have uttered them. If they were getting through to Clarrie, in spite of everything, they might be upsetting, so she added hurriedly, "There is a word for it your mother told me. It's called mirror-touch syn something…synesthopia – no, wrong, synesthetica – no! I should have written it down. It means that one person feels pain experienced by another… Oh, never mind." As she gave up, two things happened in the same instant. The correct word, synesthesia, popped into her head and Clarrie's eyelids began to move.

31 - Alec & Algy

Back in his office, the morning after leaving Sarah, Alec lifted the tape recorder out of his briefcase and put it back in the desk drawer. He could rewind it later. There was certainly no point in listening to it, he thought regretfully. Privately he would have bet money on there being a long queue of Sarah's guardian angels, falling over each other with enthusiasm to avenge the brutal attack on her daughter.

Detective Inspector Algy Green knocked and entered the open door interrupting Alec's train of thought, which was going nowhere anyway. "Any chance of borrowing your recorder, sir," he asked, "mine just bit the dust - good job I'd already been through the tape because I dropped it when I removed it and it unrolled the length of the corridor. "Dee and White between them managed to mangle it underfoot as they walked over it, so please don't suggest I rewind it!"

Alec laughed, "I admit we're trying to keep down expenses but I think we'll call it written-off assuming that that's what you did when you checked it." Rather a good pun he thought, with satisfaction. Of the many officers who had been under his command throughout the last ten years, Alec had managed to keep three men with him. They were not the most senior, but DI Algy Green and the two Detective Sergeants, John Dee and Terry White, formed a special team, and he would find an excuse to send them together to Lesser Peasey. All three had worked with Sarah in the past and, unlike the local police, would value any hints that she could hand out. Retrieving his recorder from the drawer, he handed it to Algy, and told him that it needed rewinding because he'd tried to 'record' his visit to the crime scene with Sarah – and no, she'd hardly spoken and hadn't seen or heard anything, so there'll be nothing on it, not even much traffic, he sighed.

As soon as Algy left, Alec rang the hospital and, to his surprise and relief, heard that Clarrie had shown a tiny spark of life, and the swellings on her head were going down. Without hesitation he instructed that the information must not be given out to anyone else, and not discussed outside the patients room. His next call was to Sarah.

32 – John & Terry

John Dee and Terry White were elated to be on the case, even unofficially. They knew how much district police forces resented city detectives poking their noses in, as if they were incompetent hicks… On Friday evening, as they sifted through copies of the remarkably little information gathered by Alec at Lesser Peasey, they were taken aback to discover that from Day 1, almost no progress at all was evident on any lines of enquiry.

Discovering the victim's identity seemed to have taken precedence over finding out who bashed her over the head. Originally handwritten, as notes on scrap paper, were several suggestions as to possible motives which, knowing Clarrie, they dismissed as ludicrous. The first, that she might be having an affair with somebody's husband and was attacked by a jealous wife, had been crossed out. *'Unlikely, owing to ferocity of attack'* was written against it by another hand. 'Robbery' had a question mark against it because only the painting was removed, but the first writer suggested either that it was valuable or that another artist was jealous. In the other handwriting this suggestion was crossed out twice, and just one word added alongside: *Rubbish.*

"We both know Clarrie well enough to guess that whatever she did to upset somebody was unintentional and unlikely to have happened before she started out on her trip." Terry volunteered, and John Dee agreed.

"So we need to ask Sarah what places Clarrie has visited since leaving home and if she mentioned anyone she might have met en-route,"

"According to the Super," John said, "Sarah endured everything that happened at the very moment it took place. Imagine that! The pain must have been excruciating, no wonder she passed out." Inevitably, they started reminiscing about old cases where Sarah's prowess had enabled them to wind up cases more quickly than they would have done otherwise. Often, her assurance that they were on the right track was enough to avoid wasting precious time. One thing was certain; with a wrathful Sarah on his track – the villain didn't stand a chance of escaping. There was nowhere on earth he could hide. Pointing upwards, John added, "Too many eyes on him, as we speak, all screaming for revenge!"

33 – Sarah

Before Alec's call on Saturday morning, Sarah had already heard from Polly, that Clarinda was showing a faint flicker of life. The doctors were pleased but were still not optimistic about any rapid improvement in her condition. Even so, some of the tension ebbed away from Sarah and she started to feel hopeful about restoring the precious telepathic connection they'd always shared. After breakfast, she walked back to the hill and stood looking down at the view on the other side. Before going to the police station to see the boys drawing, she wanted to check what the valley actually looked like in daylight.

Where she stood, the ground levelled off after a short downward slope from the top and then fell away again, slightly more steeply, to the grassy parkland immediately below. It was not a formal park – it was just an open space with a few flowerbeds and colourful shrubs around the perimeter interspersed with bench seats. There were several people walking their dogs in a fenced compound on one side and it struck Sarah that the fountain in the middle, where a young boy was drinking, was probably placed with intent to prevent the ground from being used as a football pitch. There was nothing to stop people enjoying the fresh air in peace and quiet. The shopping precinct and housing estates presented a pleasing aspect and were not unattractive; it was obvious that many of the old trees were incorporated into the plans rather than being felled. Wooded areas on every side sheltered the buildings and on rising ground on the opposite side of the valley, Greater Peasey was visible.

The more she studied the terrain the keener she became to see the drawing. It was obvious to Sarah that Clarinda would not have set herself up to paint a scene from life if she intended to paint something imaginative. It therefore followed that she was seeing a vision of something that appeared to her to be real. The next probability was that by being able to see whatever it was, she frightened someone so much that they were determined to prevent her from revealing it to anyone else. The scenario sounded credible so, for the time being, she would follow it through. Without further delay Sarah walked to the Police Station arriving just as John and Terry, Alec's envoys, arrived in an unmarked car. Detective Sergeants Dee and White were in plain clothes and were obviously pleased to be able to speak to her before going in to announce their presence in the village. After expressing shock at what had happened to Clarrie, and their relief when they heard that there were hopeful signs that her condition might be improving, they suggested having coffee somewhere, before reporting in.

Eventually, when they did speak to the officer in charge of the case, they agreed with him, as recommended by Sarah, that the boys' drawing was not worth preserving as evidence, and Terry volunteered to return it to them, as tactfully as possible of course, so as not to offend their parents or allowing them to lose face. "We certainly want to encourage youngsters to support us in our efforts to keep law and order, don't we?" he said, as he rolled it carefully and handed it to John Dee. They stayed long enough to discuss the progress of the investigation and evidence gathered, or lack of it, and eventually left, to meet Sarah again. It proved easy to take possession of the drawing because it was torn and smudged as if trampled underfoot. They were both outraged that evidence should have been so mishandled, just because a few people poured scorn on it – and coffee!

Not wishing to discuss anything in public, they took advantage of Doris Lynch's hospitality and were in her parlour, having been introduced by Sarah as 'good friends' of her daughter, anxious for news of her. The description was apt, although they were not in constant touch and had not seen Clarrie for over a year. Terry also asked after Polly, and was glad to hear that she had recovered fully from her dreadful experience in Wales. "She was left for dead too," he reminded Dee who was away on detachment during that investigation. Before arriving at the guesthouse, they went to the hilltop and studied the view in relation to the drawing, being eager to learn why it interested Sarah. After all, they had a witness who saw the actual painting, who said that there was nowhere near as much detail in it, even several hours after the boys saw it.

Sarah tried out her theory on them and they agreed that it was worth pursuing. They reported that all who saw the painting in progress said the view used to be like that up to about thirty years ago. Some were excited by the idea that it might be for sale when finished; it reminded them of the good old days – when they were young. "So we should be looking for someone here now, who saw the painting, and didn't want anybody to be reminded about the old days," said John, and as the others nodded, he added, "so we can rule out all the witnesses who were happy, and investigate any who didn't express an opinion."

"We also have to work out who could have seen it and didn't admit it," Terry pointed out, "plus finding out who might only have heard it described and had reason to worry why on earth Clarrie was painting it in the first place: a tall order, but probably worth a try."

Sarah was pleased by their reaction and enthusiasm and asked if, through official channels, they could look into the history of the area to see if anything significant happened there before the new town was built. They were both in digs in Greater Peasey: near enough to help Sarah without attracting too much attention. Because she didn't drive, nobody would think it odd if they collected her to take her out, especially to the hospital, so they decided to compare notes during the week and they would take Sarah to visit Clarrie next Friday evening on their way back to HQ. By that time, they should have something worth reporting to Alec and Sarah would have had time to study the drawing, and perhaps even meet the two boys who were responsible for producing it, who could describe what had been in the damaged patches.

After they left, intent on starting their investigation by gossiping to the locals in the Wench's Arms, Sarah took a phone call from Del's editor. He expressed his great concern and Sarah allowed an uncharitable thought to spring into her mind – especially as his 'man on the spot' now had more to worry about than the intelligence reports, wherever he was! She relented when he asked for her personal assurance that she would ring him at any time, day or night, if there were the slightest sign that her daughter was getting worse, not better. He had promised Del that he would be flown back immediately, if necessary by private jet, and in any case, he was arranging for someone to replace him; Del's tour would be shortened by at least two months. He also asked Sarah to look out for the junior assigned to keep track of the case. "Be gentle with him," he pleaded, "he hasn't developed a thick hide yet. I thought you'd be happier with Derek Duffy because he's on the shy side and eager to do a good job: answers to the name of Plum – for obvious reasons!"

Sarah went to her room immediately after the call, refusing the offer of lunch from Doris, intent on studying the drawing. Joe's precious offering was now a sorry mess, and much of the sketch was obscured by what certainly looked like coffee stains. As this thought crossed her mind she instantly saw it, neat and clean for a fraction of a second before an arm swept across it and the back of a hand pushed over a mug. Brown liquid spilled everywhere and the arm finished its swing by pushing the drawing away out of sight. With a surge of excitement, Sarah knew that the destruction had been deliberate and the arm belonged to the man who wanted her daughter dead. Settling down with a pad, she noted everything she glimpsed in that split second. Then, holding the spoiled picture on her lap, she waited patiently to receive whatever else it might tell her.

34 – Sonja

Sonja Norris took over the sitting-session on Saturday afternoon and, as always, had to exchange condolences and reminiscences with the previous departing relative …it was tedious and she found it difficult to maintain the pretence that she and Amy had always been close when she knew next to nothing about her family. The little she did know had been learned from Nurse Dawes who was always happy to chat. Sonja would not have changed places with her for any amount of money. She could imagine nothing worse than tending to sick people, although looking after patients who couldn't answer back or complain was perhaps not so bad. After nearly two weeks of hanging about, half-expecting Amy to recover consciousness and planning what to do if she did, Sonja would not contemplate returning to Spain leaving her in a coma.

While alone with the patient Sonja filled in the time by reading magazines silently, for her own pleasure, but whenever anyone entered, they heard her reading aloud and making asides to her unresponsive friend. She found it so frustrating. If she went home now and Amy woke up, fully aware of the circumstances that had led to her fall, Sonja would be in deep trouble. She shuddered. The alternative, making sure that Amy did not recover at all, looked more attractive with every passing day in spite of the risks. She rang Raymond every night, but although sympathetic about her sick friend, he was anxious for her to return. Their June wedding, months in planning, was approaching fast and she had thought nothing could spoil her day and her wonderful future until his wealthy, ailing father had announced his own intention of marrying. His father's coming union didn't faze Raymond, but Sonja was absolutely furious. Instead of continuing to ail, the old man would marry some gold-digger and it would be goodbye fortune... It was a situation she could not contemplate and thought she had dealt with in April, by coming over, keeping a low profile. Her parents were unaware that she was in England in April and Raymond was away himself so was unaware that she had left Spain.

Everything had gone smoothly until Amy got in her way, but Sonja had coped successfully with the unexpected and felt safe in early March, after she and Raymond were together again. His father joined them for a while to benefit from the Spanish weather and to get over the heartbreaking loss of his bride-to-be. He had been pathetically grateful for her sympathy and support and Sonja had relaxed, ready to enjoy a new way of life with Raymond, or so she thought until she received a letter from her mother:

"Hello Darling,

Do you remember Amy Weston who was in your class in school? She's had a terrible accident and is in a coma..."

35 - Polly

It was teatime at the hospital when Jenny Dawes came to tell Polly that there was a visitor downstairs asking about Clarrie. He knew somebody must be with her and was confident that they would identify him as a friend and as he had specifically asked to speak with either Sarah or Polly, Jenny thought she might like to go and check him out. Leaving the nurse to inspect the various pieces of equipment surrounding and attached to Clarrie, Polly went to see the visitor who was waiting near the information desk. Jenny said it would take her at least ten minutes to finish, so Polly need not rush.

As soon as she saw the tall, broad-shouldered back of a man wearing a 'British Warm', Polly knew it was Jack Heywood Hall - retired army major and, as they often joked, almost related to her by his niece's marriage to her nephew Dan.

"I'm not here to worry you, dear lady, I assure you." Jack said as he took her hand and kissed her cheek, "I just want to remind you that I live close by and am awaiting instructions. You must let me help in any way I can." He went on to volunteer to taxi Sarah, or run errands if they needed shopping, or indeed thrash the detestable bounder who beat Clarrie, to within a millimetre of his rotten life when he was caught. Actually, he was hoping they could find him something to do to help catch him. Polly was glad to see him and suggested he return with her to sit at Clarrie's bedside for a while. Talking to somebody who could answer would be easier than talking to herself.

After he had been brought up to date on all they knew about the attack, they spoke mainly about their first meeting and the time Polly had been kidnapped in Wales, when he began to appreciate that not all mediums were fraudulent. They hardly took their eyes off Clarrie, and several times they fancied they saw a finger twitch, or even her lips tremble. Jack promised as he left eventually that, until Sarah returned, he would keep Polly company every evening for a few hours and she promised him that she would ask Sarah if there was anything specific he could do to help.

As Polly stood in the corridor, watching Jack stride away, Amy's sister emerged from the adjacent room and beckoned to her. There was still a guard keeping an eye on Clarrie's room and Polly asked him if she could get him coffee or anything. He declined, so she went to ask Grace Weston if there was any improvement in Amy's condition. It seemed that there was no change at all and Grace looked tired. Her brother and his wife were visiting Amy now, so Polly suggested that they sat in the visitors lounge and relaxed for a while; it was obvious to her that Grace wanted to talk. Polly's instincts had not let her down; before long, Grace picked up the story of Amy's accident from where she had left off.

There was a great deal of concern when it happened because it wasn't supposed to be easy for anyone to fall or jump for that matter, from the top floor of the building, so it seemed likely that she was pushed. Prior to falling, she was not injured and still had her shoulder bag wrapped over her arm, with everything intact inside, so if the motive wasn't robbery, what could it possibly be? "I can't think what Amy was doing in that area anyway, it isn't where she usually shopped," said Grace. "We had arranged to meet at the railway station and go home together. As far as I know, she had no plans other than visiting her boy-friend, here by the way, in this hospital." In answer to Polly's question, Grace said that he was a fling of the past now, and if she was pushed over the wall, it couldn't have been him – he had the perfect alibi, being still under sedation after his operation.

The implication was that the young man was a 'fair-weather' friend Polly decided, but his surgery must have made it possible to fix the time Amy left the hospital, so she asked Grace how much time her sister would have had to fill before their meeting. The police had asked the same question so Grace said without hesitation that she would have had just over an hour to shop somewhere. That was the puzzle. As she did not have a car with her, and would need a taxi, why, unless someone gave her a lift, did she go several miles in the opposite direction from the rail station to an unfamiliar shopping Mall rather than visit one en-route to their meeting place? Grace added that, by coincidence, Nurse Dawes had been a witness; she remembered seeing Amy walk out of the main entrance alone.

Polly determined to ask Jenny for a first-hand account. It was surprising how much people remembered when there was no pressure – no police officer conducting the questioning. There was one thing in particular that worried Grace – perhaps it wasn't so much that it was really worrying, but it was puzzling and faintly irritating. "If it wasn't something of a relief having an extra sitter for Amy, I would question Sonja more closely about their friendship," Grace confided. "Amy hasn't mentioned her, or given her any thought at all as far as I know, for donkeys' years, yet anyone would think they were bosom friends, the way she devotes so much time to visiting." After a short pause, Grace added, "In fact, I would have laid odds that they were never anything more than casual acquaintances."

Grace had little to add other than the fact that Sonja lived in Spain and implied that she had returned specifically when she heard about Amy's accident. Polly could understand why Grace was perturbed and asked if Grace would mind if she somehow contrived to meet and talk to Sonja, to see if she could find out more about her. Grace was ecstatic. It was clear that having enlisted Polly as an ally she felt less fraught and she said, as she departed, that she would look forward to chatting again tomorrow.

Polly welcomed the challenge of another puzzle to take her mind off more personal worries about which she could do nothing. Who wanted Clarrie dead, and why? Her mind turned the mystery over and over ceaselessly in circles and she would welcome anything to stop it. Until Sarah returned, there was nothing specific she could contribute to solving it, so for the moment, Polly would try to help Amy and Grace.

36 – Edna

Edna had tried to conceal her impatience when her husband's immediate reaction to her plan was a flat rejection. He was never happy to leave home, even for a day – but Edna stayed calm and told him how much she longed to do something. Trying to follow in Tony's footsteps – hoping to share his last experiences on earth, they could pretend he was with them; what harm could it do? William finally gave in; holidays were something other people had, not them, but he could see how much it meant to Edna. Perhaps she was right, so he suggested they tackle the venture methodically and plan every detail before acting on it.

Edna was thrilled. No TV tonight! They would work out a route immediately after dinner and take as long as they needed to visit the places their son had described and follow the roads he walked, not on foot of course, but they would recognise the things that must have attracted him and stay as long as they wanted. If they spoke about him, some older folk might even remember meeting him. It was a tall order but even William regretted that they hadn't done years ago what Edna was suggesting now. It was unlikely that they would have saved him from whatever fate had dealt out, but they might have found who had been the hand of fate and the bastard would have hanged for it. The arrival of his meal interrupted his thoughts and in order to speed up proceedings he helped to clear the table afterwards and went to find some maps while

Edna washed up. By the time Edna joined him again William was ready to start planning the route they would take.

He had started writing notes leaving space between the lines for any changes or additions and on the floor beside him, he had Anthony's box, to jog their memories.

On the left, William listed the places from which cards were posted during the last few weeks of his son's life.

He spaced them according to the number of days between each postmark and, using the maps, they filled in all the places that linked them, which Anthony had mentioned either on the postcards or on the phone. Alongside, using an ordnance survey map, they recorded the tracks he would most likely have followed.

Finally, they tried to recall anything that Tony might have spoken of in the past as being interesting and that could have tempted him to divert slightly.

It was midnight before they finished and William had become as enthusiastic as Edna about the trip. It wasn't that their memory collection would become obsolete… Rather, it would attain added value, padded out and given substance by their personal experiences, which still lay ahead.

Edna was so excited that she couldn't sleep. In her head she was writing mental lists of all she had to do tomorrow: stop deliveries, inform friends and neighbours that they were going away, clear the fridge of fresh food and make sure they had address and telephone records with them in the car. Finally, tired but happier than she had been for a long while, she fell into a deep dreamless sleep, holding the framed picture against her heart… The following morning it was back in place on her dressing table.

She had no recollection of removing it.

Unseen, Anthony shook his head affectionately... she really needed looking after and his face broke into a smile as he drifted away.

37 – Algy

It was Saturday evening before Alec's DI, Algy Green, found time to set up his borrowed recorder, to be ready for the first job he would be tackling the following day. It was unpaid overtime, but he was anxious to clear his desk. He wanted to be out on the job with the rest of the team, tracking down the murderous villain who had beaten Clarrie. They had been friends for many years and it was through her that he had met his wife Bettina. Before he was free to help, he needed to wind up his current assignment by interviewing someone with an axe to grind about the way he was treated by traffic police when stopped for speeding. It was out of his usual sphere, but it was a favour for a friend so he could not pass the task on.

Winding back the tape to the beginning, he stopped and played it, out of curiosity, expecting it to be blank because Alec, who had been with Sarah while recording, had heard nothing other than traffic. More to the point, Sarah had not heard anything on her 'private line' either. There was a lot static-like hissing and crackling, almost obscuring the sound of a motorbike roaring along the road nearby. The background noise fluctuated. It rose and fell like jumbled voices as they might sound in the wings of a theatre, listening through a heavy curtain to off-stage clamour.

He was animated by the thought that there might be something on the tape after all, which Sarah could decipher, but he had to be sure before suggesting anything so bizarre to Alec. Re-winding the tape completely he reset the counter and played it while he sorted paperwork. At first, apart from exchanges between Sarah and Alec, there was nothing. Then his flesh started to creep as he heard a mournful wail in the distance. After mere seconds of silence, it came again and seemed to hang in the air like an echo, gradually building to a crescendo, which ceased abruptly when the Super cleared his throat and coughed. Paperwork forgotten, Algy wrote down the number indicated, and sat poised to note any other points of interest. Before starting he rang his wife to say he would be later than planned for dinner, but he had something very interesting to tell her that would make up for it... He needed only to add that it was connected to Sarah Grey and Bet would forgive him anything!

38 – Clive

Clive had been trying for days to get Joe on his own. Fortunately, he had often taken him trekking in the wood and taught him quite a lot of Boy Scout stuff, which Joe enjoyed, so the only difficulty was fixing a time. The wretched boy seemed to have a full diary of events – according to Stella, he was unable to go 'scouting' with him until a week on Sunday but Clive's hope's lifted when she said, "Unless you'd like to include his friend Bobby in your outing again? They are almost inseparable and spend hours together every day after school. Of course it wouldn't be a long enough session for a full scale camp-fire picnic." When Clive agreed, Stella promised to ask the boys if they would like to join him on Wednesday, and would let him know.

It was the best he could hope for and actually might work out to his advantage. Bobby Goswell was sharp and might have more to tell than Joe, who, he had to admit, was not the brightest bulb in the box. He would have to be more careful than ever though… young Bobby might be too sharp for his own good, and Clive's!

39 - Sarah

At midnight in Lesser Peasey, Sarah was sleeping after a day of mixed results in her search for answers. After sitting, lost in contemplation of Joe's drawing for over an hour, she felt drained, but wanted more than ever to talk to him about it. Having already obtained from Doris both the Biggs and Goswells' telephone numbers, Sarah dialled to speak to Joe's parents. She was pleased to have a phone in her room, even though it had a safety lock on it, making long distance calls impossible. She refused to own a new-fangled mobile phone. They seemed to be sounding-off everywhere these days at the most inopportune moments: church services, concert halls, in restaurants - ruining an otherwise quiet meal - no, they were not for her!

Joe's mother said she would be happy for Sarah to meet and talk to her son and invited her to visit them the following morning, immediately after church. He would only have half an hour before they were taking him and his little brother out for the day... would that be long enough? Of course, Sarah was pleased to accept. Bobby's father answered the phone when she rang his house and said he had no objections to her interviewing Bobby - anything they could do to help her, under the circumstances, would be a pleasure. Sarah made sure that she could call immediately after seeing Joe as they were next door. By the time her calls were finished it was evening and almost time for her regular update from Polly.

Sure enough, at exactly nine-thirty the telephone rang and it was almost nine forty-five before an excited Polly finished telling her all her news: Jack's arrival, his staying to sit with her, both of them being convinced that Clarrie had moved, his offer to help in any way, the mystery about the patient next door. At last, Polly suggested that if there was nothing Sarah needed Jack for yet, she might recruit him to gather information about Amy Weston. She preferred not to move away from the hospital herself. Sarah was relieved that Polly was keeping busy and not just sitting pining at Clarrie's bedside. Even so, she warned her to be careful. If she felt there was anything criminal about Amy's so-called friend, she should tell Alec, not attempt to deal with the situation personally, even with Jack's help. Polly promised and soon rang off.

Sarah sensed Polly's disappointment that she had nothing to report yet. It would have been too difficult to describe the sensations that coursed through her when she first handled the drawing and when she studied it quietly later. The arm, or hand that knocked over the beaker moved too swiftly to identify but, before the brown liquid obscured the crayon, she saw a group of people in the middle. There was something strange about the way the figures were placed and, slowly, she realised that they were all facing the same way, standing as if at attention in evenly spaced rows. Perhaps Joe would be able to remember how many people he had drawn. Sarah thought there might be more than seven. Of course, the whole group was probably scribbled in hastily and the number might be unimportant.

In bed at last, Sarah fell asleep well before midnight but, after a few hours, began to toss and turn. As she gradually awoke, she clearly felt that she was standing again at the crossroads, watching the couple nailing posters to telegraph poles as they walked towards her. This time, she allowed herself to relax and watch. When they drew near, she saw that the picture was of a young man with a rucksack on his back but she was too far away yet to read the name under it. The image started to fade but not before she read one name on the signpost... "St Helens".

Sarah smiled with satisfaction. She had been right in thinking, with hindsight, that her first dream had been a warning. Now all she had to discover was a link between Clarinda and a young man who disappeared in the early fifties. Knowing that such a thing was impossible, the connection must be with the attacker and, by some unfortunate quirk of fate, Clarinda had come between them. After writing down all she had seen and thought, Sarah lay for a while, trying to relax into a receptive state of mind without fretting over possibilities, but inspiration evaded her and she eventually fell into a sound, dreamless sleep.

40 – Polly

The level of background noise in the hospital was higher than usual; Polly noticed when she left the room to stretch her legs that there was more movement everywhere. Obviously, families and friends were better able to visit on Sundays. Nurse Dawes, who was with Clarrie, was not expecting Polly to rush back. Her other patients were all receiving visitors and she had some paperwork with her to complete. To give Polly a break she proposed sitting with Clarrie while working. Polly did not intend to stay away long as she was keen to ask Jenny about the day she saw Amy Weston, just before her fall. It was too good a chance to miss if Jenny's work was not pressing.

By chance, Sonja Norris emerged from the lift on her way to visit Amy. Her blonde hair was gathered at the back of her neck with a diamante clip that flashed in the artificial light as she walked away on impossibly high heels. Her clothes looked expensive and she wore them with style, Polly admitted, but there was an element of flashiness about her accessories: nouveau riche perhaps. Polly was eager to talk to her but first she needed to know what information Jenny had. Being imaginative, she decided to approach the problem, as Sarah once demonstrated, by creating a scenario and then trying to prove it impossible. Not standard police procedure but much more fun!

With this aim in mind, as she sipped a welcome cup of coffee, she decided that Sonja pushed Amy deliberately, from the top floor of the high-rise shopping centre. It was outrageous, her common sense chided her, but the woman was unknown to the family, so it was easy to believe that her reason for popping up was suspicious. That was the first thing to work out. Any motive would be based on a recent event – no incident at school was feasible as a reason, so Sonja must be lying when she claims not to have seen Amy for years. So what was she hiding by lying?

Eager to start probing for a solution, Polly hastened back to talk to Nurse Jenny, but all thought of Amy and Sonja went straight out of Polly's head, when she found a group of white-coated doctors gathered around Clarrie's bed and was told to wait outside. Shaking, and feeling horribly sick, Polly walked up and down wondering how, if bad, she was going to break the news to Sarah ...

41 – Sarah

"It is nice to see you looking a bit happier," Doris greeted Sarah, as she walked downstairs on Sunday morning, "does that mean there's good news about your daughter?"

Sarah was quick to say that it was good news that Clarinda's condition was stable and had not worsened. Whoever wanted her dead would try to kill her again if word got around that she was expected to recover. With less personal worry to distract her now, Sarah was becoming more susceptible to vibes in her surroundings and, for some reason she could not pin down, she had felt fidgety and uncomfortable ever since crossing the threshold. It was inconceivable that it had anything to do with Clarinda, so it could be that Mrs Lynch herself was in trouble and needed help. It was typical of Sarah that her immediate reaction was self-reproach. She had been so concerned with her own problems that she had avoided long cosy chats with Doris. On the other hand, thought Sarah, if anyone in spirit had been trying to pass on a message to Doris, they would have had to talk fast to get a word in edgeways!

Willing to make amends for avoiding her yesterday, escaping to bed practically while Doris was mid-sentence, Sarah accepted an offer to join her for coffee and they soon settled in the kitchen. The conversation at first revolved around the attack and Doris speculating about the 'villainous, murderous monster responsible for it'... Everybody knew everybody in the village and nobody could believe it was one of their own – no – it was more likely to be someone on the new estate, or just passing through – or most probably somebody who followed her here – poor girl... "Such a nice person too," Doris sighed, "not the sort to make enemies at all, I would have thought – I'd be proud to have a daughter like her but me and my Sam never had children." At last, Doris paused for a breath and Sarah seized the chance to ask if she had nieces or nephews. "Well, yes," Doris said, "my sister Mary had two girls and a boy. They are all grown now with their own families, but I see a fair bit of them, always have been close – Sammy was named after my husband and Dorry after me, the other girl is Lizzie – like Betty next door."

Before Sarah could interrupt, Doris was off again, talking about Mary meeting her husband after she left home to work in Oxford, which their parents were against, "Against her leaving home, of course, not the marriage – that worked out very well, her husband was good to her. They came back to live in Greater P when Mary got pregnant because she wanted to be near our mother, although he wasn't really keen, but they settled in alright – and of course we were a real happy family with Betty and her husband living next door; it was like having another sister. His parents moved to Oxford when they married and were killed in a car crash when he was just a kid, so he was brought up by his mother's family. He told us that he knew next to nothing about the Parkers except that his aunt, uncle and cousin had died in a fire in Lesser P. Fancy – such a lot of tragedy for one little boy. Sam and Me loved all our nephews and nieces; it was like having kids of our own with no responsibility, great fun. Life was good until my Sam died, then Mary just after – it was a terrible time for her husband too. I needed help with this place, so we decided to run it together and that's why he moved in – it works out fine because he's not too far from his grandchildren, thinks the world of them all."

Sarah gave up trying to lead the conversation. She was aware of several spirit presences who had gathered while Doris had been talking on and on, It was a safe bet that the man was Sam because he smiled and nodded when he was mentioned. The woman, probably Mary, looked less happy and Sarah expected her to communicate but figures appeared and started pushing her aside: so many restless, unhappy souls clamouring to be heard that Sarah could make out nothing. It often happened when more than one tried to claim her attention at the same time but she usually convinced them that she would listen to each in turn. Now she was overwhelmed and almost frightened by what was happening and had to stand up and leave immediately. Doris did not seem at all put out, happily accepting that Sarah had a lot to do and Sarah breathed a sigh of relief when she reached her own room.

The images and voices faded but came back in fainter and fainter waves until at last Sarah succeeded in severing communication: postponing it until she was better prepared. Only one impression lingered; beyond the unhappy group, all begging for attention, a young man stood silently aloof and he was smiling with satisfaction. Although apart, Sarah felt that he was with the others… it was almost as if he were the ringmaster, satisfied that his team was performing well. Always intrigued when presented with a mystery, Sarah made a mental promise to make contact again, as soon as

Clarinda's problem was solved. Until then, she could not afford to be distracted from her pursuit of her daughter's attacker in case, for some reason, Clarinda was still a threat to him. It took all her concentration to ignore their onslaught, but she had already concluded that their problem was related to something that happened half a century ago and was not remotely likely to have any connection at all with her own. Clarinda's safety was her first concern and had she not been so preoccupied she would have revelled in the challenge of unravelling a mystery from the distant past. Time has no meaning in the next world, so it could hardly be pressing. The most important thing she had to do now was to walk to the outskirts of the village with the drawing and talk to the two boys who had compiled it.

As Sarah walked away down the street, Clive watched her from an upstairs window. There was something extremely unsettling about the woman and he dreaded meeting her face to face.

42 – Sonja

Brightness, beyond the swirling fog that enveloped her, loomed slowly towards and away but, as time passed, lingered longer. The floating colours began to take shape and sounds echoed as they rose and fell... burbling, bubbling water... then, echoing from afar, a voice – calling: calling her – calling her name..."Amy, Amy... please come back Amy, Amy......"

Sonja stared at the motionless figure on the bed. As she turned the page of her magazine, she could have sworn Amy twitched a finger. About ten minutes ago when she arrived, she had walked in to hear Amy's brother shouting at her. His voice had actually been quite audible as she walked along the corridor, but he had the good sense to lower his volume when the door opened. They talked for a few moments before he left and she felt that he was coming to the end of his patience and, like her, wondered if the moment had come to cut off Amy's life support. She did not say as much however. He told her that Grace would be in later and they had wondered if just shouting Amy's name continually would be more likely to get through to her than endless talk. As he left the room, Gordon was gratified to hear Sonja shouting 'Amy, Amy,' at the top of her voice.

Now she started to sweat. The thought that it might be working horrified her. For the rest of her shift she scarcely took her eyes off Amy's hands but by the time

Grace came to take over, Sonja was feeling a little easier. The hands lay still and pallid, almost matching the white coverlet. Even so, the incident had shaken her and made it imperative that she find a way of ensuring that Amy would never again regain consciousness.

43 – Jack

Major Jack Hall – he seldom used the Heywood, or his rank for that matter, now that he had retired – was impatient to start helping Polly with her probing into the mystery of how Amy spent the hour before her fall. He would have been happier to be chasing after the bounder who beat Clarrie, but if this helped to take Polly's mind off Clarrie then it would be a good thing. Polly had rung him immediately after talking to Sarah, thanking him for his offer and promising to let him know if he could do anything for her. Even though it was Sunday, he had several contacts who could fill in the background and he was determined to have something to tell Polly when he visited the hospital later.

Within a few hours, he had established that the top floor of the car park, never full, was usually empty by the time most of the shops in the Mall closed at five-thirty. There had been previous falls from the same building, but several people had witnessed the first; a drunk, who was showing off to a group of equally inebriated mates, plunged to his death soon after the high rise was finished. An extra wall was then built but, in spite of this, a woman committed suicide a couple of years ago. This was also witnessed.

To satisfy his own curiosity, Jack drove immediately to the Mall, parked on the top floor and walked around the perimeter. At the spot he thought to be correct, knowing where Amy landed, he saw that it would not have been as easy to climb up as places nearer to the lifts. On the other hand, it was out of sight beyond a ventilation shaft and not so impossibly high that a strong person could not have lifted her and shoved her over. He had asked Polly if Amy was slight or heavily built and she had rung him back within minutes to say that Amy was not tall – probably a few inches shorter than Clarrie and equally slim.

Because he had nothing else pressing to do, he stopped at a coffee bar that was one of the few places open and found that most of the clientele were shift workers, employed in or near the building, relaxing before going home.

He didn't hesitate to let everyone know that he was looking into the circumstances of Amy Weston's accident and was lucky enough to find three people who were working that afternoon. Only one claimed to have seen her, having recognised her picture in the local press and he was quite happy to chat to Jack after his friends left. Unfortunately, he couldn't say whether she was alone or not.

A woman who might have been with her went into the lift first. He couldn't describe her, except to say that she had very dark short hair. He had been about thirty or forty feet away and because he was hurrying to catch the lift, knowing she'd seen him, he had expected her to hold it for him, but she didn't and he was annoyed until he saw that it was on its way up, not down. He had told the police that he had been several floors from the top and caught another lift down, almost immediately.

Jack made a note of his name and they exchanged telephone numbers, in case they needed to meet again. The man promised also to ask around. People might very well have noticed things but been reluctant to speak to the police, for any number of reasons. Talking to Jack, unofficially, would be a different kettle of fish. There was nothing to gain by staying longer tonight, but Jack was satisfied. At least he had something to relate, to reassure Polly that he was already on the job.

44 – Sarah

When Sarah was ushered into a highly polished, immaculately tidy front room by Mrs Biggs, who was carrying a sleepy toddler, she found Joe and his father already in there. They both shot to their feet and Joe's mother introduced them. "This is Joe, of course, and my husband, Seth, and I'm Stella. Please do sit down." Sarah responded by inviting them all to call her Sarah and accepted Stella's immediate offer of coffee. Seth asked Sarah if she minded his staying with Joe and, of course, she understood that he needed to protect his son if occasion arose.

It was obvious to Sarah that Joe was extremely embarrassed and she knew she would have to tread carefully, so she began by asking why he had decided to make the drawing in the first place. When he was certain that Sarah appreciated that it was Bobby's idea and they had tried to remember together what the artist had painted, Joe confessed that he had put a few things into it that he didn't think of himself. Because Bobby's memory was better than his own, he didn't feel very bad about doing so because Bobby would never lie to him. They had done their best because they knew it was important to get things right. Sarah understood and said she thought the idea was excellent. She broke the news to him about his beautiful drawing being accidentally damaged at the police station and suggested that he might like to make another one for her. She said it was a commission, just like those her daughter undertook, and she would pay him a month's pocket-money, whatever that was, if he agreed.

When she removed it from the folder and he saw how badly damaged it was he was shocked, as she knew he would be, but being commissioned to make a duplicate for real money was enough to remove his anxious frown. In the face of his father's protestations, Joe offered to do it for two weeks pocket money, as he wasn't a real artist. Catching sight of Seth's stern expression, Sarah compromised – two weeks pocket money then, and she would replace his materials. Seth smiled wryly, having been outmanoeuvred, although he still felt that Joe should be doing it again to be helpful not for gain. Sarah thought Joe should have been raising his price, not dropping it, but she would make sure he did not lose by his lack of experience in the commercial world.

The greatest damage was in the middle of the sheet, where she knew there had been a group of people. Joe said that it was one of the things he didn't actually see himself, because he ran away before they were painted. Sarah sensed his acute discomfort and knew that he found it difficult to believe that they had really been there, but he trusted Bobby, so had put them in. His faith in his friend was touching and Sarah hoped he would never be let down. She encouraged him to talk about Bobby; how long they had known each other: what did they enjoy doing best: what did he admire most about his friend? Bobby was definitely the leader, Sarah decided, but apparently never failed to stick up for him, when others tried to bully him.

There wasn't anything else Joe could tell her other than that the lady painter had been very nice to them and didn't mind them asking her questions because they couldn't understand what she was drawing. It was only when they heard that the painting was stolen that Bobby thought they should try to remember what was in it… and actually, even Bobby didn't think of doing it straight away. It was only when they were crossing the park that he suddenly said they should do it... and no, Joe had no idea what made Bobby think of it, but he liked drawing and wanted to help.

Next door, Bobby was waiting for the lady to come and talk to him. He knew she was the painting lady's mother so she was probably gaga and would be weeping all the time. He wasn't at all sure what she expected him to talk about but he would not tell her about seeing the farm and stuff just like her daughter had painted instead of the park. Everybody would think he was crazy, but if he was, then her daughter was too, because they had both seen the same thing. The old lady wouldn't want to hear that her daughter was crazy so he would do her a favour and stick to saying it was what he and Joe remembered.

45 – Terry & John

White and Dee, in Greater Peasey, had not uncovered much of significance about any part of Peasey's past – Greater, Lesser, or New. There had been an average amount of petty crime but other than a traffic hit-and-run, which ended in a pile-up and four deaths, and three house-fires over the last sixty years, it must have been a peaceful place to live. They had spent several hours of what remained of Saturday, studying official findings and left requests at the library in order to view newspaper reports on microfiche before deciding there was no more they could achieve until Monday. On Sunday, reluctant to do nothing, they decided to find the oldest pub in the area and get friendly with the oldest regulars in the bar. It was amazing that more people did not appreciate how much information these oldies had tucked away in their heads and the fact that they were often eager to have a friendly chat over a pint.

The most ancient areas in the village were now the most expensive. Thatched cottages had been restored and modernised inside and most of the older residents had been unable to resist the temptation to accept ridiculously high prices offered for even the smallest, outdated, inconvenient dwellings. However, between these now stylish properties and the council estate there were jumbled rows of terraced houses, respectable but not flashy enough to be in demand. The area boasted two grocers (one Indian), one greengrocer, one butcher, one fishmonger, one fish & chip shop, and three selling antiques. It was also enhanced by two Churches and three Public Houses. The most run-down was the Crown & Anchor and after picking up some food at the Chippy it was there, in the saloon bar, that White and Dee met Frank Brown, the answer to their prayers.

46 – Sarah

When he saw Sarah walking along the pavement and coming through their garden gate, Bobby ran to tell his mother and they greeted her at the door, together. He was surprised that Mrs Grey was not really wrinkly and was immediately wary. She might not be as easy to fool as he'd thought. Still, what could she do or say? Nothing, if he stuck to his story. Sarah accepted coffee again, as much to put Bobby's mother at ease as because she needed a drink.

While Pamela was in the kitchen, Sarah and Bobby eyed each other quietly while waiting for his father to join them. Bobby's eyes were focussed slightly beyond Sarah's shoulder and with a gasp of surprise she realised that he was clairvoyant. Ever since she left Clarrie's bedside she had felt the presence of her husband Stephen with her, as worried about their daughter as she was but, strangely enough, she had never seen him herself. So many who had passed on were visible to her, but the one person she longed to see was never revealed. The last thing she had expected was that she would come face to face with another clairvoyant – and one so young! It amazed her that in such a close-knit community he was not a subject of gossip. Flippant remarks about being psychic and knowing who did what, usually filled the air when a neighbour was reputed to have 'second sight'.

The little boy was obviously unperturbed by the ghostly presence. His blond curly hair fell across his forehead, almost obscuring his eyes but she saw them switch quickly back to meet hers, with an almost guilty start. He opened them widely with an engagingly innocent air, but blinked with alarm when Sarah eventually broke the silence with a request.

"Please Bobby," Sarah said, "forgive me for asking, but please tell me about the man who came in with me. He is my husband, who died many years ago."

Gaping in astonishment Bobby stuttered in reply… "But I can't – what do you mean – there isn't anybody with you."

Sarah smiled and promised that to be fair – in exchange – she would describe the elderly gentleman who was standing behind him. "He is your Grandfather isn't he? He spends a lot of time watching over you and often sits at your bedside, as he used to when you were tiny. He used to read to you and is so pleased that you can see him."

When Bobby got over his initial shock, he was thrilled and excited. Mostly, he was relieved to find that he wasn't the only person in the world who saw ghosts so he couldn't be sent to a special hospital, but his first words were a demand to know how Sarah could hear his Granddad speak. "I see lots of people but I can't hear them. Sometimes their lips move and I guess what they might mean – or something pops into my head like an idea and I can't stop thinking about them until I decide what they want."

Sarah reassured him that, in a way, he was hearing them. The thoughts that came to him when he saw anyone in spirit form were more than likely put there by them. She suggested to him that seeing things had probably given him enough to worry about. Perhaps hearing things would have been even more frightening for him. "I believe that being able to see glimpses of a life beyond death, is a tremendous privilege. I often used to wonder why some people can and others can't and have no answer to that, but we have to accept that the gift brings with it great responsibility. We must never exploit the spirit world for our own advantage and in quiet ways we should try to help others to understand that it exists, so that they can take comfort from the knowledge."

"I won't ever tell, don't you worry," said Bobby firmly, "not even mum and dad know, and my mates would just take the pi... ." Colour flooded his face as he looked stricken, and apologised, "Ooh-er ...sorry!"

"The day will probably come when you feel compelled to pass on a message to a friend, and I'm sure you will find the right words or a way to do it, without risking ridicule but, in the meantime, I think you should bring your parents into the secret. As you grow older, you'll need their support."

Bobby shook his head. "Mum would freak out and Dad would want me exercised," he shuddered, adding with a sigh, "and I don't want anybody to interfere. I like seeing dead people, especially Granddad."

Sarah couldn't help laughing as she corrected him gently. "I think you mean exorcised – and I quite agree, as long as you understand that the gift we both have is not to be misused for entertainment. We have to be responsible and use it only when we can help others." Looking into the child's wide blue eyes, Sarah felt deeply moved. Every emotion that swept through him was reflected there – worry, pleasure, excitement, curiosity – there was no guile or deceit in him. He was just a lovable little boy, out of his depth suddenly, but anxious to do the right thing, and Sarah determined that she would be there to support him, any time he needed her.

"You are much younger than I was," Sarah told him, "when I first saw and heard a ghost. I was about fifteen years old and doing my piano practise. I was alone and would much rather have been out with my friends. When the piece came to an end I heard the click of knitting needles behind me and turned to see my grandmother sitting listening to me, as she often had done before she died. I was more astonished than frightened because I knew she would never hurt me."

"And did you keep it secret too?" Bobby asked eagerly.

"Actually, I didn't," Sarah replied, "I told my mother and was amazed when she said she was not surprised because I took after her mother in so many other ways. Yes," Sarah nodded as Bobby's eyes widened, "the Grandma I had just seen was psychic too, when she was alive." In answer to the flood of questions, Sarah told Bobby that much of what the old lady spoke to her about, and the guidance she had always given her, had prepared her for that moment. "It would be good if you could tell your parents while I'm here to help."

Bobby nodded and seemed relieved that he was not being forced into immediate confrontation with his parents but to Sarah's surprise he glanced away and said, "Your husband is laughing now and pointing to something a long way away – I can't see where but there are people standing about in white coats. I think it's a hospital."

Sarah could have hugged him – the vision of Stephen being happy could only mean that Clarinda's condition was improving. It was strange to her, receiving a spirit message through someone else, but she decided that it was confirmation of the fact that Bobby's potential as a psychic was immense and needed to be monitored. Nobody needs to worry, she vowed, she would do her utmost to prevent his exploitation and always be there to advise him, when asked. She was glad they were having the chance to talk alone, but wondered why Bobby's parents were taking such a long time to appear. In their continued absence Bobby questioned her eagerly about the man; was he always with her, and if they were married why couldn't she see him? Sarah didn't know – but said that she hoped she would see him one day, before she died and joined him of course. The relief at having something to laugh at, sent Bobby into a fit of giggles, then he sobered suddenly and clutched her arm. "But please don't die yet. I've only just found you. I need you more than he does, he said," glaring into the empty air beyond her, which made Sarah laugh too. It was this surprisingly happy scene, which greeted Pamela when she returned with the coffee.

She was full of apologies. She had thought her husband Jake was with them, not realising that he'd been delayed by a phone call. Quite fortuitous, thought Sarah, wondering! He appeared within seconds, flustered and also saying how sorry he was, making Sarah wonder even more when he described the run-around he'd had, coping with a hoax caller, but they all settled down quickly. There was now no need for Bobby to explain how he had managed to 'remember' so much detail and Sarah was careful not to compromise him in any way, accepting that it had been a true representation of what was on Clarinda's missing canvas. Knowing that she would learn more from Bobby in private, Sarah asked if he would be permitted to walk up the hill with her to see the view. Jake and Pamela were very happy for Bobby to carry on helping Sarah in any way he could, only asking that she should return with him today before teatime, but she was welcome to call to talk to him at any time.

Bobby was halfway out of the house before Sarah finished thanking his parents, and as they watched their son walking off with her, they both commented that they had never before seen him accept a stranger so readily. They also noted a change in his demeanour. He seemed less on the defensive and happier. It was understandable that he should be buoyed-up by the attention; they just hoped he could really help and would have no need to feel deflated if nothing came of it.

Sarah felt slightly guilty as they left, regretting Bobby's refusal to confide in his parents, but she had to respect his wishes. In spite of her misgivings, she was convinced that he held a vital key and she needed his help.

47 – Polly

On Sunday afternoon, sitting at Clarrie's bedside, it was difficult for Polly to believe that her condition had improved. To all appearances, she seemed no different from the day Sarah had left, but her doctors were pleased and certain now that not only were her physical wounds healing well, but her brain was showing signs of activity. Perhaps by Friday there would be a noticeable difference for Sarah to see. Repeatedly telling Clarrie, in the otherwise silent room, how much better she was and that in no time at all she would be painting again at home, eventually cheered Polly.

Polly, eager to find a fresh way of stimulating Clarrie's brain, repeated names and random words three times each in no particular order, watching closely for the slightest twitch of a finger or eyelid... Sarah, mother, painting, easel, Del, Polly, studio, brushes, Lesser Peasey, hill, hilltop, car ...!

Hill hill hill, easel easel easel, brushes brushes brushes, painting painting painting, mother mother mother... Clarrie heard a familiar voice echoing near and far, from a long way away. She was comforted but could not respond and something other than the voice was trying to gain her attention. Even in her detached, weakened state, she sensed that it was an entity from the spirit world and that it might be dangerous to listen to it. Desperately needing help but powerless to ask for it, Clarrie instinctively did what she had always been taught to do; she imagined herself in a protective shell, repeated the Lord's Prayer and asked for guidance and protection from evil.

After almost an hour of endless repetition, without seeing a flicker of awareness in the still figure lying so helpless before her, Polly gave up, stretched and yawned. As she leaned back and her eyelids drooped, Clarrie's eyes rolled beneath her lids and her hand twitched before relaxing again on the coverlet.

48 – Sarah

Sarah, once again in her own room, sat and made notes of everything Bobby had told her. For one so young, his extra-sensory perception was very keen. His logical mind helped him to interpret his visions calmly without leaping to conclusions and he was quick to pick up the implications of what he saw. She had discussed Joe's reluctance to include the central group of figures in his drawing and Bobby grinned a little sheepishly. In his opinion, their inclusion was justified because the young man with the yellow backpack had obviously wanted them to be noticed. Bobby told Sarah that it was after seeing the man pointing at the ground near the fountain that he had suddenly thought of recreating what they had seen in Clarinda's painting. "Then while Joe was drawing," Bobby told her, "the houses and fountain and everything changed into fields and I just knew that it was what the painting was all about." He realised suddenly that he now knew two other people who 'saw' things and he threw himself back on the grass, kicking his legs in the air in sheer delight.

Apart from discussing what he had already seen, Sarah would not ask for his active support, he was just a child but, at that moment, she felt far less lonely than she had since leaving Polly at the hospital. As she walked him back home, Sarah again advised him to discuss his spiritual awareness with his parents and promised that, with their permission she would introduce him to a young man who had just found his vocation as a medium. She was sure that Simon Goodfellow would be supportive and ready to advise Bobby – after all, she would not be around forever and Simon was much nearer to Bobby's age. Sarah emphasised that Bobby should not tell anyone else, especially about his vision of the farm and fields.

She now recognised beyond doubt that she had been wrong in dismissing a connection between her dream of the crossroad and the attempt on Clarinda's life. The youth, and clamouring group of lost souls had nothing to do with Doris after all, so solving the old mystery had suddenly become crucial to discovering the identity of the attacker. Sarah thanked God that she had Terry and John to support her; they knew her well enough not to question her instincts, or the source of her information. Plum Duffy, when he joined the team, would be unlikely to question her delving into local history, when it obviously met with police approval. He might be a great help.

When Doris tapped on her door and asked if she would like to come down and join them for dinner, Sarah accepted with relief. It was about time she met the man of the house – and she was suddenly healthily hungry.

49 – Frank

It was quite late, after eleven-o-clock, on Sunday night when Terry White and John Dee returned to their Boarding House and parted for the night. They had enjoyed their sociable evening, taking it in turns to get round after round of drinks in, for Frank and his mate Vince. They were not on official duty, so had been able to relax. Not being clear about exactly what they were seeking was an advantage. They did not have to guide the conversation except for making sure that it was all about the 'good old days'. "Didn't anything bad ever happen in the Peaseys when you were lads?" John had asked. "The Police here must have had nothing to do!"

"I got my collar felt once or twice for scrumping," grinned Vince, but Frank here was always 'helping with enquiries' – you ask him!" He almost spilt his beer, dodging Frank's swinging arm.

For hours, they had been talking to no avail, but at that point the two experienced officers knew instinctively that they were on to something interesting, whether relevant to their investigation or not. It transpired that in the late fifties, there was a nationwide search for a missing person and as several people had reported seeing him in the area, more police were drafted in. All the local sightings had been on the same day except three a couple of days later – and one of the last was reported by Frank. Nobody ever discovered where the young chap had lodged for two nights but Frank had spoken to him at some length, giving him directions, and told the police that the hiker had definitely said he was heading for Swindon.

Vince said that everyone thought Frank was going to be arrested, he spent that much time at the nick. The problem facing the police was that all the other witnesses gave descriptions fitting the official description but, apart from the clothing being the same, Frank insisted that the boy had dark brown eyes, not bright blue. Only when sightings of him twenty miles away were reported before he disappeared completely, did the police leave Frank in peace. "Anyway," Frank said, "they had more important things to worry about around the same time, because they were still investigating the farmhouse fire over at Lesser P, where three people were burned to death."

They did not imagine the information could be relevant – there was no reason to believe that the missing boy and the fire were connected, but it was a line they could follow up with the local police and at least they had something to report to Sarah, so they ended their day tired but happy.

50 – Edna

William and Edna Daniels went to bed early on Sunday night, eager to be up and away early, on the first leg of their holiday. In spite of the heart-rending reasons for taking it, they referred to it as such, not only to neighbours and friends, but to each other, in an effort to buoy up their spirits.

Anthony had walked away in 1951 to catch a bus at the top of Croppers Hill, which would take him within walking distance of Thatto Heath Station. He had refused a lift, saying it would be a lot shorter stretch than he intended to cover on foot when he reached the Cotswolds. Even such a minor thing had caused anguish later. If only they had driven him to catch the train, they would have had a few more precious memories to store.

At Lime Street, Liverpool, he had changed trains and headed for the Midlands. They knew he had broken his journey to go to Moseley Old Hall, near Wolverhampton, because the story about Charles II, hiding there in 1651, after the Battle of Worcester had always fascinated him. He had mentioned it on his first postcard, but they did not want to go there themselves; they were on a mission to discover where his trip had ended.

He intended to walk when the route was countrified and ride local buses through built-up areas. His second postcard was posted in Coventry, after visiting the Cathedral. He wrote that he was looking forward to seeing Kenilworth Castle, and walking more from then on. Apart from Tony's interest in history, Sir Walter Scott's novel about it had been his favourite book. Neither William nor Edna had been there, but their guidebook said that it was '...probably one of the finest ruined castles to be seen in Britain today, dramatically portrayed amidst the gentle rolling countryside of Warwickshire.' This then, was definitely on their list.

Neither wanted to be away from home for more than a week or two but by joining his route, before his trail had grown cold, they might perhaps be able to tune into his thoughts and feelings about what he saw. They could also imagine that they were really on holiday, doing what most people enjoy doing – seeing sights and taking photographs of each other in front of famous landmarks.

After spending the night in Leamington Spa they would drive to Banbury – Tony must have gone there to see the Cross and Broughton Castle, where there was armour or something from the Civil War. Edna had kidded him, saying that it sounded incredibly boring and Anthony had laughed and shown her a picture. The grounds certainly did look beautiful, so they would go there too.

Next, he was sure to have gone to Blenheim, near Oxford, but from then on, they would have to guess where his fancy might have taken him.

As Edna's eyes slowly closed in sleep they rested on William's briefcase, hoping it contained everything they might need relating to their son's disappearance. As well as the postcards and poster, they had other photographs of him and copies of all the correspondence that had ensued up to a year after he had left home. Filled with hope, that the promise was about to be fulfilled, Edna prayed that all their questions would soon be answered.

51 - Sarah

Sarah was restless and unable to sleep, in spite of the fact that she had spoken with Polly for well over an hour after dinner and the news that Clarinda was responding to treatment should have calmed her. Perhaps the meal had been over-rich but she had enjoyed it at the time; Doris was a good cook. Sarah had had a tiring day and it had been a relief just to exchange small talk. They carefully avoided any mention of the dreadful incident that had brought her to Lesser Peasey and entertained her with their own family anecdotes and yet she felt disturbed; perhaps it was something that was said that jarred, because remnants of the conversation had floated on the edge of her consciousness ever since her head touched the pillow. The substance still eluded her as she arose and prepared to face the day but there was no point in fretting, whatever it was would come back to her in time, and it was probably not important, certainly not worth the sleep she had lost! Perhaps she was just not thinking clearly.

It had always been Sarah's habit to make copious notes when trying to solve a problem and the thin writing pad she had brought with her was already used up so after her morning coffee, before walking round to the police station, she went into the post office next door to buy a bound note book. Later, she would sort through her flimsy jottings and make sure that she was more organised when she next conferred with Terry and John.

Betty Parker was serving a boy who could hardly see over the counter and teasing him... "Now, young man, how much change shall I give you from this one-pound coin?"

He couldn't have been more than eight years old, but he was more than a match for her. "I don't know, but you'd better make sure it's right 'cause my mum's a real whizz at counting." His worried frown disappeared when Betty roared with laughter and handed him some loose change along with his bag of sweets. She greeted Sarah and tipped her head towards her husband who was at the stamp counter, "Our grandson is good few years older than that one but not half as sharp! You've met Joe, haven't you? He's a lovely lad."

Sarah pleased them by agreeing and adding how impressed she had been by his drawing. In answer to their enquiries about her daughter, Sarah managed to restrain her impulse to smile and inform them that Clarinda might at last be coming out of her coma. Instead, she accepted their commiserations, looking suitably worried. It was a relief to get out of the shop. At the Police station, she would be able to phone Alec Holmes and talk more freely than she could from her bedroom. As she left the shop, she almost bumped into Doris, who was beckoning to a young man she had left standing at her own front door. "You're in luck," she called to him. "This is Mrs Grey, I thought she might still be here."

It was a safe guess that this must be the reporter assigned to help her and Sarah was not surprised when he introduced himself as Derek Duffy. Shaking his hand, she smiled and invited him to call her Sarah. "Would you prefer being Derek or Duffy," she asked, "I must admit I would not feel happy calling you Plum, your nickname I understand." He was not much taller than Sarah and at first glance appeared to be as wide as he was high.

"I'm told that being a Michelin Tyre baby, I acquired the nickname very early in life, so if you don't mind, it would be a nice change to be Duffy – not saddled with Plum, or more often Plump!" He grimaced as he gazed down at his girth and added that he had actually lost several stones since he joined the paper and at this rate his mother wouldn't recognise him when he went back to visit her. As they walked to the Police Station, he explained that it was principally to lose weight that he had left home. His mother was a fantastic cook and took offence if food was left on the plates. Eating out to avoid upsetting her was costing him too much, he said, so his only escape was moving a few hundred miles away. As they reached the entrance, he stopped in mid-stride and turned to her, looking more serious. "I haven't lost sight of what we are both doing here – the way your daughter was attacked was diabolical and I really hope I can help to track down who did it." As she walked in through the door that he held open for her, Sarah smiled her thanks and said she appreciated all the help she could get.

To her surprise, Detective Sergeants White and Dee were already there, working, searching through old files. Apparently, they had found what they first sought after only a few hours at Greater Peasey and were now following a hunch. "Working on your theory that the motive for the attack on Clarrie was based on something that happened between thirty and sixty years ago," Terry explained, "we looked for unsolved cases. The worst incident might not have been a crime, but three people died in a house fire – and we think it was the farmhouse that was in the missing painting."

"We need to talk it through," John interjected, "so we have the use of an empty cell. There is a table, and we can soon find a couple more chairs. Don't worry they've promised not to lock us in!"

Introductions didn't take long but the two men exchanged meaningful glances. Sarah didn't need ESP to know what they were thinking. With young Duffy, a stranger, present, they would not be able to refer in any way to her being psychic. It would certainly restrict the scope of their deliberations, so she suggested straight away that if they went through the highlights of the case so far, to put Duffy in the picture, they might be able to decide on an aspect that he could start researching straight away, through his newspaper archives and connections.

Understanding immediately, and having gone quickly through the background, they reported their meeting with Frank Brown and what had been discussed. If Duffy wondered why their interest should have been sparked by a missing person passing through the village – hardly a riveting event – he showed no sign. They soon got round to suggesting that any news reports written at the time about Anthony Daniels might be more helpful than anything in the local police files, which were purely factual. Duffy, eager to get started, stood and grabbed his jacket. He looked nowhere near as tubby without it flapping around him and it seemed that every one of its many pockets was stuffed with all his working tools and overnight needs, in lieu of a travel bag.

"Where are you lodging?" Sarah asked, suddenly wondering where he had spent last night.

"Oh, I was going to ask if your landlady had another room, but I forgot! Never mind, I'll be OK. I have the telephone number – I'll ring you there later." His voice echoed back along the corridor as he hurried away and for a moment the three friends eyed each other, holding their breath...

Gradually, they all relaxed and Sarah lifted out her new notebook. Leaving several pages blank, to be filled in later, she wrote the date and time at the top of the page, and sat with pen poised. "Now," she said, "who goes first?"

52 - Clive

Clive Parker, having come face to face with the loathsome young woman's mother, doubted that she was party to the blackmailing plot.

She had been quite pleasant, if a bit distracted, which was understandable as her daughter was in a coma; there was nothing to suggest that she was coming out of it and he was still disinclined to make sure she didn't – it would be too risky. He had no excuse to visit the hospital, so could not afford to be seen there. Anyway, there was sure to be a guard on her door.

He felt helpless and frustrated, unable to put his predicament out of mind and get on with his chores as efficiently as usual.

He had not heard any up-to-date gossip. It had been rumoured several times that she was dead but he now knew for certain that she was hanging on to life and he hoped it was by a thin enough thread to snap soon. He could not stand the strain much longer.

As he worked he worried about episodes from his past, wondering which gory detail had surfaced to be used against him and who, in those days, could have known about the terrible things he had done. He corrected himself mentally – the terrible things he had been forced to do! Only the Gleaseys knew and even if they had survived the fire, they were guiltier than he was and would never have divulged any of their secrets to anyone.

The more he tried to think clearly the more puzzled and confused he became; perhaps he had jumped to conclusions about being blackmailed. The girl had actually said nothing threatening, but then, he hadn't given her time and she didn't need to put it into words; her picture said it all.

Clive, or Ben as he was then, could remember the exact moment captured on the canvas.

He was digging two more graves, swearing to God that they would be the last and thinking it a fitting place for Glenda and Art Gleasey to finish up – alongside their victims – when a hiker came through the gate and sauntered down to the farm.

Being covered in blood, Ben could hardly intercept him although aware that the two bodies, even in the gloomy kitchen, were easy to see between the broken planks of the front door, which had been smashed during his fight with Art.

If only he had reached the hallway in time to close the kitchen door, he might have been able to explain the blood by saying he'd been killing chickens, but he was too late.

By the time he reached the kitchen through the back door, the boy had pushed his way through the broken one and was kneeling next to Art. Looking up in horror, he said, "I thought I could help, but I think he's dead. What on earth happened here, there's blood everywhere?" His gaze fell to take in Ben's clothing and he obviously guessed that Ben was responsible. He had risen and turned to run but fell over the body of Glenda. He was unlucky enough to be stunned when his head hit the iron fender round the open fire. It was a scenario not unfamiliar to Ben and almost by instinct he seized a poker from the hearth and smashed it down repeatedly on the intruder's neck and chest.

Ben lost track of time as he sat staring at the grisly scene before him. His first thought then, was that Art wasn't around anymore to cart the bodies outside for burial; nor was Glenda around to clean up the mess. They had been a formidable team. He was suddenly quite alone...

53 – Polly

Clarrie's condition continued to improve according to the medics but Polly would have been more reassured if she had been moving, opening her eyes or even twitching something. Keep talking, the doctor advised: not so essential now perhaps, but it might bring the patient back more quickly.

It was difficult to decide what to talk about; in her improved state, Clarrie might actually be listening, even though unable to reply. With a notebook open, occasionally recording her thoughts, Polly decided to relate all she knew about Amy, still in a deep coma in the room next door. "It seems to me," Polly began, "that somebody tried to murder the poor girl. Jack is helping me by finding out more about the shopping Mall where she fell and searching newspaper reports. He already has a witness – someone who works there says he saw her go up in a lift and the woman with her had short black hair." She started to write a few notes, but stopped and put the book hastily into the bedside drawer. She had heard Amy's door open and voices in the corridor.

Grabbing her handbag, Polly went to the door, opened it and walked out casually; Sonja had been sitting with Amy for over an hour and might be leaving. This could be an opportunity to talk to her – about what, God only knew, but Polly had instinctively disliked the woman and needed either to confirm her feelings or be able to put them aside. She was right.

Sonja Norris bade goodbye to Grace who also waved a salute to Polly, as she passed the open door. It was natural then for the two of them to walk to the lift together. In the few minutes it took them to reach the car park, where Polly pretended also to be leaving the hospital, she reached at least one conclusion. She distrusted Sonja even more than she had before.

In the sudden silence, Clarrie drifted back into a deeper sleep. The panic she had felt when feeling helpless and under attack from unseen forces had passed quite quickly because a sense of remoteness enveloped her. Some tiny part of her brain knew that it should be making an effort to function but another just couldn't be bothered. There were two worlds in her head and without the necessity of separating them she accepted both, giving them equal importance. Voices floated pleasantly in one and the other was literally haunted by ghostly figures, all trying to communicate with her. Their clamouring had at first frightened her, but when her father appeared, keeping others at bay, her mind slowly accepted their presence as normal. One woman stood silently apart. Clarrie was vaguely aware that she belonged neither to the spirit world nor the one she could hear, but it didn't matter. Nothing mattered to Clarrie as she relaxed and slept again.

After Polly returned and retrieved her notebook, she started recording her grave misgivings about Sonja. The woman had talked quite openly about her fiancé and their coming marriage. Polly commented on how upsetting it must be, Amy now being so ill, she might not recover in time to attend the wedding. Sonja seemed to be taken aback slightly but said she hadn't actually sent out all the invitations yet, but of course she was on the guest list. "You must have been looking forward to seeing her again, I hear you have not met for many years," Polly said. An immediate flash of irritation crossed Sonja's face, but she answered pleasantly that keeping up with friends was not as difficult as it must have been in the old days on the Costa Blanca, when telephones were hard to get.

Sonja happily related anecdotes about their schooldays, but seemed to have nothing to say about recent events in Amy's life. Rather boldly, Polly asked if Sonja was familiar with the Mall where Amy fell, and Sonja said she shopped there at Christmas when she last came to England to visit her parents. "There is a huge fish tank in the restaurant on the top floor. I love the Angel Fish and Kissing Gouramis ...so calming to have coffee there after an exhausting shopping session. I must go again to see if it still works its charm: I feel quite stressed these days."

Although engrossed in her notes, Polly had lined herself up so that she would not fail to see the slightest movement of Clarrie's hands. How she longed to be able to ring Sarah with good news... but, until then, at least she felt she was being of use to somebody. She had always hated being idle.

54 - Edna

Edna and William were tired after driving all day. They had followed the most direct route to Coventry and enjoyed a late lunch there before visiting the cathedral and marvelling at the beautiful carvings. From there they drove to Warwick. They were sure Anthony would not have missed looking around the castle and were eager to see it themselves. The day had been full of, "Oh, he must have loved that," and "Look there, he would not have left without going in there," and the freedom to indulge in speaking their every thought aloud was having a therapeutic effect on them both. Instead of spending the evening doing nothing fruitful, they agreed that it was better to head for Banbury, find a hotel and have a good start the following day.

William reflected, as he lay awake on Monday night, that although there was no chance they would succeed in finding any trace of their son, undertaking the journey was bringing them closer to putting the past behind them. After seeing the Cross, and Broughton Castle, they would probably push on towards Oxford. Being reasonably sure that Tony would have avoided the city centre, they planned to spend an hour or two at Blenheim. From then onward, the route he might have followed was mostly guesswork. One thing was sure - Tony would have avoided main roads, so that is what they also would do, stopping only where they imagined he would have been tempted to spend time.

Edna fell asleep almost immediately. Her inner

conviction, that they were being guided in their search, made her calmly confident that wherever their journey took them, they were doing the right thing. Several times during the day she had felt that they really were seeing things as Tony had seen them, standing in the same places. Sometimes she even thought that she sensed what he must have thought about them. She could almost hear him sighing with pleasure at the beauty all around, and laughing aloud when a girl in a Minivan, who looked about thirteen years old, beat William to a parking place. Her last thoughts were satisfaction that they were at last doing something positive; this is what they really should have done years ago...

55 – Sarah

Duffy spent so long researching that he'd had no time even to think about where he would sleep that night, but Sarah had anticipated his needs and had persuaded the police to hand back Clarinda's room keys to Doris, on the understanding that she would be occupying the room herself leaving hers for the young reporter. When he rang the police station in an attempt to contact Terry and John, he found that they had left a message for him. Not only did he now have the telephone number of their lodging, which he had failed to note down when he dashed off earlier, but he received the welcome news that there was a room waiting for him with Mrs Lynch if he needed one.

He reached the guesthouse well in time for supper so, before the four of them sat down to eat, Duffy and Sarah went into the parlour to look through their notes. Divested of his baggy coat with its bulging pockets, Duffy was quite a respectable size, not at all fat. He would certainly be able to enjoy Doris's cooking without worrying about dieting, Sarah thought.

After leaving the station that morning, Sarah spent the day strolling around the village, trying to pick up impressions by gossiping to anyone and everyone who seemed to be approachable. Most people knew who she was and were obviously sympathetic: willing to talk, if it helped. It was apparent that although some had watched her painting or seen her in her car, very few had in fact spoken to Clarinda. Two of the few had actually been in the Wench's Arms on the Saturday night. The barman (who was off-duty when he and Sarah chatted at a bus stop) told her that her daughter had arrived alone and sat alone. He saw only one other customer talk to her and that was Postie Parker. Sarah knew from Doris that Mr Parker had helped to carry Clarinda's gear back earlier, and she had already met him herself. He seemed very pleasant and harmless enough, so she was no further forward. Duffy, on the other hand, had had a much more fruitful day. He was eager to talk about what he had to show and Sarah was just as eager to listen.

56 – Polly

Polly was at last successful in being in the same place as Jenny Dawes when the nurse had time to spare. A few minutes earlier, when Jenny finished checking and tending to Clarrie, she invited Polly back into the room, saying she was now off duty and looking forward to resting her feet. "Give them a rest in here for a while – I would welcome some company," Polly said hopefully, with a smile. "There is something I would like to ask you, if you have no objection."

Jenny was intrigued enough to agree and she sank into the easy chair, which Polly always disdained; according to her it was far too low for comfort. Without wasting time, Polly explained that she was trying to help Grace Weston who was anxious to solve the mystery surrounding Amy's accident. "I believe you saw Amy leaving the hospital the day it happened, and although you must be tired of talking about it officially, would you mind describing everything again, to me?" Polly asked with fingers crossed and was relieved when, instead of jumping up and leaving, Jenny settled herself more comfortably.

To Polly's disappointment, the account was no different from that which she had already heard, but she was careful not to betray her feelings and began to talk about the boyfriend who had been a patient. Jenny spoke to him often, before and after Amy's fall and commented that he seemed to recover quite quickly from the shock, but must have missed the magazines and fruit. She then added that the police had been less interested in Amy that day, than they were in the death of the Ward Sister on geriatrics. Polly's pulse raced, intuitively feeling that there could be a link. Letting the subject of Amy go and gossiping about a new angle, encouraged Jenny to relax completely. "It was a real shame. I didn't know her well but she was a really nice woman and due to be married soon – then she suddenly collapsed and died." Jenny sighed, "A hypodermic syringe lying near her must have stuck into her right forearm as she fell and was nearly empty. Because she was right-handed it certainly wasn't suicide so they suspected foul play at first, but who would have wanted to kill her? Anyway, the tray with others on it, ready for the ward, had been knocked over, so she must have dropped it and fallen on it."

Polly would have to ask Jack to check the official police report. She could not believe that they would have closed the case without investigating it more thoroughly than Jenny implied. "Perhaps the future husband was having second thoughts," she said flippantly." It would have been one reason for murder, although a lamentably poor one! Even so, he had to be eliminated from suspicion, according to the way Polly investigated.

Jenny shook her head, having taken the remark seriously. "Oh no. he was in Spain; convalescing with his son in Valencia. He was a patient here, that's how they met."

Bingo! Polly thought, that was one coincidence too many. There was no need to probe more, the police must have interviewed everyone remotely concerned but it was difficult to know where to stop, so she asked how long the Sister had been on the geriatric ward and which ward had the husband-to-be been in. Jenny grimaced, rather sadly, and told Polly that he was an old man, nearly eighty, at least twenty years older than his bride-to-be but very well off. According to rumour he had a son who was only ten years younger than his fiancé – and wasn't it a shame, his son was also getting married soon; they could have had a double wedding.

Polly had a lot to add to her notes when Jenny left. She was convinced that the son, or his wife-to-be, or both, were unhappy about the father's coming alliance. She had no doubt that Sonja was the son's bride-to-be in June, and was the murderer of the Ward Sister. Amy had fallen within an hour or so of the time the Sister was discovered dead in her office. Amy had not seen Sonja since high school, but must have seen and recognised her in the hospital, and Sonja certainly would not have wanted a witness to the fact that she had been in the building when her future Father-in-law's future wife was found dead. Jenny said Amy walked out to the car park alone, but Polly knew she had no car with her so she must have arranged to meet Sonja there. Is there a school photograph with them both on it, she wondered. She could ask Grace. It would be interesting to discover how different Sonja appears now – or is perhaps basically unchanged.

She was so engrossed that she was startled when she heard Jack's rap on the door and it opened slowly.

Their voices, raised in greeting, echoed in her head, drawing her away from the gloom and the dark figure that still hovered nearby.

The unsmiling woman, dressed in white, was beckoning, pleading for help. Clarrie wanted to go to her but felt trapped.

Where was she?

Now the woman was speaking.

The other, more familiar voices were closer, drowning out the words. A figure appeared beyond the woman. Joyfully she recognised her father and when he moved between them she felt suddenly calm, ceased her mental struggle to move, and fell again into a deep sleep.

57 - Alec

D C S Alec Holmes listened to the tape and agreed with Algy that there was something on it that he hadn't heard while standing with Sarah on the hill. Experts who examined it confirmed that the sounds were within the human voice range but in spite of all their gadgetry, they were unable to distinguish words. He was therefore keen to let Sarah hear it, even though she heard nothing at the time. Undoubtedly, she had been through a stressful few days and was not perhaps as receptive as usual. Anyway, he could not delete it without first playing it through for her. When he rang her and explained, she was clearly intrigued and excited and readily agreed to have dinner with him on Wednesday evening. He was in touch with Polly regularly and knew that Del rang her daily, even though he had been assured that Clarrie was out of danger. His two Detective Sergeants in Peasey reported that Duffy was fitting in. They were all getting along well and making progress.

At last he felt able to tackle the mountain of work that still awaited him knowing there was no more he could do to help his friends for the moment. Who knew what Wednesday would bring?

58 – Edna

By lunchtime on Tuesday, Edna and William had already seen Banbury Cross and were on their way to Broughton Castle. They had picked up more information and some pictures from the tourist office and Edna was reading passages aloud from a local guide book. She was speculating about places that would most likely have attracted Tony, unable to decide. She suddenly stopped mid-sentence and after a few seconds silence William looked sideways to discover why. Seeing tears rolling down her face he pulled the car over to the verge and stopped, alarmed, wondering what was wrong.

A piece of paper had fallen out of the book as she turned the page. It was not related to the locality and there was no reason other than by accident that it should have been there. William took the paper from Edna's shaking hand and read:

The Mistletoe Bough by Thomas Haynes Bayley (1884)

The mistletoe hung in the castle hall, the holly branch shone on the old oak wall.

The Baron's retainers were blithe and gay, keeping the Christmas holiday.

The Baron beheld with a father's pride, his beautiful child, Lord Lovell's bride.

And she, with her bright eyes seemed to be the star of that goodly company.

Oh, the mistletoe bough. Oh, the mistletoe bough.

"I'm weary of dancing, now," she cried; "Here, tarry a moment, I'll hide, I'll hide,
And, Lovell, be sure you're the first to trace the clue to my secret hiding place."
William read on, about the young bride's disappearance and how her friends failed to find her. Years passed and Lovell grew old.
At length, an old chest that had long laid hid was found in the castle; they raised the lid.
A skeleton form lay mouldering there in the bridal wreath of that lady fair.
How sad the day when in sportive jest she hid from her lord in the old oak chest,
It closed with a spring and a dreadful doom, and the bride lay clasped in a living tomb.
Oh, the mistletoe bough. Oh, the mistletoe bough.

William was puzzled until Edna composed herself and explained. Only the day before he left home, she had heard Tony singing the old Victorian ballad and he told her that it was true and not the only horrific happening at Minster Lovell. He had spoken with such enthusiasm about the place that she was now convinced he would have included it on his planned route.

The poem was hand-written on paper torn from an exercise book. They stared at it, and each other. Their son had filled many such books, noting down anything that caught his interest, but neither dared say aloud the outlandish thought that crossed their minds. Without another word, William took their half-planned route from the glove compartment and, after consulting the map, wrote in another port of call.

59 – Duffy

Duffy's enquiries had started by 'phone with his own newspaper archives – a friend searched them for him while he went to the local newspaper offices. There were two local papers, but only one had existed for more than half a century, The Peasey Reporter. The front staff, at first suspicious, and a bit bored, became more interested when he showed his credentials and invited them to ring the police to confirm his legitimate interest. The receptionist, after doing so, asked the doorman to conduct him to the lift and rang ahead to warn her boss's secretary that he was on his way. By the time the boy stepped out of the lift, the secretary knew all about him and had had time to tell the editor. "Admittedly," Duffy laughed, "It was an ancient, slow, creaky old lift, but still impressive communication."

The editor was not quite as old as the paper or the lift but looked it, and actually remembered the search for the missing hiker. He insisted on taking Duffy personally to dig out the story, informing him on the way that his staff would have to cope without him completely in a few weeks as he was retiring. He was quite eager to go over the records – mostly his own reports – and happy to reminisce about the old days. "We didn't have all this modern technology when I was your age," he said. "It was just as well that I had a good memory because my shorthand was lousy! On the other hand, the job wasn't as glamorous as it sounds nowadays, so I didn't have a lot of competition from other would-be reporters."

As well as photocopies, Duffy had acquired one of the original posters, which Sarah recognised instantly as the one she had seen in her dream. The news reports named the missing youth as Anthony Daniels and outlined his possible route as far as it was known. They asked anyone who had information or may have seen him, to contact the police or the paper. It gave the name of his parents and stated that Anthony would not voluntarily have gone missing because he had been looking forward to starting his new business. The last postcard they received was from Reading, and they could not understand why. Having been away three weeks, he should definitely have been heading back home – not retracing his steps but circling, perhaps visiting places of historic interest. His parents were therefore convinced that something untoward happened to him after leaving Oxford.

It seemed that several local people had come forward to say they had seen the boy with the yellow knapsack, as they used to be called in those days. The poster was not coloured, of course, but he was described as having bright blue eyes and all the earlier sightings mentioned them, as also did at least one person who had spoken with him here. All the witnesses were quite sure that he must have been the missing boy. The police called off the local search after several reports came in of his being seen miles away, heading south towards Swindon. The first was dismissed immediately because although the description tallied in all other respects, the hiker had dark brown eyes. When the two following sightings confirmed that the hiker was twenty, then thirty miles away, everybody stopped worrying about him.

Sarah thought this was strange and asked if the

eyes had been mentioned in all the accepted sightings, but Duffy could not confirm this without seeing the witness statements. She then told him that White and Dee had actually spoken to the man who insisted that the hiker had brown eyes and she voiced her own suspicions that the blue-eyed boy might never have left Lesser Peasey. He might have died in the farmhouse fire, which had always been accepted as an accident. It might actually have been set deliberately to cover up the murder of three victims.

They agreed that tomorrow Duffy would see what facts he could dig up about the farm and its occupants. Sarah said she would have another walk-about and see if any of the locals remembered the people who had lived and died there in 1951. They had not closed the door and Doris walked into the room in time to hear the gist of their conversation. She said that she and her brother-in-law were not around then but Betty might well be able to give them a list of all the people who had lived in the area for more than fifty years. When they bought the post office they had taken over all the old records and Betty rescued them after her husband put them out to burn. Doris was so aghast that a triple murder might have gone unpunished on her very doorstep that she spoke of little else throughout supper, but it was nevertheless a good meal and she basked in their appreciation of her excellent cooking.

After climbing into bed at last, Sarah felt more at ease with Clarinda's familiar belongings around her. The clothes in the wardrobe, the makeup box on the dresser and a book on the bedside table, all made her daughter feel closer – not lost in a haze of unconsciousness. She relaxed, trying to visualise Clarinda, lying in her hospital bed, hoping to reach her in thought.

Sarah drifted to sleep eventually, barely aware that her mental picture of the room now included the figure of a stranger, touching Clarinda's shoulder, as if trying to wake her. It was not a nurse. It was a young woman, in a flowing white gown.

60 – Betty

From time to time Betty Parker kept remembering the family grave she had discovered, but always when her husband was not around to be questioned about the stupidity of saddling cousins with exactly the same two names. She could appreciate that one, little Andy who died, was known by the first, and Clive used the second, but whatever were their parents thinking of? Could it have been done deliberately, for fun, because they were born close together? The thought struck her that they might even have been born on the same day; she would have to ask. If they were, it was even more weird to give them the same two names.

She was having coffee with Doris tomorrow morning – she must remember to tell her. It would be a change from always talking about her house guests – and that was something else she must tell her husband; there was suspicion now that the farmhouse fire in the early 50's, was started deliberately to cover up a triple murder! He would be out for the rest of the day, but it was unlikely anyone else would tell him first. Doris spoke to her in confidence; she would not have gossiped to anyone else.

61 – Clive

Clive tried to assess his situation calmly with a complete lack of emotion. He had distanced himself so successfully from his beginnings that he no longer felt like Ben and could hardly believe that he'd had the guts to do what he had done. The unfortunate hiker had been so close to his age and build that he had seized the chance to escape not only the immediate horror but to change his whole life.

Before he became party to the Gleaseys' diabolical deeds, long before the war when his movements were not as strictly monitored, he wandered into the cemetery. An older boy drew his attention to a gravestone, which recorded three deaths in the Parker family. He held Ben enthralled with a graphic description of the terrible fire that had killed them all. Hearing the alarms and shouting in the street below, he looked from his bedroom window and witnessed the blaze. The vividness of his description lived with Ben ever after. He actually remembered Art and Glenda talking about the fire when he was a small child because they overhauled their own electrical wiring after it was said to have caused the Parker fire.

Fearfully, that night, he had pictured what it must have been like for little Andy. The horror was too much so in his imagination he pretended that Andy had escaped and, being the same age, was his friend. A year or two later, when he no longer had any real friends, and hardly ever left the farm, he wished he really had been the Andy who survived ... he would still have been adopted because his parents died in the fire, but not by the Gleaseys. His stepparents could not have been worse or even as bad. During the war, lots of people disappeared – perhaps taking advantage of the chaos to escape their drab lives or dodge the law. It seemed as though you could call yourself anything and claim an incendiary bomb landed on your house and your papers were lost. In those days, in his early teens, it sounded plausible and he thought, if he ever had a chance, he would be Andrew Clive Parker. He was familiar with the local family names and was sure that there were no remaining Parkers in the village. The telephone directory had none listed anyway so it would be easy.

At eighteen years old, he still longed to escape to a new life but was not so naive. He couldn't just pick a name and use it but he planned in detail what he would have to do. All he needed to assume Andrew's identity was his date of birth and the names of his parents, all of which were on the headstone. He could then claim his papers to be lost and apply for a copy of Andy's birth certificate. It would be simple then to acquire a national registration number so that he could take a job, but it was all just a pipedream until the night he burned his old identity with the unfortunate hiker. His chance to escape his old life and the consequences of all his misdeeds came at last, and he was ready.

As he had expected, by allowing himself to be seen in the distance leaving the village the following day and, after walking for miles until almost sunset asking directions to places even farther away, nobody suspected that the hiker had been anywhere near the farm. After it burned down and the three bodies were found there was no reason for anyone to suspect that they were not the people who lived there. His plan worked perfectly.

When he had time to examine the contents of the hiker's bag, hoping to find something of use to him, he found two postcards. One with a message already written was addressed and stamped and for the first time, as he read it, he felt remorse. The boy obviously had caring parents and because of him they would be crushed. Then he corrected himself, unwilling to take on the terrible burden of guilt; he had not expected the stranger to come to the farm and had certainly not invited him in. If the boy had not been so nosey he would have walked away and still been alive! No – it was just fate.

62 - Bobby

When Wednesday came round, Joe and Bobby were only mildly interested in the promised scouting trip. What was the point of it when they couldn't go until after school? Still, Bobby pointed out, not many grown-ups were willing to give up their free time to take a couple of kids out - and they would still be able to have a campfire and cook something. Anyway, what else would they have done if Joe's mother hadn't arranged for them to go?

Even as he spoke, Bobby had an uncomfortable feeling that going out camping with Mr Parker wasn't really a good idea. He rarely saw Joe's ghostly great-grandfather, other than in the bus shelter, but he was with them now, looking worried and shaking his head. Not being able to hear him, Bobby tried to read his lips, but couldn't. Then he had a bright idea. He concentrated hard and in his head he kept repeating, "Go and tell Sarah, go and tell Sarah, please, I can't hear you! Go. Tell Sarah."

"What's the matter with you?" Joe demanded, "You look all funny with your face screwed up! Are you hurting somewhere?"

"Oh, I'm OK," Bobby said hurriedly, "just trying to remember what we were supposed to learn last time we went out." He was actually a bit shaken because the old man must actually have heard him. He had gone. When he got home, before they left to go scouting, he would ring Sarah and find out if she'd had a visitor! It would be great if she had – not just because she could pass on what the old man was saying, but it would prove that he was not helpless. Instead of just having to put up with seeing people without knowing why, he might be able to take control sometimes.

Now that he was looking forward to ringing Sarah, the day passed inexorably slowly for Bobby.

63 – Sarah

Sarah was also finding the day dragging. The thought that the tape Alec was bringing to play for her might have something significant on it, was intriguing and exciting. She always enjoyed Alec's company, but the tape was definitely the main attraction that night.

Postie Parker and his wife had been most helpful in her search for old inhabitants and she had a list of well over thirty. Because most were married couples, it was not too daunting and it was even more convenient that the majority of them might be at the Day Centre for lunch. There were two couples and three single people who never, ever, went to the Centre; perhaps they regarded it as charity and wished to retain their independence. Whatever the reason, Sarah chose to call on all seven during the morning. She would then go to the Centre and talk to the other old people there, in a group. Obviously, some people now in middle age might also recall the farm and its inhabitants, but it made sense to start with those who were contemporaries.

Duffy offered Sarah a lift on his motorbike to the farthest out of the addresses but, seeing the look on Sarah's face at the very idea of riding pillion, Doris suggested that if she hurried, there was a bus in five minutes that went past the place. There was no official bus stop at the farm gate, but the driver would stop to let her off if she asked. "It will be Ted on this morning," Doris said, "and he's always helpful, so you'll not have to walk far and there will most likely be people coming and going at the farm all morning, so you're bound to get a lift back."

True to his reputation, Ted cheerfully stopped to let Sarah off and waved as he drove off. His last remark as she descended the step was to take no notice of the dog warning; the farmer's wife was ten times more fierce! Doris had telephoned ahead, at her own suggestion, so Sarah was greeted halfway down the drive by an elderly gentleman, who looked as if he wouldn't know one end of a spade from the other. He introduced himself as Robert and said he did not usually join his wife when she entertained friends for coffee, but he understood that Sarah wanted to speak to them both. Valerie, his wife, welcomed her at the front door with a warm smile, looking anything but fierce, to Sarah's relief.

It was evident from the way they lived that they were no longer running the farm and they confirmed as much when they said it was now in the hands of their three sons, although Robert was CEO. Doris had obviously regaled Valerie with the full story of who Sarah was and the reason for her visit so having already commiserated about the 'dreadfully cruel attack' on Sarah's daughter, as soon as coffee was served she launched into the subject eagerly. "I did wander up the hill to see her painting because I was so intrigued. I went into the village library that morning to change my books and heard that an artist was sitting there, apparently drawing the estate, but actually depicting the fields as they used to be before the Gleasey smallholding was destroyed by fire. It was terrible. They and their son died in it – well he was really their stepson, but it doesn't alter the fact that it was an awful thing to happen, does it? And the artist was very young so how did she know? She wasn't copying from a photograph or anything"

Sarah wondered how Valerie and Doris managed to exchange so much information, when neither seemed to leave conversational gaps for interruption. She could hardly tell them that Clarinda was psychic, so she glossed over the question and asked if they had known the family. They had.

Robert took over and said he had liked neither Art nor Glenda. Art wasn't much of a farmer nor obviously was he a good boss; his labourers never lasted long. "Not that I had occasion to call there much but, whenever I did, there was always a new face about and Glenda always looked sour. I felt sorry for the boy. He started at my school just before I left it and must have had a problem making friends because I never saw him with mates around the village. The fire made me think about him a lot. I couldn't recall the last time I had set eyes on him, except at a distance as he worked around the property. Everyone I asked said the same thing – not one person had actually spoken to Ben for years. I must say, we all felt very guilty; he must have had a miserably lonely life."

Robert certainly looked stricken at the thought that he had been found wanting in caring about a fellow human being – not putting himself out to wonder if the boy needed a friend. Sarah was not sure it was relevant, but asked if there had been other adopted children before the boy, Ben. Neither had heard of any others and Valerie had always understood that they only gave Ben a home because he was related to them in some way. Valerie was two years behind Robert at school and confirmed that Ben was a loner. As such, the other children regarded him with suspicion. None was ever invited to his home or he to theirs, as far as she knew. They could tell Sarah no more and they could not name anyone who might have been close to the strange pair.

Sarah changed course by mentioning the mystery of the missing hiker. They had only vague memories of the newspaper reports, but two of their sons had spoken to him when he was several miles away, walking towards Greater Peasey. It was late afternoon and rain clouds looked threatening, so they stopped their car and offered him a lift. He accepted and they dropped him in the middle of the village. The sky had brightened so he asked how far away the next village was. They told him that it was only a few miles to Lesser Peasey and formed the impression that he was considering going on after having something to eat.

Sarah was well pleased with this information because if he did continue in the same direction he would have reached the smallholding in the early evening and might well have called there, seeking a bed for the night. The place had gone up in flames before morning so, if he stayed there, there should have been four bodies in the ashes, not three.

64 – Clive

Now that the day of the ramble with the boys had come, Clive was not at all sure what he hoped to achieve. His need to discover if and where they had seen any sketches of the planned painting was now less urgent because the police had dismissed their memories of it as rubbish anyway. He had heard that Bobby pointed out to the police the way the attacker had fled and that was a facer because he was right, yet there was no way the boy could have known. They had still been well out of sight when he heard them coming and he certainly didn't hang about waiting for them to reach the top of the hill. So, the subject of his session with them this time would be how sounds carry in woodland – in other words, how easy it is to be deceived about the direction of sounds when they are bounced from trunk to trunk. It might get a reaction from Bobby. Still, he would have to be careful how he probed for answers – Bobby was far cannier than Joe.

He had always enjoyed taking Joe and his friend out before, but something about Bobby these days made him feel uneasy. The boy had a habit of staring and narrowing his eyes, looking thoughtful. Perhaps he was short-sighted or something, but it was disturbing. He was less worried about Sarah Grey than he had been – so consumed was she with anxiety about her daughter that she scarcely seemed interested in anything else. He was angry when he discovered her interest in the farm and the fire; exactly the kind of speculation he feared that the damned painting would rake up. With the painter likely to remain comatose forever, only the person who had given her the information could now reveal it. That person was obviously not her mother but if he found out from her who the girl's closest friends were, he might discover which one would have been close enough to her to drag her into a blackmailing scam.

He had expected the one responsible to threaten him directly before now and as the days passed, he grew more edgy. He was desperate to find the real blackmailer so that he could deal with him too; he wanted his good, quiet life back again, it was so unfair. After years of building successfully a new life, his old one had come back to haunt him.

How right he was.

As he worked through the afternoon, unseen watchers drifted around him, grim-faced and unforgiving. So long undisturbed, they had now found a conduit to the world they had once walked in life and could no longer rest in peace.

65 – Bobby

It was almost four-thirty when Bobby phoned Sarah. Uncle Clive and Joe would be arriving within minutes and he was anxious to find out if Joe's great-granddad had really understood him and been to talk to her. Doris told him that Sarah was not available and said she could pass on a message. All Bobby could think of saying was that he had thought of something else that had been in the picture. Doris was immediately intrigued and asked what it was. Bobby's mind instantly went blank then, to his own surprise, he blurted out, "The farm was on fire!"

He was so shocked he dropped the phone back on the cradle and stared at it, horrified; he had lied to Sarah. To add to his discomfort, the doorbell rang and Joe was shouting through the letterbox. Bobby could do nothing other than ring up again later and tell her he had not meant it. Now he had to go out. If ghostly old Mr Parker showed up again he would just ignore him. It was his fault he was in a mess. Bobby was fed-up.

66 – Sarah

Although well on the way to being convinced that the hiker perished and Ben had walked away, Sarah was responsible enough not to accept her theory without more evidence. One of the sons had driven Sarah from the farm but not, unfortunately, either of the two who had met Anthony Daniels, so after being dropped off in the village she continued her scheduled visits. The other old people she interviewed lived within walking distance of each other, just outside the village, so with nothing more to add to her store of knowledge, she eventually arrived at the Day Care Centre.

More commiserations and hopes that her daughter would soon get better and more regrets uttered by Sarah, saying it was too soon to tell – they could only pray – were followed by more confirmation that Art and Glenda Gleasey were a strange couple, who should not have been allowed to adopt a child. "The trouble was that if they hadn't they would have had to contribute money for his care in an orphanage until somebody else took him on." A woman who looked about ninety contributed in a high tremulous voice. "I was his health visitor, and although they didn't really want a child they did take him in. I think they thought if he was going to cost them money anyway, they might as well adopt him. They had him working around the place even when he was just a toddler. He fed chickens, collected eggs and weeded vegetables, but I must say that they made sure he went to school when he was old enough. After that I didn't have any reason to visit."

"Did you ever see him anywhere again outside the house, perhaps as you moved around the village?" Sarah asked. The negative answer came as no surprise. Further questioning indicated that the official visits were only an opportunity to ask the child how he was. The answer, "Very well thank you," was invariably accepted at face value because there were too many visits to make and too little time. The child had been given an opportunity to say, 'I hate it here, I work hard every day but have no toys and am never allowed to have friends' ...as if! What could they expect? Would an unhappy child admit that he was miserable, in the presence of the people responsible? Sarah did not blame the Social workers, who had always been in short supply, but the system had a lot to answer for.

A glance at her watch told her that she had better head back and prepare for her dinner date. Alec would be early, as he wanted to play the tape through before they went out, and she had a lot to add to her notebook before he arrived. When Doris greeted her excitedly and gave her Bobby's message, Sarah could only reply that he was such a helpful boy with a truly amazing memory. She knew that it was not a memory that Bobby had reported – it had to be something he had 'seen' since they last spoke. Because it fitted perfectly into the scenario she had already suspected, Sarah made up her mind to speak to the little boy again as soon as possible. He must not talk about the fire to anyone else – it was a pity he had told Doris.

Sarah immediately telephoned Bobby but in his absence asked his mother if she could walk to school with him the following day. Of course Pamela agreed – and told Sarah again how pleased she and Jake were, that Bobby regarded her as a friend and seemed much less jumpy these days, since she had allowed him to feel that he was helping her. Sarah said that he really was helping, because he was so observant and able to describe things without elaborating or speculating about their meaning.

A few hours later Alec arrived, and was soon inside, closeted in the parlour with Sarah. Doris's brother-in-law, who had let him in, walked straight into the kitchen and asked Doris, "What's that copper doing here again? Not staying for supper, is he?"

After saying that the man was not just a policeman, he was Sarah's friend, Doris added, "But I expect she'll tell him that young Bobby has just remembered something else that they should have put in that picture of theirs. The farmhouse was on fire!" She was bubbling with self-importance as she sent her latest piece of gossip on its way.

67 – Bobby

Bobby had not enjoyed the scouting expedition as much as usual; in fact, he could hardly stop thinking about the lie he had made up. When his mother repeated to him what Sarah had said about him he felt even worse, but was buoyed up by the thought that she would be coming to see him in the morning. He would explain and was fairly sure she would understand. He would be able to ask her about the old man. He decided to ring and tell Joe not to wait for him if he didn't want to be late for assembly. That would make sure they could have a proper talk because being late frightened Joe; he was weird. Sarah must have something really important to say if she was walking with him to school. Adults didn't like getting up early if they didn't have to!

The game they had played today, trying to guess where Uncle Clive was when he shouted or banged a saucepan with its lid, was stupid. After guessing wrong several times, he had been laughed at, and asked how come the police had believed him when he told them which way the man had run away after attacking the artist. Something about the laughter stung Bobby... And Uncle Clive had talked about their drawing several times and always seemed to be scoffing at them for thinking that it might be useful to know what the lady was painting. He said they should confess that they had seen an old photograph of the valley, nobody would be upset with them – it had been a clever prank and after all, they had not meant any harm.

As Bobby listened with mounting anger, the man before him almost disappeared in a darkly glowing haze. It was fascinating the way a muddy blue blur surrounded him. It was yet one more thing he would ask Sarah about. Anticipating tomorrow, his anger faded to irritation and when they parted company, they all appeared to be on good terms but Bobby knew he would never go 'scouting' again. Joe could if he wanted to, but Bobby was thoroughly bored with the whole idea; enough was definitely enough.

68 – Alec

Alec was amazed that Sarah and her few helpers had come up with a plausible reason for the attack on Clarrie, even though the villain was still at large. He had already received separate reports from Detective Sergeants White and Dee so was completely in the picture.

Closing the parlour door, to aid Sarah's concentration, Alec at last switched on the tape recorder.

Closing her eyes, Sarah relaxed and was transported back to the evening when they walked to the top of the hill together.

She listened to the sound of traffic growing more distant, rising and falling in the background and felt again the cool night air on her face as they rounded the top and stood on the far side, where Clarinda was attacked.

The faint sigh of a light breeze was all there was to be heard and the hands on the mantelpiece clock crept forward for almost ten minutes before the slow susurrus rustle increased, as if many voices were communicating in hushed whispers.

They merged with the soughing wind but even to Alec they sounded human.

As he watched anxiously, he saw Sarah tense slightly; she raised her head and tipped it a little as if straining to hear. The technician had reported that the significant part of the tape content lasted for twenty minutes and he was watching the counter, waiting until he was sure that it was safe to switch off. Before it reached that point Sarah opened her eyes and spoke to him.

"Well, that was fascinating," she assured him. "I heard many voices that I certainly was not aware of at the time." Before he could ask, Sarah went on to say that although she could not distinguish everything that was said, one or two words and phrases repeatedly reverberated in the frantic clamour to communicate.

As she listened, she imagined she could see the restless spirits drifting around her, their faces sometimes looming close – pleading, angry and some bewildered – but all eager to be heard. "Without having caught one whole sentence and identifying the words out of sequence, I still formed the impression that everyone in the group suffered the same fate, in the same way. None expected to die; promises made were not kept; they worked hard but were cheated. It seems far-fetched, talking it over now, but I'm sure I heard the words, cellar and chains, several times from different directions."

Alec listened attentively, looking more and more worried, then asked Sarah how all this could relate to the attack on Clarrie.

It was clear to Sarah that the people she heard were those who Joe sketched, reluctantly – the crowd that Bobby had seen near the farmhouse.

She remembered that Bobby also mentioned that the hiker with the yellow backpack tried to tell him something by pointing to the drinking fountain in the park.

She explained her suspicions about the site of the fountain being where the vegetable patch was in the picture and because she had obviously been communicating with the 'other side' only minutes before, Sarah avoided having to reveal Bobby's secret.

Together, they reached the conclusion that someone recognised the old farm, had something to hide about his connection with it, and could not understand why it was being painted unless it was a veiled threat, a threat that only he could understand. He probably concluded that he was about to be blackmailed.

If several people met their deaths there at his hand, should they be looking for someone who must now be very old?

It was understandable that at any age he would want to silence a blackmailer, but he could be in his early sixties – there have been children who murdered in their early teens.

Sarah told Alec that the word she heard more often than any other was 'sorry'. She assumed they were aware that, in their need, they had put Clarinda in danger. They took advantage of her clairvoyance to reveal the valley as they'd known it; before they could rest in peace, they wanted the world to know what had happened to them and where their bodies lay.

"It's obvious," said Alec, "that we'll have to excavate the area, and to do that we'll have to provide a very good reason." He had no doubt that they would find human remains and was also confident that he would be able to come up with an adequate excuse to dig there. It was, after all, open parkland; nobody would be inconvenienced or even care as long as the County bore the cost rather than the local authority.

When they eventually drove off to enjoy their evening meal, Doris phoned Betty and said they both looked very happy. "She's had good news, I'm sure. Wouldn't it be wonderful if her daughter is out of her coma and on the way to a full recovery?"

There was a click on the line as Clive put down the extension. His eyes narrowed and grew icy with fear. He too thought that Mrs Grey didn't seem quite as worried as she was when she first arrived. They were deliberately trying to conceal the fact that the girl was getting better but the truth was out now! He had no idea how he would be able to get at her in hospital but somehow, it must be done...

69 – Polly

Clarrie's condition continued to improve according to her doctors although to Polly there had been no apparent change in her since Sarah left. It was now more important than ever to Polly that she should stay close to the bedside. Clarrie might wake at any moment they said. When she did, she must see a friendly face, not just a mass of plastic piping in an empty room.

In her endless dream, Clarrie drifted in and out of places where strange things were happening. Sometimes, voices she recognised pulled her away from wherever she was and she felt frustrated, wanting to stay. Accepting the shifting scenes was effortless. Shutting them out to listen to words without pictures required concentration. Something was changing though. More and more, it seemed important to see who was talking. As her awareness increased, so did her terror ...where was she? Why couldn't she move? The voice was Polly's; Polly would help her ...she must stay and listen to Polly...

At the bedside, Polly picked up and stroked Clarrie's pale hand. "You will wake up very soon, my darling, don't be frightened, you are getting better and better every day and we are all praying you will be able to come back home soon." Pausing only to take a sip of water Polly continued, "If you can hear me, please give me a sign. Try to open your eyes or move something – a hand, a foot ...anything!"

Feeling a little calmer, Clarrie listened. She had to

move. She tried, and seemed to have lost all connection to her body but, gradually, she sensed pressure under her where her weight pressed against the mattress. After a few more minutes, she also sensed that a covering was over her. When she realised that Polly was holding her hand, she wept...

At first, Polly could hardly believe that Clarrie was responding, but there was no doubt about it; steady trickles of tears were running down both her cheeks. Polly was so excited she pushed the call button for the nurse. Surely, tears would not show up on a monitor, and this was something they would never believe if they only had her word for it. Polly launched immediately into another one-sided conversation with Clarrie – as though, if she didn't hang on to her attention now that she was showing signs of life, Clarrie might slip away again beyond reach.

The frustration of not being able to move when she wanted so much to see Polly, ebbed away when she realised that something in her had changed... She listened and heard Polly say that she was crying, although she felt nothing ...or did she? Concentrating on her eyes and face, she gradually did feel a slight coolness where her cheeks must be wet ...then the tickle of another teardrop. Once she started to feel she became almost clinically interested in what else she could do, and the excited voices around her became less important than focussing on different parts of her body. If she could feel, she must be able to control and move something. She gradually realised that instead of resting, cabbage-like, totally accepting what was happening around her, she was thinking – wondering – trying to remember what had happened to bring her here, presumably to a hospital.

The last thing she remembered was sitting at her

easel, painting. She was watching someone digging near a farmhouse, as he had been when she started the painting. He stopped and looked away towards the road. The hiker she had also seen the day before was still only halfway between the farm gate and the building. How strange, she remembered thinking, and at that instant, as a violent blow felled her, the last thing she registered was an astonishing change in the valley below. The pain exploding in her head obliterated her vision of green fields. What she saw was imprinted on her brain and, in her mind's eye, she saw it again. A maze of streets, busy with cars and people, had replaced the quiet countryside.

As if to confirm her train of thought, a young man appeared a few feet away from her. He was the hiker – still carrying his yellow kit bag – the symbol of his identity. Clarrie was not afraid; this must be how her mother saw people in spirit, but it had never happened to her in quite this way before. He looked anxious and said, "We waited so long, but I'm sorry you got hurt. Please don't forget us," he added as he turned away. The strain of the last few minutes took its toll and she slipped away to sleep again, thinking about him and wondering what it was that she must not forget...

The duty nurse was duly impressed by the evidence that Clarrie was showing signs of emotion but tried to calm Polly down, impressing on her that although any indication of brain activity was good, they would not know whether the brain was fully, or only partially recovered, until the patient came round properly. Polly was glad when the woman left the room to get on with her other jobs – she wanted someone to be optimistic with her, not dampen her spirits.

Polly noticed that the tears had dried up, so she moistened a tissue and wiped Clarrie's face before settling down. Was it her fancy or did Clarrie look more normal? She had seen her sleeping hundreds of times as a baby, a child and as a young woman and ever since the first night in hospital, she had seemed unreal, like a stranger. Now, she felt that she really was looking at Clarrie, and her heart sang.

70 – Frank

On Thursday, White, Dee and Duffy met for a pub lunch. By chance, Frank Brown and his friend Vince were there, so they were soon included in speculation about the fate of the missing hiker. There did not seem to be any harm in talking about the case openly, in fact it might bring out more memories. Other customers joined in and a voice suddenly piped up from behind the bar. "Hang on a minute – I'll fetch my mum – she'd enjoy chatting about meeting him. She was a real pain at the time though – talked of little else for months!"

When they looked surprised, Vince told them, "This is old Aggie's pub. She served behind the bar until she was nearly eighty and her eyes got so bad she kept giving us back too much change." When the laughter died down he added under his breath, "Made up for her old man short-changing us – God rest his soul."

A seat was vacated for the extremely robust, elderly Aggie, and Dee bought another round of drinks, which brought a huge smile to her face. She appeared to have no difficulty seeing who was talking and wanted to know all about the three strangers before getting back to the point. She said she told the police at the time that he was a very nice young man. He talked about his parents and the new business he was setting up. When Aggie asked him what his girlfriend thought about him going off hiking for weeks without her, he said he didn't have a steady girl-friend, but he'd met a nice one at Minster Lovell and he was on his way to Bourton-on-the-Water to visit a friend with a gorgeous sister, so he wasn't giving up hope.

The three exchanged looks. If he had intended to go there, why had Anthony Daniels headed for Swindon? Everybody laughed loudly at Frank's expense, when Aggie wagged a finger at him and said, "Young Frank there, didn't even noticed that the boy had blue eyes, but I gave them a complete description of him and everything he wore."

"Boxers or Y-Fronts?" shouted a wag at the bar.

Glaring in his direction, and then ignoring him pointedly, Aggie said the poor hiker would have been lucky to find a girl who understood his northern accent. Being pushed on this point by Terry White, Aggie sniffed and said that it was not that broad really, but he was quiet-spoken as well, and she was a bit deaf, so it was difficult to follow his every word.

Frank Brown remained quiet for a time, while others chatted on, but when the subject changed, he beckoned Terry and nodded towards the door. Outside, he declared that even at the risk of being laughed at again, he needed to say something. "It didn't seem to matter if I'd been mistaken about the eyes not being blue because others saw him afterwards, but there is one thing now that certainly doesn't fit. The hiker I spoke with was a local for sure – no way was his accent northern. Everything else about him was exactly like the poster and it seems to me that it would be too much of a coincidence if two young men, so alike, were in the same place by accident."

Terry decided to be straight and admitted that they were following up that possibility. He asked if Frank could remember whether the boy he had met looked at all familiar; could he have seen him in the area before that day. Frank thought not, but was content to know that his theory was not ridiculed. Terry had spoken to the Chief Super a few hours earlier and being well aware that they might now be looking for more than one body, he decided to rope Frank in to help. "It is possible that other missing people have passed through this area – not recently, of course, but you might ask around and see if anyone can recall anything, even rumours, about familiar faces suddenly not being around anymore, at any time in living memory." Frank's jaw dropped but he recovered and looked serious. It was clear that Terry had done the right thing because Frank shook his hand and promised to be discreet, before they went back inside.

71 – Sarah & Bobby

Sarah was up early on Thursday morning and, not wanting to be a nuisance – remembering what it was like getting a child off to school – she waited at the garden gate for Bobby to appear. Within minutes, Joe walked from the back of the houses and waved as he hurried off to school. He wouldn't suspect that she was waiting for Bobby; Bobby would not have wanted to hurt his friend's feelings by letting him know he was meeting Sarah privately by arrangement.

Pamela walked out with Bobby to greet Sarah, but did not have a chance to say much because Bobby clutched Sarah's arm and hurried her away. Both women exchanged looks of surprise, but shrugged and laughed at the boy's behaviour. "I wish he was always so eager to go to school," Pamela shouted as she waved them off.

As soon as they were out of earshot Bobby slowed down and explained to Sarah that he had not meant to say anything about seeing a fire in the picture, but had been startled when Mrs Lynch asked him to leave a message. "I didn't want to be rude," he said, "and have her thinking I didn't trust her, so I said the first thing that came into my head. But I'm really truly sorry; I didn't actually remember anything else about the picture at all." Sarah surprised him by telling him that there really had been a fire there so, by accident or intuition, he was right. She could tell that there something else bothering him and was amused when he explained that he had 'sent' Joe's great-granddad to talk to her because he was unable to hear what the old man was trying to tell him.

Bobby was disappointed to hear that she had had no visitation from old Mr Parker, so Sarah explained that there was such a lot happening in her life at the moment and so many people on the other side trying to give her messages that it might have been difficult for him to make himself heard. He accepted her explanation and suddenly stopped. They were opposite the bus shelter and he told her that Joe's great-granddad was inside, sitting on the bench. Sarah saw no one there immediately, but she turned and approached the apparently empty seat. As usual, she made a mental plea for guidance and soon, he materialised to her. He acknowledged that Sarah could see him, nodded towards Bobby and said, looking grave, "Tell him to be careful, he isn't Andy." With that, he vanished abruptly. Sarah repeated the warning and Bobby stared at her in astonishment. "Of course I'm not Andy! Who is Andy anyway?" Sarah had no idea what the message meant, but managed to convince Bobby that the advice must be important and might be for Joe. She was sure he would understand the rest of the message when the time was right and, in the meantime, he must be careful and more guarded than ever in his dealings with other people, especially strangers. She hesitated after adding 'strangers', well aware that putting too much trust in 'friends' was often more hazardous. She asked, casually, if his parents had many friends who came regularly to their house, and Bobby shook his head. "I go round to Joe's when they go out. Dad says it's cheaper to meet people for bowling or eat out 'dutch' than it is feeding them at home. He isn't a cheapskate, but he doesn't like being late to bed and if people visit they never know when to go."

Bobby's little face looked so stern as he passed on the oft-heard phrases, parrot-like, that Sarah had to smile. When they were passing the woodland, Bobby remembered to tell Sarah about seeing Uncle Clive covered with a weird, dark mist. She explained that everyone has an aura that is invisible to most people, which children more often than adults are able to see. It is usually an indication of a person's mood, or even their state of health. Of course, he then wanted to know what muddy-blue meant and Sarah had to disappoint him by saying that it might only have been an indication of the man's mood at that moment – perhaps he was upset. Bobby said that he and Joe were the only ones who had any right to be angry, and explained how Clive had been mean and made fun of their picture.

Sarah was surprised, because she had thought from something he'd said that Clive had not seen Joe's drawing at all. It was after she took possession of it and she considered showing it to him but the moment passed and she forgot. She had even more cause to ponder when, as they parted company at the school gate Bobby turned round abruptly before running off and said, "By the way, it must have been the police who told him. I never said anything to anybody, just like I promised." There was no way she could question him now about what he meant but it sounded as if Clive knew more than he should about something!

72 - Polly

Polly had just put down the 'phone after bringing Sarah up to date with the latest news about Clarrie and hearing how the investigation into the attack was progressing when Jack arrived. After expressing his relief, that Clarrie's injuries seemed now to be healing he tried to let Polly down gently by saying they must now pray that when she woke up she would be able to talk to them and that her memory would not be impaired. He feared that Polly was unaware of how rare it was for patients who had been comatose after brain injury to recover completely. He had discussed the problem at length with one of the surgeons, who belonged to the same lodge, and was afraid that Sarah and Polly might yet have more sorrow to bear. He would be on hand to support them whatever happened, and the best way he could do that now, was to distract Polly by helping to solve the mystery of Amy.

Jack was fascinated to hear all her latest findings and agreed with Polly absolutely that Sonja must have been responsible for the Ward Sister's death. "We must prove it to our own satisfaction before going to the police with your theory," he advised, "and it will not be easy. She probably made sure she was noticed when she came from Spain this time, but would have avoided doing so when she nipped back to off her future mother-in-law." He laughed at Polly's reaction to his turn of phrase. "You can tell that I'm making an effort to modernise my language! Sonja would have disguised herself in some way, yet was still recognisable to the unfortunate Amy so in all probability, although she changed her current appearance, she ended up looking more like she did at school. Do you think there are any school photos knocking about? Perhaps you could ask Amy's sister."

Polly said the same thought had occurred to her and that if Jack had no objection, she would go next door to see who was Amy-sitting. Within minutes, she was back and happy to report that Amy's brother Gordon and his wife were there and he had rung Grace to ask about photos. She said there were several, which she would find and bring with her to the hospital. Gordon said they would be off-duty and handing over in thirty minutes, but had told Grace that they were in no rush, so to take whatever time she needed. It was obvious, Polly remarked, that Grace had told him what Polly suspected and, having no more liking for Sonja than the rest of them, he was keen to help.

While they waited, Polly reminded Jack that Sarah would be returning tomorrow, early evening. After staying for only a couple of nights Alec would take her to dinner on Sunday, when he drove her back to Lesser Peasey. "It all sounds very well planned," said Jack. "It wouldn't do you any harm to have a break too, so might I suggest that having spent a few hours with Sarah, you consider leaving her alone with Clarrie on Saturday evening and allow me to take you to dinner – please say you'll come." Polly admitted that a change of scene would be nice and Sarah would probably welcome a few hours alone with her daughter, so she accepted with only the slightest hint of confusion.

To get back to the problem of proof, Jack pointed out that while Sonja was in England, her absence from Spain must have been noticed: by her future husband, for instance and his father who was visiting to recuperate. They had to consider that Raymond might have known what she was up to and would lie about her absence. If she had kept quiet about going to England, where did her friends think she was, if not at home? To find out, Jack came to an instant decision – he would fly over to Spain and ask. When Polly demurred about his time possibly being wasted, not to mention the cost, Jack dismissed her protests, saying that a break from routine wouldn't do him any harm either, and it would be a chance to brush up on his Spanish.

A knock on the door interrupted them and Polly opened the door to Grace. After accepting an envelope, in which, Grace said, there were several snaps in addition to two official annual group photographs taken in successive years – fifth and sixth form, she sat with Jack and they examined them together. Sonja was not as slim then but in spite of her hair colour, they had no problem picking her out. Now she was a striking blonde, with sweptback curls. In those days, her straight dark hair was short and a sharply cut fringe reached her eyebrows. As soon as he saw the picture, Jack slapped his thigh with delight. He would be careful to find pictures of other girls similar in appearance, but when he showed them all to his witness at the Mall, he didn't doubt which one would be picked out as the woman seen entering the lift with Amy, no doubt at all.

73 - Clive

The more he thought about the abortive scouting excursion, the more worried Clive became. It was a mistake to have taunted Bobby as he had; it was obvious that his remarks about Joe's drawing upset them both, but when he referred to Bobby's knowing which way the attacker had fled, the boy's expression froze and his whole demeanour changed. Shortly after that, it became clear to Clive that Bobby would not be camping out with them again. Everyone knew that Bobby told the police which direction to search, so what had he said to ring alarm bells? If Bobby suspected him of being a would-be murderer, is it likely that the boy would keep quiet about it? He could not afford to attract any vestige of suspicion, but what could he do to prevent it. If he could talk to Bobby alone, he might be able to assess how much of a threat the boy constituted.

His only chance of doing so was to separate him from Joe and be there to walk home with him, so tomorrow he'd ring the school and tell them he would be collecting Joe early, on some pretext; he was well known to the staff so that bit would be easy. He could take Joe shopping for a birthday present before leaving him at home, then drive back in time to park his car, meet Bobby as if by accident and walk home with him. Offering Bobby a lift was out of the question - too risky. It might lead to outright rejection and bring things to a head, in public! During the first ten minutes of the twenty-minute walk, Bobby had better give him no reason to feel threatened otherwise he wouldn't make the last ten.

Clive still had the woman in hospital to sort out; time was against him and his patience was wearing thin. He decided to say he had business in Oxford and he would suggest to Doris that knowing Mrs Grey pretty well now, perhaps she would like to take her daughter some flowers and do some shopping. If she accepted, it would give him an excuse to be in the hospital making a few acquaintances he could use later. At worst, he might at last find out the exact state of his victim. Every day that passed increased the danger he was in. He must act soon.

74 - Edna

Edna and William were actually enjoying their tour. They both felt that their son was with them in spirit. Such an easy phrase, and so often used, but especially in Edna's case, she really did sense his presence. The comments she made about what Anthony would have thought or said about some of the things they saw rang true to William and even he was beginning to believe that there was a life after death and that one day, when they both passed on, they would all three be reunited. For now, he subdued his reservations and accepted cautiously that Anthony was travelling with them and possibly guiding them along the route he had taken so long ago.

They thoroughly enjoyed Blenheim Palace, where there was so much to see that they spent many more hours there than planned. In contrast, they need not have spent more than an hour at Minster Lovell, but the romantic ruin of the old Hall was near a pretty village, surrounded by lovely countryside. They walked in and around, exploring, for the whole afternoon, knowing that they were doing what Tony must have enjoyed doing on possibly his last day on earth. Pausing to admire a particularly attractive cottage, they found themselves blocking the gateway when an elderly woman tried to enter. Their apologies and the exchange of a few pleasantries resulted in an invitation to see inside it and share a pot of tea.

Edna admired the array of family photographs on a

sideboard and one in particular caught her attention. The young man was about nineteen or twenty and remarkably like Anthony. When their hostess said that it was the last picture she had of her son, who had died in an accident nearly fifty years ago, the coincidence was too much for Edna. Before long, she was talking about their personal tragedy and the countrywide search that took place when Anthony did not return home. Jessica Mycroft was full of sympathy. At least she had known how her son died and she could only imagine what it must have been like living for so long with the faint hope that he might be alive somewhere, perhaps having lost his memory. When she saw the poster, Jessica remembered hearing a plea for information on the radio and in fact, a friend of hers was about to go to the police to say she had met him, when they heard that the search had moved to Swindon, so there was no point.

Before they finished their tea and biscuits, the doorbell rang and, within minutes, Jessica ushered in a much younger woman who smiled warmly and introduced herself as the friend who had met their son. Jessica had telephoned her and invited her over to speak with her guests. William and Edna were both close to tears as they listened to the only person they'd ever met who had spoken to Anthony after he left home.

"I was seventeen," said Francesca, "and loved talking to visitors about the stories you must already have heard. At the ruins that day there was quite a large group travelling together and just one other lone visitor. He was standing near enough to hear what I was saying, so as they wandered off to explore it was quite natural for us to carry on talking about the old legends. He was a lovely boy, so handsome, and I confess now, that I was enjoying his company and badly wanted him to stay longer. We walked around the village eventually and several times he could have 'made a pass at me' as we used to say, but he was a real gentleman and to my great disappointment, he didn't."

They all smiled at her frankness and she pleased them by going over in detail the things they had talked about and the views he expressed about life in general. He mentioned them, his parents, and the business he was setting up. Finally, to her delight, he had asked for her address and promised to keep in touch. She wept when she heard of his disappearance and it had taken her a long time to get over his loss. She said she'd never fallen for a boy so quickly before and, with typically teen-age over-dramatisation, she felt that her life was ruined. She was sure he liked her too and, who knows, they might have become close friends and lived happily ever after.

It was unusual for Edna to relax and discuss her innermost feelings with strangers but she said that Anthony must have been equally attracted to Francesca, otherwise he would never have promised to write to her. William was even more astonished when Edna told them the reasons for the journey they were making and said she was firmly convinced that Anthony had been with them in spirit for most of their trip and had guided them to this place. She sounded so sure of herself, when she declared that his reason for doing so must be to prove to them both that there really is a life after death, that they have not lost him forever and must stop grieving for him. Only after they had said goodbye and left the cottage did Edna, bursting with excitement and joy, tell William that when Francesca had been describing her afternoon with

Tony he had appeared, standing between him and the young woman and had put his arm round William's shoulders.

For many years, ever since Edna had seen the medium's features transformed into those of her son, she had longed to see him again, vowing that next time she would be better prepared. It had happened at last and she was able to look into his eyes and smile. "Did he tell you where we should head for next," William interrupted her thoughts with a wry smile, not sure whether or not to believe her.

"Silly man," laughed Edna, not at all offended. She made it clear that planning their route was pointless; they would just drive and see where they ended up. When it came to choosing which turn to take, she was absolutely convinced that William would choose the one that would eventually lead them to the place where Anthony had died and could only hope that they would also learn how he had met his end.

75 - Sarah

As her head touched the pillow on Thursday night, Sarah had an instant flashback to the scene she had been concentrating on the night before, when trying to reach Clarinda telepathically with no apparent success. Now she remembered the figure in white, the stranger at the bedside, glimpsed briefly as she fell asleep. This sign that there was now some contact between Clarinda's mind and her own made her want to shout the good news to the world, but she knew she still had to let everyone assume that her daughter was still in a deep coma.

With renewed hope, Sarah tried to rid her mind of preconceptions and sent out her thoughts as she tried to picture the hospital ward where Clarinda lay. Within a few moments a picture began to form in her mind's eye; she was seeing things as though from the bed, through the eyes of another and the woman in white was still there. Sarah heard the words, *"Where are we? I'm so frightened; I feel lost; Why is it so dark?"* Then Clarinda answered calmly, *"Don't worry, you're not alone. We have to sleep quietly until we are well."* *"Please come with me; I'm afraid,"* came the reply. Again, Clarinda tried to reassure her, *"Go back. Please don't come to me again. I'll come to you if you need me. Go now. Rest and sleep."*

Sarah was astonished. She had often wondered if people in a coma could hear what was said around them, even if unable to respond, but now it seemed that although still comatose, Clarinda was not just hearing, she was thinking. The knowledge that Clarinda's brain was functioning thrilled her, even though it presented another problem. Clarinda had offered to help, but the only way she could go anywhere was if her spirit left her body. This had happened several times years ago, without harming her, when she first discovered that she was psychic, so Sarah accepted that it was possible. Her concern was that the woman was an unknown quantity. Who was she? Did Clarinda know her, and if so, how? Mustering all her willpower, Sarah asked for a name and felt faint with relief when she heard Clarinda say, *"I'm Clarrie, who are you?"* Echoing back as the woman faded from sight, the answer came, *"Amy, Amy, Amy..."*

Now Sarah understood. She had heard all about Amy and hoped that she would heed the advice and return to where her own body lay, in the room next door. Polly had said she was not responsive and how could there signs of response if her spirit kept leaving her body. Amy must be hovering between life and death, out of control. Sarah wondered how much control Clarinda had, in her weakened state, but now that Sarah was aware of the problem, she would be able to help. Even though it was after ten-o-clock, she rang the hospital to speak to Polly.

Polly, after Sarah rang off, sat again at Clarrie's bedside and took her hand. "Your mother knows that you are concerned about Amy and she says you must not worry, she will help her while you rest and get better yourself." As if the last few minutes had not been exciting enough for Polly, what happened next was enough to make her ring Sarah back, in spite of the time. "Sarah! Dear Sarah, I cannot wait to tell you – Clarrie opened her eyes and I swear to God, I'm sure that, as she closed them again, she mouthed the words, 'thank you'..."

Sarah very rarely instigated communion with the other side of the veil, it went against all her instincts, but now she summoned to her mind everything she knew about Amy and asked for guidance. Even though nothing specific happened, a sense of calm consumed her and she fell asleep knowing that, should her help be needed, those concerned about Amy knew where she was and would be sure to let her know!

76 – Frank

Frank Brown was determined to help the police. He still smarted at the way his description of the missing boy was derided by his mates, in spite of the fact that the local Bobbies thanked him. They said his description of the encounter was useful. He knew all the most ancient inhabitants of the Peaseys and lost no time in starting to call on them. There were about thirty of them in the Home for the Elderly, so he biked round there on Friday morning and asked the Superintendent if they would like him to come and entertain them, on Sunday perhaps, with a singsong. He played the piano and had sheet music for all the good old tunes. As he expected, he was assured of a welcome; he could come at around three-o-clock and have tea with them at four-thirty. It would be no problem to get them talking, Frank guessed, many of them rarely had visitors.

Still in their own homes, there were five married couples lucky enough to be growing old together and before midday, he had spoken to three of them. It proved quite entertaining, because they all welcomed their surprise visitor and were happy to answer his questions without asking any awkward ones of their own, about why he wanted to know. He did hint that he was thinking of writing a history of the area and hoped to discover some interesting facts he might include. What about when you were just little kids," he asked the Coopers who he was currently interviewing, "Can you remember people talking about anything of unusual interest?" It was always his first question, and he had a few scribbled notes, which listed a train derailment, several road accidents, and a drowning in March 1947 after a severely cold winter. In addition to heavy rain, the resulting thaw caused serious flooding all over England.

Mr Cooper immediately mentioned the floods – he told Frank that the boy who died was a cousin of his... "Colin was only seventeen and had set off walking to a farm at Lesser Peasey, where they were offering work for labourers. We never did find out how he drowned."

"You don't know whether he drowned or not," his wife interrupted. "His body was never found, was it? Just because his coat and knapsack were floating in the river, everyone thought he'd been swept away."

"He must have drowned else he'd have come home, wouldn't he?" Cooper pointed out. "Anyway, I was mad as hell because I told him not to go – even if he'd got the job it wouldn't have lasted five minutes. They never kept anybody long at that place, must have been rotten employers – always advertising for workers they were."

Frank decided that the possible non-drowning might qualify as a mysterious disappearance, so before his next call he wrote down the name and date and known facts. The back of the used envelope where he had so far written all his jottings was covered, so he pulled back the flaps and eyed the stark blankness of its inside with satisfaction. His lack of foresight in not bringing a proper writing pad annoyed him, but it didn't really matter, he would re-write it nice and tidy before he presented his findings to Terry White. He did wonder if it was significant that the smallholding, which the fire destroyed, had cropped up again and decided to ask more questions about the owner.

His last call was on old Mr Blake, who was still as sharp as a razor at eighty-eight and knew Frank better than most people as he taught him all the way through secondary school. Because he knew he could rely on the schoolmaster's discretion, he explained the real purpose behind his interest in the old days. It certainly would not have been believable if he kept up the pretence of writing a book! English grammar had never been his strong point. Mr Blake recalled the suspected drowning, and said he'd always felt dubious about that, because Colin Cooper was a jolly good swimmer, but the earlier vanishing of one man in particular had always puzzled him.

"The disappearance of Louis Laroque in 1940 was more worrying to me personally," he said. "We had to take older people onto the cleaning staff and to tend the school grounds when war broke out in 1939. All the able-bodied people were called up to join the Armed Forces. It was a difficult time for everyone." He paused to fill his pipe with tobacco and refill Frank's glass with home-brewed beer, which was remarkably good; his latest hobby he explained. "Displaced Persons, as we called them – those who had escaped from their own countries – had a more difficult time in some respects. Native communities often mistrusted them. They were unknown quantities who might turn out to be spies!"

Frank was old enough to remember what it was like then. Posters everywhere warned that 'Walls Have Ears' and 'Careless Talk Costs Lives'; his favourite was 'Be Like Dad – Keep Mum'. Apparently, when Laroque turned up looking for a job, he made a good impression because not only did he speak perfect English but, also, his profession before the war had been landscape gardening and even better, he was younger by a good ten years than all the other applicants. The man in the post still had three weeks' notice to work out, so Blake promised Laroque the job if he could wait. He was delighted because not only was the head gardener's pay better than anything else he could have expected, but it was work he would enjoy doing. He filled in, signed all the necessary papers, and said he knew where he could get casual work on a farm for a week or two and would be back in time to take over from the man who was leaving.

"He didn't say where he would be working," Blake said, "and the people at the hostel he'd been staying at had no idea either. Anyway, as it was late afternoon when he left me to collect his bag, it must have been a local farm because he had no transport and very little money. If it had been a long walk away, he would have stayed in the hostel for the night."

It made sense to Frank and he tried not to be distracted by the thought that the farm at Lesser Peasey was in the frame again. It transpired that when the Frenchman was reported missing, his absence was of little concern to the authorities. They said nobody had seen him so he must have moved on. Pointing out to them that the man had set out for his destination just before nightfall cut no ice. He had not been spotted walking anywhere in the district, day or night, since leaving the hostel and not figured in any accident reports so, as there were no weeping relatives demanding a wider police search, he might as well not have existed. The old man was obviously still upset, remembering, feeling that he should have done more at the time, but Frank assured him that more could not have been expected of him. He was overworked, short-staffed with a school to run, "A school full of unruly kids like me," he laughed, trying to lighten the mood.

After they had chatted around the subject for a

while, Frank asked for his earliest memories of the area, particularly the smallholding and the people who owned it. Blake had never met the owners but remembered hearing that they were unfriendly and often rude to anyone who tried to get to know them. The farm dogs that had the run of the place discouraged callers. When they hired workers, the owner picked them up in his truck, at the roadside. He was amazed when the place burned down and the paper reported that they had a stepson called Ben. He had no recollection of the boy ever attending school, but supposed he must have done.

Frank was happy when he left. It might have been due in part to the amount of home-brew he had consumed, but he had a feeling that Detective Sergeant White was going to be pleasantly surprised by all he had discovered so far and he might have even more to report after Sunday tea at the Old Folks Home. It would take him hours tomorrow to write it all up neatly, but it was worth it – he had not felt so useful for years.

77 – Sarah

The first thing Sarah had intended to do on Friday morning was see Bobby again before school; she wanted to know what it was that Bobby had not told Clive. Her lateness to bed had caused her to oversleep, so it was doubtful that she would be able to talk to him about it at all until she returned. Today's meeting with her fellow sleuths was likely to be long and, she hoped, fruitful. They must plan their next moves too. She would have little time to prepare for her two nights away but her mood was buoyant; Clarinda was getting better and that was all that really mattered.

Even so, she decided it would not hurt to have a casual chat with Clive about his scouting trip with the boys and see if anything odd cropped up. She had nothing to lose except a few minutes of her time and she was not due at the police station for another twenty, so having decided on a plan, Sarah closed her door firmly and went in search of Clive.

78 – Edna

It was the eleventh day of June. When Edna woke up on Friday morning, the first thing she thought was that it would have been Tony's birthday. She couldn't picture what he would have looked like in his mid sixties – to her he would always be eighteen, confident that he was a man and capable of taking care of himself. They should never have agreed to his going off alone but how could they have argued against something he regarded almost as a symbol of his being grown up and independent.

In spite of the satisfaction that she and William were experiencing, following his journey, the knowledge that they must be nearing the place where Anthony died was beginning to put a strain on them both. William, at eighty-seven, was coping with all the driving well enough, because they were careful to stop every couple of hours, at least for a drink and a snack, but it would have been easier if she also was able to take the wheel. William was going to teach Tony to drive and they had saved to buy him a second-hand van as a coming home surprise. It was such a shame he never knew. The seller offered to return their deposit but they refused it and donated it instead to charity. It was their last gift to their son and it was beyond bearing that they should take any part of it back.

Pulling herself together, she directed her thoughts to the woman who was so young when she and Anthony walked together in Minster Lovell. Edna met

William on his fifteenth birthday and even though only fourteen she knew that he was the boy she would marry. Four years later, against the advice of her parents, but at least with their support, she had been a bride and within a year Anthony was born, the light of their lives. He would have been sixty-seven now, and she might have been a grandmother; what a wonderful life was lost to them. Still, William and she had each other and were still lucky enough to be in good health, and now, in a funny kind of way, they were finding their son again.

They intended to drive on towards Broadway because among their memorabilia was a letter to Tony from a friend who moved there with his family the year after leaving school. The two boys were close friends and had kept in touch for a while. Neither William nor Edna could recall Tony talking about him for several years, but they found a letter with the address on it and Tony might have intended to look him up. Although they knew Tony never reached the boy, they both felt that it could well have been where he was heading. An hour or so after leaving Minster Lovell, as darkness approached, they dined and spent the night in a private boarding house and enjoyed a leisurely breakfast there, before shopping at a local market. Much refreshed and in good spirits they set off again and after driving for two hours they stopped in a lay-by to enjoy the fruit they had bought.

It was a country lane and the traffic was not heavy so, because the verge was wide, they walked a little way back and forth, enjoying the fresh air. Had they been in the car and not on foot they would have missed the signpost to Greater Peasey. It was set back and almost hidden by low hanging boughs and they commented simultaneously that although not mentioned in any of their guidebooks there was something familiar about the name. Anthony might never of heard of it either, but if he had seen it, and it certainly looked as if it had been there long enough, it might well have piqued his interest, as it had theirs. Was finding the sign Divine Guidance? Without hesitation, when William took the wheel again, he turned it in the direction of Greater Peasey.

Edna's mood was euphoric; she felt so tuned in to what her son had seen and thought about during his last hours, that she told William that although they hadn't covered much ground, she preferred not to journey any farther today – nor perhaps even tomorrow. She told him that whenever she looked at the map, considering where their next overnight stay would be, her mind went a total blank. No direction seemed obvious and she was reluctant to leave the area in case her confusion was a sign that Tony's journey ended here. As they entered the town, a large notice, claiming that it was the home of the Peasey Reporter, fronted almost the first building they saw. They suddenly realised that some of the accounts in William's briefcase were cuttings from that very newspaper! No wonder the name rang a bell: a bell nearly fifty years distant.

William started to shake. His stomach churned. Now that they might be within reach of discovering the truth, he felt sick and frightened. The truth would not be pleasant and he feared he might not be strong enough to support Edna through the ordeal. He regretted that he had been so against her seeking to know more about how to use and develop her psychic awareness.

She had always been almost fragile, so acquiescent, relying on him to take the lead and make decisions.

Now, while he felt lost and fearful it seemed that she had found an inner strength. Perhaps it would be powerful enough to support them both. He could only pray that the truth really would bring them peace and not add to their regrets.

79 – Sarah

Although Terry and John would be driving Sarah back to the hospital at around five-o-clock and they could talk on the journey, they decided to have a meeting at the police station at three-thirty, immediately prior to the trip to include Duffy. They needed to compare notes with him and decide on his next step. Her attempt to locate Clive at lunchtime was futile – apparently, he was sorting out a problem with a supplier so Sarah convinced Doris that she only needed a light lunch and was resting in her room.

There was still a chance that Clive would return before her meeting so she set her alarm clock in case she fell asleep. Sarah felt strangely uneasy about leaving the village without having a chat with him although, on reflection, she could not think why. Whatever he said or did to upset Bobby, he was unlikely to have noticed at the time, let alone remember ...and how could she ask? The answer was that she could not. Having come to a decision of sorts, Sarah turned over, shut her eyes and soon slept.

80 – Edna

William and Edna booked into a hotel near the centre of the village and spent the morning browsing around a shopping precinct. While enjoying several breaks for coffee they initiated conversations with other customers that always led to the reasons for their visit, although it was a long shot that anyone would recall meeting Anthony so long ago. An elderly woman, whose dachshund allowed Edna to pet him (at which the owner professed astonishment), invited them to sit with her. "Beltane is a darling," she said, "but he doesn't make friends easily", and they were soon showing her the press cuttings. She looked at the by-line and informed them that the young reporter was now the editor but about to retire. "You really must call on him. He is delightful and would see you anyway, but do say that Millie sent you, along with her regards."

It would surely do no harm, they decided, to ask if he remembered the search for Anthony so, as soon as lunch was over, they strolled round to the Newspaper offices. The receptionist was at first reluctant to disturb the editor, but when they explained their reasons for wishing to see him, the girl hesitated. She remembered that Boris Thwaites had recently been quite pleased to discuss the old reports with a dishy young man she wished she could meet again. His phone number must be somewhere and this would be a good excuse to ask for it! Ringing the secretary she said, "I think his name was Duffy. If you could give me his telephone number,

I'll pass it on to Mr and Mrs Daniels who are here making enquiries about the same case."

There was a long pause before the editor himself came on the line and asked for the visitors to be sent straight up to see him. He would like to talk to them himself. Hiding her disappointment, the receptionist directed them to the lift and decided to get into conversation with them afterwards – she was not one to give up easily and they might know the young man.

"Please call me Boris," smiled the wispy-white-haired editor as he invited them to sit down, "I was a very raw whippersnapper when I reported on your son's disappearance. It was my first important assignment and now, in my last few months with the paper, it has come to the fore again."

William and Edna had no idea what he meant but like the true newshound that he was, Boris had unearthed quite a lot of information about the official enquiry since Duffy's visit. They were unlikely to tell him anything he did not already know, but that did not bother Boris. He was glad that the elderly couple were likeable, so he would not have to suffer in his pursuit of a good story. They accepted his offer of help with obvious relief, so he spent the next hour explaining to them that there seemed to be a connection between their son's disappearance and a recent attack on a young woman in Lesser Peasey. He knew the local police chief well and promised to introduce them to him as soon as possible. He naturally assumed that they would keep him informed of any new developments in return.

It was well after teatime when they returned to their hotel and they were both hungry but too tired to consider going down to the dining room to eat so they ordered room service. Sitting in front of the television, snugly wrapped in their voluminous hotel towelling robes, they grinned happily at each other as they ate. In spite of everything, they were calm and relaxed. It suddenly felt as if they really were within reach of answers to questions that had plagued them for most of their lives.

81 – Clive

The scenario devised by Clive was working well. Joe had needed some persuasion to leave school without Bobby, even to collect his own birthday gift but the opportunity to choose a game for his new Game Boy Color was too tempting – he desperately wanted the latest Super Mario Brothers. As it turned out they'd had to place an order for it as the release date was July lst but to make up for the disappointment and to assuage Clive's guilt, he had allowed Joe to select Gex to take home. It was a very happy boy who was dropped off at home, clutching 'Enter the Gecko'.

When he returned to the school and parked the car Clive was just too late to make meeting Bobby look accidental. He was probably halfway home, Clive thought with annoyance; his timing was well off the mark. He almost ran through the woods and caught sight of his quarry sooner than he expected. Bobby was crouching and appeared to be poking at something with a stick. He heard Clive coming and sprang to face him looking quite aggressive Clive thought, the way he held the stick, but he curbed his imagination. "Hello there. What have you found then?"

Clive tried to sound friendly as he approached and stared at the half-hidden object. It was crockery, a little white dish bordered with blue flowers and distinctively shaped like a shell... He was appalled. Even with only half the earth scraped off, it looked remarkably like one from the Gleaseys' kitchen. It was only a few hundred feet from the site of the farmhouse and it was not beyond the bounds of possibility that he had left it there himself. He was often in trouble for putting out milk to feed hedgehogs and losing plates. Clive paled; it was a direct link to his past and seemed like a sign that he could never escape the consequences of his actions and perhaps it was a warning not to make things worse.

Bobby abandoned his attempt at scraping off the hardened earth to reveal the pattern and stared at Clive with wide-eyed concern. "I was going to take it home but do you think that would be stealing?" he asked. On being assured that it had obviously been buried a long time and it was unlikely that the owner was still around, Bobby smiled happily. It might be chipped or cracked but he was sure his mother would like it more than the flowers he had been looking for.

Looking down at Bobby's face framed in a tangle of curls, Clive felt shame; however could he have considered harming the boy. His anger would be better directed at the woman who at this very moment might be coming out of her coma and denouncing him to the world. He took the dish from Bobby and wrapped his handkerchief round it, suggesting that they should wash off the dirt at the stream. Even though he had his heavy schoolbag to cope with, Bobby was difficult to keep up with as he ran ahead to the stream. Clive's careful probing with a stick soon loosened the dirt and revealed that the dish was in perfect condition and Clive polished it with his handkerchief as they walked on.

There was a strange, awkward moment at Bobby's gate as Clive handed him the now shining trophy. The boy's gaze went beyond him for several seconds during which the smile left his eyes. Was something wrong?

Clive asked him, but Bobby shrugged and said it was nothing. He thanked Clive abruptly for helping him and hurried to the house with his treasure.

All Clive's worries about what he had done to arouse suspicion returned. In a weak moment, he had blown his chance of finding out. When it came to dealing with the woman, he would not be so stupid and he would certainly have to do something about her soon.

82 – Duffy

The meeting had gone well and Sarah's only regret as she left Lesser Peasey was that there was no time to see Bobby again. She was so excited about being with Clarinda soon that she resolved not to worry about it. Doris had noted the hospital and hotel numbers but it was unlikely that she would need them. If only Duffy could have told her about the hiker's parents being in the vicinity before she drove off with Terry and John, perhaps she would have postponed her trip.

Duffy was thrilled to hear from the editor that incredibly, after so many years, the missing hiker's parents had turned up. The editor suspected that they'd somehow had wind of the renewed interest in the case and Duffy was inclined to agree. What else could have persuaded them to undertake a driving tour at their age? As Boris pointed out – following in their son's footsteps, so to speak, would have been easier when he first disappeared. Duffy was offered an introduction to them, if he could be at their hotel at ten-thirty the following day and of course, he agreed. It seemed that depending on what they discovered, their stay in the village might be short, and by befriending the elderly couple Duffy would discover more about the timing of their trip. He was not stupid enough to think that Boris's gesture was anything other than a business deal; he knew Thwaites would expect to be kept abreast of developments in the investigation, but he was sure he could handle the matter discreetly without compromising himself with his own paper.

It was a shame that Sarah and the police team were absent but Mr and Mrs Daniels were sure to stay around to meet them – after all, what was one weekend to people who had let close on fifty years pass before taking steps personally to discover what happened to their son. In the meantime, he would learn everything he could about them and their tragedy. It would make a terrific story; bi-lines in the Nationals were suddenly in sight!

83 – Polly

Polly was sitting stroking Clarrie's hand, still talking to her almost non-stop.

"Your mother should be here in less than an hour. I know you can hear me and it must be lovely, just lying there, not having to worry about anything, but you really do have to make an effort and wake up." After changing the gentle stroking to a few sharp slaps on the pale, listless wrist, Polly resumed even more firmly. "Try hard now, open your eyes, smile or cry – anything – we need you to come back to us." There was no response and tears gathered in Polly's own eyes as she stared at Clarrie's still form under the crisp unwrinkled sheets.

Beyond the throbbing and humming that seemed almost part of her she heard a familiar voice ...Polly, angry with her, telling her what to do. She could not understand. She could see people all around her so were her eyes open, or not? Most of them were strangers who faded in and out of her vision but she was comforted that her father was still near. She longed to go to him and it would have been so easy but he wouldn't let her. Raising an arm in warning he told her to stay and rest, it was not yet time – she still had work to do. Part of her understood that, unlike him, she was alive and she wondered about the woman in white who was no longer pleading with her for help. Answering as if she'd spoken aloud, her father told her not to worry, Amy was not alone. Slowly she began to separate her visions from the reality of her hospital room and the curiosity to see it grew.

Thinking was becoming easier and she guessed that if she could not move then her injuries were serious.

Surely, she thought, her mother and Polly knew she wasn't dead but they must be frantic with worry. The sob in Polly's voice filled Clarrie with an overwhelming desire to comfort her and drove her to summon every ounce of her strength in an effort to speak.

It was no use – she felt nothing, but then, amazingly, Polly stopped talking, burst into tears and started to thank God. Exhausted, but content that she must have achieved something, Clarrie slid into sleep again.

84 – Duffy

Friday nights were always busy at The Crown & Anchor. Older regulars who could not stand crowds stayed away and others arrived early to make sure of their usual seats, with good views of the dartboard. Most of the players came in only for matches and they usually brought noisy supporters with them so a party atmosphere prevailed. Greater Peasey was a magnet anyway for Duffy, bored as he was by the same faces at The Wench's Arms. Lesser Peasey did have a cinema but the film had been unchanged for a week.

His first thought as he mounted his bike and strapped on his helmet was that he might go for a drink to the hotel where Mr & Mrs Daniels were staying, but common sense told him that they were more likely to be in bed than in the bar. As he rode off, he remembered that Terry and John had struck lucky at the Crown, meeting Frank Brown; he might find other company there even if Frank and Vince were not. Ten minutes later, he was inviting the barman to drink with him and asking if he had seen Mr Brown. He was in luck – the barman nodded to a corner table where Frank and Vince were deep in conversation, looking serious, passing between them sheets of paper. Ordering another round of whatever they were drinking, Duffy made his way over to re-introduce himself.

Frank shook hands cordially enough but he obviously doubted the wisdom of discussing his connection with the police investigation. Duffy heard enough as he approached, to guess that the papers were written notes to be handed over to Terry next week. Vince hastily gathered the loose sheets together and pushed them into an old briefcase, which Frank was using again after its long sojourn in the attic. Trying to reinforce his credentials, Duffy told them that he had just come from a meeting with the police and they all appreciated Frank's support. "I'm the only one of the team here this weekend," he said, "and I had an important call just after they left – too late to tell them about it." The two older men raised their eyebrows sceptically, with side-glances at each other.

"Not too late to tell us though," Vince queried with a contrived, innocent air. Frank grinned widely, but nudged Vince, prompting him to move round to make room at the table.

"Do let the boy sit down, then we can hear all about it!"

Duffy thought it unlikely that Frank gossiped carelessly so, as Vince was obviously a trusted confidant, Duffy scored several points by referring to the latest theory, that Frank's description of the man assumed to be the hiker was accurate. Still confidentially, he said it was beginning to look as if the poor young man's journey had ended in the vicinity.

Now that their attention was riveted on him and they were more relaxed, Duffy was not surprised when they fired questions at him eagerly about how the investigation was going. He was careful not to mention the possible connection with the recent assault on Sarah Grey's daughter because, to be honest, he was not too clear on the point himself. His brief, as well as helping Sarah in any way he could, was to send full reports back for Del Delaney's benefit. He had seen Del once. While waiting in an outer office for his interview, Del walked through, in earnest conversation with a junior and his words often came back to Duffy, *"Always remember, if you can't write the truth, write nothing. Anything in black and white can be misinterpreted or twisted to hurt someone and will come back to haunt you."* Probably little in his current reports, if anything, would be published but if they helped Del he was satisfied.

"What was it about then?"

"You sure you should be telling us before them?

Duffy was startled to be brought back instantly to the present with two eager faces staring into his, waiting for an explanation. Ever since being invited to meet Anthony Daniel's parents, although excited by the prospect, he could not ignore the feeling that the age gap might make them regard him as too young to understand what they had endured. Having someone with him who was part of the original enquiries, a witness no less if he put it across to Frank properly, was one of his more brilliant ideas. They were bound to be surprised and pleased to talk to someone of same generation and would be at ease, increasing the likelihood of getting answers to his own questions. Before putting his idea forward, Duffy assured them that the call was to him personally as a reporter and it was not a police matter. Even so, because he was wearing two hats, so to speak, he would not do anything to upset his friends in the force. His aim was to gather specific information with Frank's help, if possible.

It was clearly an invitation that was impossible to turn down and it was several hours later before the party broke up. As Duffy biked back, he reflected that he could not remember having enjoyed an evening as much. After his first two beers, he stuck to Coke so it was not the alcohol. He hated to admit it but compared with his usual crowd, the two oldies were refreshingly undemanding. There was no competition to see whose joke got the loudest laugh or who knew the latest gossip. They treated him like an equal and he felt comfortable with them all. Instead of making him happier, the knowledge worried him. Would he now be less acceptable to his peers?

Beer or no beer – Duffy went to bed at last, with a headache.

85 – Polly & Sarah

When Sarah walked into Clarrie's hospital room, it was to find Polly in tears. "Oh, my dear Sarah," she gasped, "it is wonderful to see you again – and at just the right moment."

"What happened? Is Clarinda worse? For goodness sake, tell me!"

Immediately contrite, Polly said that Clarrie was definitely getting better. "I'm afraid I grew impatient! After days of talking to thin air, I so badly wanted any kind of reaction that I shouted at her and slapped her hand just like we used to do when she was naughty, when she was little, but I wasn't really angry! Then I was sorry and angry with myself – and then, you know how she used to stamp her little feet and screw her face up when she was frustrated? – Well, that's what she did! No, no – not stamped her feet, for goodness sake! What is the matter with me? It was her face... From being completely blank and still, it changed to that dreadful frown. She is trying hard, I know, and is upset not being able to come back, but she will," Polly added hastily, "this is a good sign and we now have more reason than ever to believe it will be soon."

It was only eight-thirty when Sarah finished updating Polly with details of the investigation but knowing that Sarah needed to be alone with her daughter, Polly gathered her belongings together and stated her intention of driving to the hotel for the night. She could have been spending every night in a comfortable bed, but Sarah guessed that she had slept instead in the bedside chair, and was touched to have such a good, caring friend. Even so, once alone, she was relieved to be able to relax. Placing her hand on Clarinda's forehead Sarah tried to keep her own mind empty of everything except a prayer for Clarinda's complete recovery. It was not easy. Her thoughts drifted and stray notions passed through her head – concepts that came unbidden with no apparent logic or relevance.

Not allowing her mind to dwell on any, she continued to pray and a recognisable picture slowly formed in her mind's eye. It was the view of the valley in the painting; someone was digging and a young man with a yellow rucksack was walking towards the farmhouse. As Sarah recognised it, the scene seemed to explode and for a fraction of a second, it appeared as it really is in the present. Without a doubt, she was seeing into Clarinda's mind, reading what must have been her last moment of awareness before the brutal blow felled her. Sarah was glad this time to have escaped the terrible pain of the blow, which stunned her too, simultaneously.

It was sickening to have it brought so clearly to mind, but it was also something to celebrate. It proved that Clarinda's brain was working and that they could still communicate.

Telepathy didn't come anywhere near to being as reliable as a telephone, but feelings and moods are often picked up by like minds, even when miles apart. People answering a call sometimes say they were about to ring the caller.

Not all lied. What else could it be but telepathy? Even this limited contact comforted Sarah and she felt optimistic as she tucked herself up on the chair.

The motley images and thoughts, which had drifted through her mind whilst praying, returned and disturbed her slightly but still made no sense. Eventually tiredness overcame her and Sarah relaxed into oblivion.

86 – Polly

It was midnight before Polly went to bed. It was so early when she left the hospital that she decided to go for a snack somewhere. According to Jack, some of the café bars in the Mall, where Amy fell, stayed open late and she badly wanted to see the place for herself; so why not eat there?

Now, comfortably settled in the hotel watching TV with the remote control clutched in her hand, flicking through the channels, she regretted not having returned earlier. The meal proved adequate but there was nothing to see in the car park, except confirmation that the wall at one point was slightly lower and someone reasonably strong, tall and determined could easily have lifted Amy's weight over it. Having driven up to the top floor, Polly started her search for food one floor down and almost immediately saw the restaurant with the fish tank that Sonja described as calming. The place was closed but the tank, just inside, was well lit and the fish certainly were beautiful. She was not the only one almost hypnotised by the display. A young woman standing nearby startled her by saying they were certainly colourful enough but there too many guppies. "The fantails and neon tetras are okay, I suppose, but I liked the big gold ones better..." Before Polly could answer, she waved goodnight and hurried off to join a group spilling from the bar opposite.

Perhaps they could have a tank at home, she mused, the fish were so pretty. Polly knew nothing about tropical fish or how difficult they were to look after but they would be a lovely homecoming gift for Clarrie when she left hospital. First thing tomorrow she decided, as she switched everything off and closed her eyes, she would pick up a book and find out: colourful, with lots of pictures. One was never too old to learn!

87 – Edna

Edna was awake before William and because they were in twin beds she succeeded in leaving the bedroom without disturbing him, to luxuriate in a hot foam bath. She first tried to wash her hair under the shower but the elaborate unit defeated her so she shampooed it under the tap! The bathroom was much bigger than theirs at home and far nicer than those in previous overnight stops but the hotel was selected because they planned to stay longer – however long it took until they were satisfied there was nothing more to learn in the area.

She was looking forward to meeting a young reporter called Duffy – such an unusual name, who knew something about the police looking again into Anthony's disappearance. If true, it was amazing that it should be happening now.

What could have triggered their interest after such a long time?

Although after all, she sighed, why should she and William have chosen to act differently this year from the way they had for years past?

Perhaps there really was a Grand Design somewhere; all the loose threads of the tapestry were being pulled together and it was time for the pattern to be revealed. The discreet warble of the telephone interrupted Edna's thoughts and she was relieved to hear William answer it immediately; he must have been awake, thank goodness.

Over breakfast, William explained that Duffy was bringing someone else to meet them. The man was one of the witnesses who probably spoke to their son, but Duffy was reluctant to get their hopes up, because the identity of the hiker he met was now in doubt. Edna's hopes could not get any higher. Talking to anyone who remembered the search was satisfying but the promise of meeting anyone close to the investigation excited her so much she hardly tasted her food.

An hour later, they met Duffy and Frank Brown in the lobby and took them back to their suite. Edna instantly liked Duffy – such a nice boy, she whispered to her husband as they went into the lift. The 'nice young boy' was well aware that he'd made a good impression so he took a chance and asked if they would mind if he kept his tape recorder on. Later, he was glad he had – nobody would have believed what prompted them to make the trip. He liked them both, and hoped they would not be disappointed if they learned nothing more about their son, but they, especially Edna, were so gullible – did they really think that their son was guiding them from beyond the grave? Terry and John would be amused and even Sarah would have to smile when he told her. He would give her advance warning before she met Mr & Mrs Daniels; he would not like their feelings to be hurt.

Resting in their room later, before lunch, William and Edna were happy, especially to have met Frank. He lived within walking distance of the hotel and expected them for tea at four-o-clock. He also suggested that they might like to go with him tomorrow to the residential home where he was going to play the piano for a sing-song. It would be more interesting than sitting around the hotel and less tiring than sight-seeing, Frank promised, with the opportunity to meet other people who might remember their son. On Monday afternoon Duffy was going to arrange for them to meet what he called the official team – the people he was working with on behalf of his newspaper. One of them was a woman whose daughter was mugged recently, but what that could have to do with their Anthony was a mystery.

William was collecting together and putting away all the cuttings that were spread out on show and Edna knew something was worrying him. "Come on, out with it ...what are you thinking?" she asked him.

"The young man Frank spoke to," he answered, almost reluctantly, "you know it couldn't have been our Tony, don't you?"

"I agree absolutely," Edna assured him, "and don't worry, I do realise what that means. It was somebody pretending to be him and because they were wearing his clothes, it means that they must have taken them from him. It means that the man probably harmed Anthony – most likely killed him and left his body somewhere, having stolen all his belongings. It means that Tony did not send the last few postcards, which we have treasured for years. More to the point, it supports our belief that we were guided here so that the evil man who has enjoyed his life and profited by murdering our son will be found and justice will finally be done."

William thought how right he'd been. Edna had reserves of strength he would never have expected. Even within days of acknowledging his disappearance, they each privately faced the fact that given a choice, Anthony would have come home, so he must no longer be alive to choose. For the first time they now spoke aloud of his death as an indisputable fact and in a way it was a relief.

William was still not as convinced as Edna about being 'guided' but if it kept her happy and optimistic, he willingly went along with the idea. It was a fascinating concept though, and he wondered what disclosures the next few days might bring.

88 – Algy

Although tied to his desk by other cases, Detective Inspector Algy Green was well briefed about the case and pored daily over all the written reports as they came in from Lesser Peasey. Now he was free to take a more active part and his first assignment was to arrange the excavation of the area where a drinking fountain stood on parkland. The paperwork was already completed and permission granted by the local authority. DCS Alec Holmes proved to be right – their only concern was the cost; who was footing the bill? When they were convinced that it would not be them, and assured that the area would be restored to whatever its former glory was, they signed their assent.

Work would start on Monday and several teams would be standing by, on call, according to what was uncovered at the site. The dwelling, according to old ordnance survey maps was about forty feet from where the fountain now stood and, in Joe's drawing, there was a shed between it and the farmhouse. Algy thought the site of the house was likely to be more interesting, but if Sarah wanted to know what was under the cabbage patch, he would not argue against her. He was looking forward to working with Sarah again and, knowing that she was spending the weekend at the hospital, he and Bet intended calling in to visit Clarrie. It was not their intention to stay long but when she was cataloguing several hundred books, gifted to her Antique Book Shop, Bet came across a very old volume that she knew would interest Sarah and wanted her to have it. It was not particularly valuable apparently, but was sure to intrigue her.

Bettina's son Adam was less than a year old when they married in 1992. Now seven, he was old enough to understand why his middle name was Bane. It was his father's family name and he would be able to use it if he wished, when he grew up. To Adam though, Algy was his Daddy and they adored each other.

He was going with them to the hospital so that he could meet Sarah, to whom they all owed so much.

Whenever possible on outings, Bet encouraged him to choose to wear what he liked and was trying not to laugh as Adam studied his wardrobe. Having decided that Sarah must be very old, he had already selected black trousers instead of jeans, commenting that when he first wore them to a wedding, all the wrinkly people said he looked very smart.

The white frilly shirt that went with them, he instantly rejected as being too sissy and he whittled his choice down to three – his Oxford United pullover, a bright green polo neck sweater and a striped cotton shirt with long sleeves. He stopped wearing the football one when United sold Matt Elliot, his favourite player, and it proved to be too tight anyway, so that simplified things. Since seeing Algy in his DJ, Adam had fallen in love with bow ties and, selecting a blue satin one from his collection, he held it up for approval. Trying to keep a straight face his mother suggested that he should place it against the red and white stripes of the shirt to see how it looked.

To her relief, he frowned and tried several others before asking if he really needed a tie. Bet hugged him and said he would be more comfortable if he left his shirt open at the neck, and Sarah would be impressed enough that he had chosen to wear long trousers instead of short.

With the most important decision of the day made, the trousers went into the press for half an hour while they enjoyed an early lunch. For different reasons, they were all looking forward to seeing Sarah again and hoping there would be good news about Clarrie.

89 – Polly & Sarah

Polly and Sarah, having parted early the night before, talked non-stop for most of the morning, exchanging news, bringing each other up-to-date in a way impossible by 'phone. Apart from the stream of disconnected thoughts, which Sarah felt were coming to her from Clarinda, she assured Polly, she could not claim to have communicated with her during the night. Polly was happy to have confirmation that Clarrie still had a mind and that things were going through it.

"What kind of thoughts did you have?" Polly asked. "I suppose you knew they were not your own because they were strange."

"Clarinda's vision of the valley, followed by the brief sight of the new town and the park convinced me that we were in touch," said Sarah, "but after that there was nothing coherent to hear and just darkness. It was quite uncanny and frightening and made me realise how far she still is from recovering." Although almost overcome with emotion, Sarah rallied when she saw tears in Polly's eyes. "Come on, show me what you shopped for on the way here this morning, I can see it's a book by the name on the carrier bag." As Polly handed it over and began to explain why she bought it, Sarah interrupted, "Good Lord! Now this really is weird. It reminds me of the two words that kept going through my head in my dream …gold and fish." One look at Polly's face reassured her; the tears vanished. Polly was agog to hear more but first Sarah wanted to know what sparked her interest in fish.

Starting at the end, Polly explained that she was considering setting up a fish tank for Clarrie but as she mentioned seeing one in the Mall and went over her reasons for going there, Sarah began to feel remote from everything around her and could not banish what followed her brief communion with Clarinda. Other words came back to her mind: green, swaying, floating, falling, shimmering, shining. All wrong: all wrong, why?

Polly's voice receded as Sarah tried to recall phrases that murmured in the darkness of the night and, beyond Polly, standing at the bedside, she saw the ghostly form of her own Grandmother. She was smiling reassuringly but shaking her head as she used to when Sarah failed to grasp something.

With a cry of surprise, Sarah startled Polly by exclaiming, "That explains it – the words have nothing to do with Clarinda! I have just been reminded that I promised to help Amy!"

She understood now that although the valley she glimpsed was in her daughter's memory, her mind had been a channel connecting Sarah to Amy. The ways of the Spirit world were certainly mysterious and never ceased to amaze her. Polly was only too willing to go over everything she knew about Amy, which was lamentably little, and the theory developed with Jack, which she was confident was plausible. "There does seem to be something significant about the fish, because we are continually drawn to them," Sarah admitted. "The phrases I heard could merely be descriptive of Amy's last conscious thoughts, just as the valley was Clarinda's.

"Do they have to be significant," Polly looked doubtful. "She might just have seen the tank in passing and thought they were pretty. It would be more helpful if she pictured the person who helped her over the wall of the car park. Why should she remember something so trivial?" Sarah saw her point, but now surmised that they were not meaningful to Amy at the time. Only now were they relevant – but she could not imagine why.

Picking up Polly's new book, Sarah turned the pages and agreed that a fish tank would be an attractive addition to their decor at home. "The fish are beautiful," she commented, "but I have no idea if or why they have any importance. Write down everything you can remember about your conversation with Sonja and the woman last night. We will go through the details with Jack when he comes to collect you tonight, but only briefly, as I do not intend to spoil your evening. It will do you good to have a decent meal and a change of scene."

Polly hastened to say that the only reason Jack was taking her out was to discuss the case with her, and tried not to look flustered by the implication that it was a 'date'.

The fact that Jack was planning to visit Spain surprised Sarah but she agreed that there was no other way they could confirm Sonja's absence from home, and possible presence in England when Amy fell and nearly died. Feeling more hopeful than earlier about her daughter's mental state, Sarah allowed herself to put her personal worries aside as she considered how best she could help Amy, who showed no sign of coming out of her coma. She had never seen Amy in life but she now dimly recollected a vision that drifted through her mind several nights ago, when half asleep.

It was Amy, seen through Clarinda's eyes, so the connection was already in place; the task suddenly seemed less daunting.

90 – Clive

Clive abandoned his plan to offer Doris a lift into Oxford to visit Mrs Grey's daughter when he realised that Sarah was spending the weekend with her in hospital. He would stand no chance of carrying out his plan to put the patient out of her misery with her mother watching. In any case, he was out of his depth when it came to disposing of someone by subterfuge; it was never necessary before.

Perhaps he should do nothing and just bluff it out if she came round and accused him. After all, it would be her word against his and he was well known and respected in the village – had been for years. She, on the other hand, was unknown and must be brain-damaged – whatever she said would sound like the ravings of a lunatic. Young Bobby was bothering him more; the way the boy cyed him was unnerving...

Could Bobby possibly have seen him running away that day? How else could he have known which way he went? An impression might be lingering in his brain and at any moment, Bobby might denounce him! Yes – there was more to fear from the boy than from the stupid woman who thought she was clever enough to blackmail him. Clive seized on this notion almost with relief.

His lack of action was driving him mad and Bobby Goswell was a much easier target than the woman would be. First, he must decide on the method – then on the time and place.

Most importantly, he would need an alibi and another visit to Dave would do the trick.

As Dave's wife always pointed out, anything over three beers addled the man's brain, but he never stopped at less than four.

As long as she saw them leave and return together, Vera would never suspect that they'd parted company, while Dave was in a drugged stupor in the car! Clive resumed his chores, whistling happily. At last, he had a plan.

91 - Duffy

One of Duffy's interests was photography, but there was seldom time to take pictures for fun. His camera was nothing special - just point and click, but everyone said he had a good eye for lighting and composition. When he could afford the time, he intended to go to night-school classes and become a pro. Articles accompanied by pictures might earn him something from the glossies. Officially he was off duty and it was Saturday after all, so he decided to stroll around the common and parkland, camera at the ready in case an elephant crossed his path! Grinning at his own joke, (spoken aloud for the benefit of Doris as he left the house) Duffy headed out of the village.

As he reached the hill, where Clarrie was attacked, he saw two boys about halfway up and recognised one as Joe, who drew the now famous picture and guessed that the other was Bobby because Sarah said the two boys were inseparable. She said both boys were likeable and had praised Bobby's keen observation. Perhaps he should take a few snaps of them; if ever he wrote about this case, shots of them together might come in useful. Already, work was more important than pleasure and he hastened to catch up with them. They were unaware of his approach and Bobby's voice was raised in exasperation; "You must know the names of your own relatives!"

"I told you I don't know anybody called Andy. I'll ask my Mum, but she'll want to know what it's all about and

I can't understand either – why the sudden interest and how can it matter to you," Joe protested.

Not wanting to sneak up on them, Duffy cleared his throat and called, "Hi there!" They turned and responded suspiciously to his greeting. Joe moved slightly behind Bobby and, as usual, let his friend take the lead.

"Are you following us?" Bobby asked. His tone was not aggressive, but neither was it friendly. He stood in the centre of the path trying to look tall, taking advantage of the fact that he was on slightly higher ground. Duffy smiled, thinking fast, and decided to use Sarah's name as a reference.

"You're friends of Mrs Grey, aren't you?" Duffy queried, adding quickly that he could not actually claim to be a friend himself, but he was working on a case with her and the police. If he thought this might impress them, he was wrong, but Joe looked happy when Duffy said that his picture had been a tremendous help to them all. Bobby remembered seeing Duffy with Sarah, so he relaxed a little, but was still wary. He accepted Duffy's reason for wanting a photograph, but made a point of saying that before it was ever used, they would have to give their permission, wouldn't they? With a serious face, Duffy agreed and asked if they would like him to put the clause in writing before taking the photo. Eager to please, Joe held out his drawing book – he never left home without one – and offered a black crayon. Turning down the offer, Duffy wrote in his own notebook, tore out the page and handed it to Bobby, who read it carefully before folding it and putting it in his pocket. "We're off to the wood to search around," he said, asking if Duffy wanted to go with them. "I found a dish there, not even scratched, and my mum thinks it's pretty, so there might be other useful stuff lying about."

"Fine, I'll take your photo by the fountain with the hill behind you, then I'll come and help you look – I'm not working today. But I'd quite like to hear first-hand about the way you saved Sarah's daughter." Seeing the suspicious looks they exchanged, he tried to redeem himself. "I mean, you must have disturbed whoever attacked her and if you hadn't he might have killed her." After a few minutes, walking in silence, Bobby relented and said there wasn't much to tell. A thought struck him; if Duffy was with the police, did he know which way the mugger had run off and, if he did, had he told anyone? He must find out if his suspicions about Uncle Clive were wrong. He hoped so and with that in mind, he launched through the story again.

To Bobby's disappointment, when he reached the point where, standing alone, he apparently heard someone running away, Duffy held up a warning hand, cautioning him not to say more. "You never know if anyone is within hearing. We don't want details to get around, do we?" He misinterpreted Bobby's distress as irritation at being interrupted, but Bobby's concern was for Joe – someone in his friend's family might be a real villain, and nobody else suspected him. To save Joe being shamed, perhaps he should keep his thoughts to himself, just in case he was wrong; he would not even tell Sarah he decided, until he was really sure.

92 – Clive

Clive was unnerved. His thoughts continually shot back to the farm – when he started digging a new grave, vowing it would be the last – and the ill-timed arrival of the boy who turned up and never left. He had scarcely given him a thought after posting the last of the cards, satisfied that his ruse had been successful. The intruder's shocked face, staring at the carnage in the kitchen, now haunted him. It was the hedgehog's dish and that damn picture, which brought back images blocked for years, he decided. Even burning the painting failed to banish them. He would never have come back to the area but he met, fell in love and proposed to a girl within a few weeks and only when he was shown the wedding guest-list, did he discover that many of her relatives lived in Greater Peasey. Although he rarely left the farm when a boy, he was afraid he might be recognised even after a ten-year absence, but many locals came to the wedding and nobody did.

When visiting later, he ventured over to Lesser Peasey and saw that the farm no longer existed and a housing estate occupied the fields below the hill. Luckily, the ground where the bodies lay was undisturbed; it was parkland. He began to feel safe and, to gain acceptance, claimed to be related to the Parkers who perished in a house fire. It established him as a local because older people remembered the family and he'd been right, nobody recalled the toddler's full name

– why should they? He did not intend to show anyone his birth certificate so he was just Clive – cousin of the unfortunate child whose identity he had assumed. Life went smoothly until Doris and Sam moved to Lesser Peasey, into the terraced house next door to the post office. It made him sweat at the time, but he held his nerve and survived.

His life always had been more about survival than fun. His years with the Gleaseys were never more than tolerable even when he was too young to understand the monstrous way they preyed on people. At times, he wondered why some labourers left without saying goodbye. At first, all were friendly, talking about their families and writing letters and he was in his teens before it dawned on him that those who left unexpectedly were all loners without connections. A row he once heard confirmed his growing suspicions. A worker was demanding several weeks pay... "You said you'd keep it safe for me until I wanted to move on, so where is it?" Art managed at last to calm the man by handing over a wad of notes, saying he would have the other half for him the following afternoon, without fail.

That night, Ben saw Glenda tipping powder into the man's stew from a rusty tin. It was from the barn and he almost cried out to stop her, but realised suddenly that she must have brought it in herself and wisely made no comment. Instead, he lay awake in his attic room, jumping at every sound, sure something terrible was happening. He was right. Unfortunately, as Glenda and Art carried the man downstairs, she saw him peeping round the door. "Don't just stand there," she ordered, "Give us some help."

He did, of course, and when they reached the vegetable patch he saw a deep hole similar to many he had helped to dig for compost. He was horrified and screamed about telling the police, but they laughed and said he'd dug more than one grave and would swing with them if anyone ever found out. Before rolling the victim into the hole, Art handed Ben the spade and demanded that he smashed it on the man's head. Ben hysterically refused, but Art said, it would come down on his own then – there was room enough in the grave for two. Knowing that Art was not joking, Ben complied and Glenda made a show of wrapping the spade in sacking to preserve his fingerprints, saying they could afford a new spade with some of the wages they'd saved. She probably was joking, but forever afterwards, they held the threat over him.

After reaching eighteen, he begged to be freed, promising that with a few pounds he could get well away; he would never speak of them or the farm. He'd been fed and clothed but never paid a wage. The meagre amount of money that came his way went unspent because he rarely went out, but he knew it wasn't enough to live on for long. They refused, saying there was no money to spare, but he saw them gloating one night, over piles of banknotes spilling from an old tin trunk and in a fury, he demanded a share. He raged when they laughed at him and he could scarcely remember who hit out first. His only clear recollection was seeing Art in a pool of blood and Glenda screaming that he was a murderer – that she'd kill him and see him in hell. So he'd had no choice; he picked up a fire iron and hit her and hit her until she was silent and he slowly became aware of the grisly scene around him.

It was a long time before he could think clearly enough to pick up the money and pack a few things from his room. Why he decided to bury them both instead of leaving them where they lay, in the kitchen, he couldn't think. Either way he would have been number one on the suspect list, so the arrival of the hiker was fortuitous, a real stroke of luck. Lucky escapes had featured high throughout his life, so why should his luck run out now? He stirred the ashes of the canvas in the incinerator and added more burnable rubbish before lighting it again. Eying the fierce blaze with satisfaction, he smiled; yet again all traces of his crime were destroyed by fire. The wretched painting was gone forever...

93 - Clarrie

Having told Sarah everything she knew and a lot that she suspected about Sonja, Polly said she'd already arranged for her to meet Amy's sister Grace and have a few moments alone with Amy. Laying stress on Sarah's great faith in prayer and empathy with the family, Polly assured Grace that Sarah would be happy to sit with Amy while she took a tea break. Sarah laughed but agreed that Polly could hardly reveal the real purpose behind her wish to visit a non-communicative stranger. Their voices and their words drifted and echoed in the quiet room. Clarrie was dimly aware of their presence and her breathing quickened slightly.

Must try to speak ...move ...have to show them.

The woman in white was calling her and the silvery ribbon that seemed to float behind her sparked Clarrie's interest. She remembered it happening to her, a long time ago. How frightened she was, until she found that it was her lifeline, tying her to her physical presence, dragging her safely back after allowing her spirit briefly to roam free. Clarrie's thinking was clear enough to register that this time her father was not with her but she knew he would come if she called – he was never far away. Remembering that woman was Amy, Clarrie guessed that Amy's hold on life was fragile because the shiny thread wavered loosely. She urged her to go back; Amy seemed not to understand. Don't die ...don't die ...please go back. A growing sense of panic made Clarrie exert every nerve to go to her and, amazingly, she suddenly found herself holding Amy's hand, leading her back to her bed. The ghostly Amy sank thankfully onto her bed and Clarrie hoped that she would not venture forth again, voluntarily. Her own lifeline was taut and she felt it pulling her firmly back. She was standing. She could feel the floor beneath her feet and it was so good to feel. If she returned she would not feel anything. Did she really want to go back or would it be better to cut adrift? She felt so free. For a moment she was tempted – it would be so easy but, knowing how devastated her mother and Polly would be if they could read her thoughts, she could not willingly inflict more pain on them. Slowly, she allowed herself to be drawn back to what she now regarded as a useless shell. Her thoughts revolved around Amy. Who was she? What had happened to bring her here? There were no answers and she began to question her own position, wishing she knew what was wrong with her and wondering if Del knew she was ill. It was with a flood of relief that Clarrie suddenly knew that something had changed. Sensation really was returning to her legs and arms. She could not move them yet but the sheet over her and the pillow under her head now had substance. It was a wonderful moment...

"Sarah!" Polly gasped, "Do look – she's crying! It's what I've prayed for – a sign, something for you to see yourself, to prove that our darling girl is coming back to us!"

Wiping away her own tears, Sarah could only agree that it was a relief to have witnessed something personally but, although she didn't voice her thoughts, she would be more optimistic about a complete recovery if Clarinda's mind did not seem so closed to her. She would never wish to read it, even if such feats were possible, but she craved the old, comforting feeling of not being alone. Aware that it was not the time to express doubts she put her misgivings aside and agreed that they had every reason to hope for a full and speedy recovery. Now it was time to go next door to meet Grace. What she might be able to achieve, she couldn't imagine, but she was willing to try and it would certainly do no harm.

94 – Sonja

When Sonja saw Grace reading a magazine, obviously taking a break in the visitors' lounge she kept out of sight, if Amy was alone her chance had come sooner than she could have hoped. After some research and hours of mixing and boiling to make it more concentrated – careful not to use any of her mother's pans – she was now ready to act; time to say 'Goodbye Amy'!

Trying to decide how best to finish the job she'd bungled months ago had been incredibly difficult, because anything obvious like suffocation or stabbing was impossible. Poison by mouth was also out of the question – and introducing a lethal compound into a drip, when it could only have been done on her watch, would have been ridiculous. At last, looking up 'poisons', she discovered that pesticides containing Organophosphates could be fatal on contact with bare skin. Wearing a mask and rubber gloves she pumped a cupful from a commercial spray-can to work with. All she had to do on the point of leaving, was contrive to pour it onto Amy's skin without being observed because, although colourless, there might be an immediate visible reaction to it. While pretending to adjust the top-sheet, concealing a small phial of the liquid, she would empty it over Amy's bare feet. There was no risk to her own skin as she always wore gloves and would make sure her skin was protected by plastic inside them. It was unlikely that Amy would survive in her weakened state, even if they detected the toxin.

Sonja was sure her plan was perfect and if Amy was alone this was the time to put it into action. It was worth going to find out. There was no knowing how long ago Grace left the ward but she was showing no sign of moving, so Sonja hurried away as fast as her high heels would allow – excited by the prospect of being able to return home soon.

95 – Algy

Algy Green and his family arrived at the hospital room door within minutes of Sarah returning, so Polly's stream of questions went unanswered. He had telephoned ahead for permission to bring Adam up but he popped his head round the door and suggested that they might like to draw the curtains around Clarrie's sleeping figure while the boy was present. Bet handed Sarah a huge bunch of flowers together with fruit and chocolates for both her and Polly, and surprised Sarah even more by giving her the book. "As soon as I came across it, I knew you must have it," she said, "I hope you'll find time to dip into it – you lead such a busy life, but it isn't something you would need to read from cover to cover at one sitting!"

Adam had already found Polly's book on fish and asked if he could please look at it. While he was happily absorbed, Algy told Polly that Adam was crazy about fish and they never came shopping in this direction without taking him for a meal in his favourite restaurant, where there was a big tank. It became clear that it was the one in the Mall and Polly was soon telling Algy about Amy's almost fatal fall. He did remember the case and was fascinated to hear that Polly was looking into it – convinced that it was a case of attempted murder. He became seriously interested when she gave him all her reasons for suspecting Sonja, agreeing that they were feasible. After echoing Sarah's admonition not to risk putting herself in danger he gave her his card and scribbled his home number on the back, urging her to keep him informed if she and Jack made any progress. Polly was delighted because she would have been reluctant to ring DCS Holmes with anything less than incontrovertible evidence. With Algy she could talk things over more freely

She awoke to the sound of voices, conversing quietly, forcing her to concentrate to hear what they were saying: pulling her away from the shadowy world that was no longer real to her. As her mind became clearer and a new potency entered her body, Clarrie opened her eyes. She saw that she was lying in a narrow metal cot and gazed fearfully at the drip-feed stand nearby with tubing connected to her wrist. There were curtains on the other side and people out of sight. Who were they? Trying to stay calm, she listened and recognised her mother and Polly talking, but not to each other... Were they with friends or doctors? Then she heard a child laughing and curiosity gave her the impetus to move. Stretching out her arm, shakily, she clutched the edge of the curtain and peeped through the narrow gap.

As Adam lifted his gaze from the book, their eyes met. He waved shyly and smiled. Startled, Polly turned, wondering who was behind her. Sarah and Bet were beyond Adam, facing the other way, so what had the boy seen? She was just in time to see the curtain sway back into place and couldn't hold back a startled cry, "Sarah – Sarah do look!" By the time she finished the sentence, "I think Clarrie is awake", Sarah was at the bedside sobbing with relief, cradling her daughter in her arms.

Algy and Bet insisted on leaving immediately, sensitive to the need for privacy at this fantastic, wonderful moment. Polly did not try to dissuade them; she was too overcome with emotion to say anything other than that she would ring them tomorrow. She stood in the doorway for a moment, before deciding that she too should stay outside rather than intrude but, just before it closed, she heard Sarah calling for her to come back. "You silly goose! After all you have done for us, how could you possibly think that we would not want to share this moment with you?"

Within seconds, they were joined by several medics; they had quite forgotten that the monitor would have revealed the change in Clarrie's body rhythms. After a quick check, the doctor was kind enough to allow them to stay in the room for a few minutes, while the nurse carried out her duties – adjusting the drips, straightening sheets and pillows, and making Clarrie comfortable. Before departing, he warned them against asking probing questions that might excite or upset his patient; the less she spoke or moved before a thorough examination was completed, the more likely it was that she would make a full recovery.

They didn't care about seeking answers to anything, or even talking to Clarrie. It was enough to be near her, marvelling at the miracle of having her restored to them and seeing her smile.

When Jack arrived to find a small crowd standing in the corridor and heard the constable on duty talking urgently into his 'phone he was at first alarmed, then relieved, when he realised that the news was good. It was lucky it had been Algy, with his family, who witnessed Clarrie's emergence from her comatose state. Others might not have appreciated the importance of observing secrecy about her condition. It was difficult not to look happy as they left the hospital, although having a child with them made it easier – Adam needed constant warnings, not to run ahead; completely unaware of the recent drama, he was eager now to go to the Mall, his first visit since Christmas.

Polly recognised Jack's voice at the door and went outside to give him the latest news about the investigation in Peasey before bringing him in. She wondered if, before they went to dinner, Sarah would feel up to talking to them both about Amy. Jack was keen to hear her opinion before going to Spain – he was probably leaving in the early hours. The doctor said there was no need for anyone to sit with Clarrie but, as long as visitors were not noisy and spoke more to each other than to her, she might enjoy the company; he suggested wryly that they could always ask her!

Before the door closed behind Polly, the young constable entered and apologised for intruding but said his instructions were to stay in the room in case the victim said anything relevant to the attack on her. He was obviously embarrassed but Sarah understood and suggested he brought his chair in with him. He sat near the door as far away from the bed as possible, out of Clarrie's sight. The drawn curtain did not prevent him hearing what was said, but there was little they needed to say and Clarrie eventually fell asleep, holding Sarah's hand.

96 – Edna

Edna and William thoroughly enjoyed their teatime visit to Frank's cottage and were looking forward to going with him tomorrow, to join in the sing-song at the Residential Home. He even ran through his repertoire for them and added a few of their favourites. William's voice was surprisingly strong for his age and he liked harmonising alongside Edna's descant, leaving the main vocal to their host, who was ecstatic. "We will certainly wow them tomorrow – we could go on tour with our talent!"

Anthony was not mentioned during the few hours they were there but there was one weird moment when Frank was leafing through his piles of music. He hesitated at one sheet and commented, "Pity this is a Christmas thing – I really like it." When Edna saw that it was 'The Mistletoe Bough' she smiled; surely it was another sign that they were doing the right thing.

97 – Jack

It was almost six-thirty before Polly and Jack rejoined Sarah so in order not to disturb Clarrie they all went to an anteroom to talk; they could hardly speak freely in front of the constable anyway and he took up his position outside again with obvious relief.

Jack had been busy putting together as much information as he could find about Sonja and her future father-in-law. His records, and those of the Ward Sister who died were held by the hospital and it did not surprise either Sarah or Polly that Jack was able to gain access to them. He seemed to have useful contacts everywhere. Sonja Norris was engaged to Raymond, the only son of Cedric who still maintained a firm hold on the reigns of his business empire in spite of being in his mid-eighties. "Cedric has a little pad in Wroxton Regis, only fifteen acres or thereabout," Jack told them. "He lets Raymond handle branches in Spain and Italy but probably has little confidence in him as he pays him regular visits. Raymond lives on the Costa Blanca, south of Valencia. Sonja occupies the guest suite in his villa – for the sake of appearances I suppose."

Sarah started delving in her handbag and produced an address book. She reminded them that Del's parents lived near Jávea, halfway between Valencia and Alicante and they might be able to help him in some way. In any case, they were very fond of Clarinda and rang Polly for news every few days. They would be pleased to connect with anyone who had first hand information about her condition. Jack checked the map he intended to take with him, on which Raymond's villa was already marked, according to the address he'd given as Cedric's next of kin. It was in the hills inland from Gandia, only about an hour's drive from Jávea. Instead of flying to Valencia, Jack promised Sarah that he would use Alicante airport and drive north, breaking his journey to visit them if convenient. It would be a slight diversion but worthwhile if there was the slightest chance that they knew anything about Raymond Butler.

Sarah questioned Jack about the fish tank at the Mall and he could think of no reason why it should be relevant to Amy's 'accident' except that she must have seen it on her way up to the top floor. When he returned he would call at the cafe and drop a few casual questions to the staff. News reports of Amy's fall all included photographs of her and her face was sure to be remembered, so he would ask if anyone saw her with a dark-haired woman. It was something the police would not have asked at the time and might jog someone's memory. If he returned with reliable information that Sonja was absent from Spain on the day Amy fell, they would have good reason to take the case back to the police and any evidence they could get to back up their theory would be worth pursuing.

Before leaving for dinner, Polly asked anxiously if anything of note happened when Sarah sat with Amy. She intended returning to the hotel for the night and could not bear to wait until Sunday morning to find out. Sarah shook her head and smiled as she saw Polly's face fall. "Now cheer up, something worth telling did happen, although not at all what we expected." Jack had been ready to leave but immediately sat down again, looking interested but puzzled. Polly perked up and waited expectantly. "Well," Sarah resumed, "I was comfortably settled within about ten minutes, sitting quietly and actually feeling that Amy is not beyond hope, when the door slowly opened. I was sitting in the corner of the room so that I could see every part of it, in case anything worth seeing happened, so was out of sight to the woman who entered. She closed the door furtively and behaved so strangely that I didn't immediately let her know I was there."

Polly leaned forward as if afraid to miss a single word and held her breath as Sarah continued... "There was no mistaking her for a nurse – she looked more like a fashion model."

"Sonja!" Polly exclaimed, "What did she do?"

Sarah said she guessed that the intruder was Sonja although they'd never met. If Sonja had merely removed her outdoor clothing and sat beside the bed Sarah would have spoken, but she went straight to the bottom of the bed and lifted the sheet off Amy's feet. She removed something from her glove without taking it off and, as she leaned towards the bed, Sarah clearly heard a man's voice. *Stop her*, he commanded. Startled, she blurted out the first thing that came into her head – a question – "What are you doing?"

98 – Doris & Betty

When Doris popped into the shop just as it was closing for the day, she was the last customer and Betty invited her to stay for a cup of tea. After a particularly busy day, having coped on her own, she was tired out and any excuse to put her feet up was welcome. They hadn't had a good gossip for days so the teapot was almost empty before Betty thought about the gravestone with Andrew Clive Parker's name inscribed on it. "Have you ever heard of cousins born in the same year being given the same name?"

"I don't see why not if it was a family name," said Doris, "and it was only a second name for little Andy."

"Yes, but I mentioned it to our Stella and she says she was helping here in the shop one day and remembers distinctly that Clive signed for a registered letter addressed to Andrew Clive. It was years ago and she only remembered it because the names were backward; it should have said Clive first. I see her point and yet he never uses two initials – I'd almost forgotten he had a second name."

"I suppose we could ask your Albert," said Doris, "but his parents weren't around to tell him all that family stuff, were they? Anyway, it might just have been a coincidence if the parents were living in different places and the babies were called after the same ancestor."

Betty was still unhappy and told Doris that the subject only came up because Stella asked if anyone in the family was called Andy, having quite forgotten about baby Andrew and the fire – it was a long time before Stella was born of course. "The strangest thing is," Betty added, "that it was actually little Bobby Goswell who wanted to know."

Doris frowned. "Don't you think there's something strange about that boy," she asked. "He's a good kid – always polite, but I often wonder what he's thinking – he's quite deep."

"Well, he's a good influence on Joe, who thinks the world of him – the first thing he always asks when we suggest taking him anywhere is can he bring Bobby!" Betty added that she'd promised them a day out to visit Didcot railway centre. "It sounds great – I think the engines still run up and down, showing off!"

"Rather you than me," Doris commented, pouring the last of the tea from the pot, "Never did like the old trains; all smoke and nasty smells. Dangerous too, too easy to get pushed under one. You be careful!"

99 – Clive

Clive, in desperation, was even considering that his best option might be to take Joe and Bobby to the cinema – they both wanted to see 'Pig in the City'. 'Babe', the first pig film, held no appeal at all for him personally, but it would have been an opportunity to make sure that Bobby ended up under a bus. He could hardly believe his luck when the trip to Didcot came up. Betty was really excited about the idea – he was astounded that she felt so nostalgic about smoke and steam; he couldn't understand the craze for train-spotting either, although he supposed that, like fishing, it was an excuse to sit around doing nothing. He'd have to get over to the railway centre to check the layout before they went on Sunday; today he was supposed to be bidding at a furniture auction – but if he came back without the chest of drawers, so what? He'd been outbid! Things were definitely going his way.

100 – Polly Jack & Sarah

Polly and Jack were both questioning Sarah, drowning each other out, in their keenness to confirm what happened in Amy's room next door.

"What did she say?"

"What was she holding?"

"Whose voice was it?"

This interested Polly the most. Jack was more eager to discover what Sonja held in her hand and what she intended doing with it.

Sarah teasingly reminded them that if they did not leave soon they would be late for dinner and, taking her seriously, Jack said that the restaurant would hold his table however late they arrived. Sarah gave in and carried on by describing the look of consternation on Sonja's face as she swung round and saw that she was not alone. "But she recovered very quickly and said that on her last visit when the nurse changed the bedding there was a swelling on Amy's foot, and she wondered if it had gone down." Sarah added that the woman was quite disarming and sounded so concerned that under other circumstances she might have believed her. As for the unearthly voice, Sarah had no idea who the man was, but it was good to know that someone was watching over Amy. Whoever it was would be sure to make contact again if necessary.

"Whoever it was must know exactly what happened and could save us a lot of time if they just told us how to prove it," Polly complained. "Oh, alright, I know I'm being unrealistic, but it is galling, feeling that those on the 'other side' could help more. It's exactly the same with Clarrie's attacker – Stephen must know who he is – why doesn't he tell you?"

"I truly believe that we are being helped," Sarah assured her, "but although an imperfect vessel I do have integrity and must approach solutions to problems with care. I need to be convinced, at every step, that I am being logical. If the answer were dumped in my lap I would not accept it until proven so nothing would be gained. Anyway, you became suspicious of Sonja very quickly, before you knew much about her at all; isn't it possible that someone planted the thought and prompted you to act on it?"

Looking a little sheepish, Polly conceded the point and before she could discuss it further Jack reminded Sarah that she still must tell them what was in Sonja's hand.

Unfortunately, Sarah explained, Sonja turned away too quickly for her to see what she pushed back inside her glove. She left the room quickly, saying there was no point in two people staying, so she would come and take her turn tomorrow. "After she went," Sarah told them with a smile, "I examined Amy's feet and they looked fine, but the sheet near them, where Sonja hovered, was wet. Don't worry," she assured them, "I had the sheet replaced and kept the wet one to hand to the duty constable, who will make sure Alec gets it personally. I am afraid your book is now minus its plastic bag – I needed it to protect the evidence and make sure it was not compromised before being analysed. Heaven only knows what it is and what it might have done to Amy's skin.

"Which is where I came in," Polly laughed. "Why doesn't Heaven tell us?" Before the point could be argued again, Jack stood and retrieved Polly's coat and they soon left, leaving Sarah resting, waiting contentedly for her daughter to wake from her now natural sleep. It was going to be very difficult trying to mask her happiness in Lesser Peasey on Monday but, for now, she could relax and enjoy every precious moment.

101 – Jack

Jack sighed happily, as he gazed at the Spanish coastline below. The plane was about ten minutes away from landing at Alicante so he was flying over the place he was about to visit. Unimpeded by cloud, the brightness of the early morning sun revealed mountains and valleys below, stretching from far inland to the Mediterranean Sea. The scattered villages with their whitewashed dwellings looked sparklingly clean and magical. He watched the sky change from velvety blackness to purple and for several minutes they flew through an all-red world until the edge of the sun's disc emerged from the horizon. Peach and yellow streaks soon stretched and widened until, for a few seconds, a glorious intensity obscured everything. Then, as if the effort proved too much, the splendour lessened and day started, as bright and promising as it usually did on the Costa Blanca.

After landing and retrieving his suitcase from the carousel with nothing to interest Customs officials, he was soon waiting in line to complete the paperwork and collect the keys to his hire car. There was still dew on the vehicles in the shade of the car park and even after the short walk, he was hot enough to appreciate the air conditioning in the car. It was an easy drive away from the airport straight onto the dual carriageway, which, after a few kilometres, became the motorway. After plucking a ticket from the machine at the tollbooth, he tucked it safely away before driving past the raised barrier and heading for Valencia. It was a region he knew well until a few years ago and, when not in a hurry, he used to take the coast road but he suspected it would be much busier now and he was, he reminded himself, not on a sightseeing trip.

Unlike the UK motorways, the traffic was not heavy and after driving comfortably at his own pace for a couple of hours, he exited at Ondara. It was one leg farther north than he need have travelled but was nearer to his destination, so worth the extra charge. When he called George Delaney from the airport and been given directions to the villa he was sure it would be easy to find and was looking forward to enjoying his first coffee of the day with George and Grace. Leaving the motorway behind, he turned onto the old Alicante road, immediately recognising given landmarks and less than fifteen minutes later was slowing down at the villa gates. They opened before he could leave the car – a clear invitation to drive straight in and he was relieved to be so obviously welcome.

The gravel drive, edged with flower-filled rockeries on each side, soon widened and continued to circle the house, so he drove round until he reached the front entrance and parking area. There was scarcely time to enjoy the spectacular view of the mountain and valley before George greeted him. "Come on in, you made good time from the airport, coffee is ready and breakfast or brunch – whatever you can face at this time of day – don't suppose you've eaten, have you?" It was a rhetorical question; apparently, they were determined to feed him something, and he suddenly realised that he was, in fact, hungry. Wide shallow steps, edged by a gentle concreted slope, led up to a covered terrace where Grace suddenly appeared in the open doorway. On her arm was a pile of newspapers and magazines and she hurriedly put them on a garden chair while she greeted him. Her first words made it clear that they were hoping he would not rush on to Gandia – in fact, he would be welcome to spend the night. It was a tempting offer and he admitted that he would enjoy staying for a few hours, but needed the whole of Monday clear, to start his investigation.

Uppermost in their minds were Clarrie's condition and the doctors' prognosis after her being so near to death. In spite of frequent calls from Del and Polly, it was clear that talking to someone who had just left her bedside gave them the reassurance they needed. He eventually explained the reason for his sudden visit to the Costa and they immediately wanted to help. "Why don't you leave your car here and we'll drive you," Grace suggested. "We don't mind staying overnight somewhere – and we could cover more ground than you could on your own." To Jack's surprise, George was enthusiastic and insisted on talking-over Jack's plans.

They had heard of Raymond Butler and actually met his father Cedric many years ago at a wine-tasting, but knew nothing about the family or Raymond's place up in the hills. Searching the local telephone directory proved unhelpful because they did not have a company name to look up and Raymond Butler appeared to be ex-directory. Jack was surprised when George suggested looking it up on the internet and led the way into his study. With some amusement George assured him, that not only was technology available in Spain, but Jávea Computer Club boasted a membership of over 500 – much bigger than most. "Any excuse to switch on his toy," Grace joked as she went to prepare the meal. "You might do better searching through these local papers before I throw them out," she advised. "There are also two or three copies of a new magazine

– a freebie that has just started up, 'The Grapevine'. No," she added when Jack perked up, "they are nothing to do with wine-making – they are full of articles and ads. I pick them up when I go shopping and I kept the May issue to show George because some abandoned puppies need homes. I thought we might take one." Before George had time to protest, Grace continued, "I'm sure I read something recently about the grape harvest. If we ring whoever wrote it, they might know the Butler family. They are big growers I think, so it's worth a try."

George agreed and added to Grace, "I've heard that another paper is launching in October – I think it will be called 'Round Town News'. It might not be free, but it will be a tabloid, so keep your eyes open for it."

"Don't worry, I won't let you miss the first issue," laughed Grace. Winking at Jack she said, "George always likes to be on top of local news."

By the time Grace reappeared on the patio with their early lunch, George put aside carefully a list of telephone numbers to ring the following day, including those of several reporters; no point in irritating people by disturbing them on a Sunday, they decided. Of course, Jack knew the address of Raymond's property and where it was located but he explained that he wanted to talk with as many gossiping contacts as possible, before calling on the occupants. Grace mentioned that there were several bodegas and cooperatives within a few miles of Jávea, which might well be open. One in the Sierra Bernia hills even served Sunday lunch but they would be too late for that. George suggested that they tour the area in the afternoon, which would be a pleasant drive even if they did not pick up any useful information about Raymond Butler's Company. "We need not come home again, we can drive straight on to Gandia," he said, "We'll find a decent hotel, enjoy dinner, then tomorrow we'll start our investigation proper."

While the men talked and planned as they sipped the last of the wine, Grace was busy packing overnight cases. She and George were both fluent in Spanish and Jack was pleased to have their support. He felt a stab of guilt when he heard Grace on the phone as he walked back into the villa ...she was cancelling a meeting. When she realised he was in the room, she assured him that her presence in the Charity Shop was hardly vital, but they might worry unless warned not to expect her. Grace made a few more calls to neighbours to inform them that the house would be empty overnight – it was a custom developed over the years; whether on foot or wheels any strangers in the vicinity would be noted, and watched.

When they set out for the Jalon Valley, it was after three-o-clock. Jack had needed some persuasion to take a siesta; his hosts insisted that a short rest, even without sleeping, would set him up for what might be a late night and after all, he had been on an early flight from Luton. The guest room window opened onto a balcony, but he resisted the temptation to sit outside and read. Instead, he stripped and showered, donned a voluminous towelling robe and lay on the bed.

To his astonishment, he slept for almost an hour.

Somewhat shamefaced he admitted that they were right – he had needed to relax and felt much more ready to enjoy the rest of the day. He wondered briefly, what Polly and Sarah were doing. They were probably content to be watching over Clarrie, even if she was not awake. The rhythms of natural sleep, together with a sigh or the movement of a limb, were very different from the eerie stillness of an unnatural coma. So far, his worst fears about possibly permanent damage to Clarrie's brain had not been realised, thank God! Now he worried that the swine might not be caught before news of her recovery leaked out. The need to silence her, whatever it was, must still exist and, in all honesty, Jack would rather have been back at home in England now, helping to protect her. Still, if he carried out this assignment successfully, it would be less for them all to worry about; while Clarrie was still in danger, the fewer distractions there were the better.

l02 – Pamela

Bobby's mother, Pamela, was waiting impatiently for her husband Jake to finish using his computer. Since returning from church after communion, he had been dealing with emails, mostly jokes she suspected! She had always been interested in porcelain but owned few books on the subject. In one that was specifically about old, collectible pieces, there was a dish very similar to the one Bobby found, so she was keen to search the web for an exact match. Seeing him arrive home from school with Clive that day had puzzled her, especially as Clive brought Joe home by car over an hour earlier. Bobby was strangely reticent when questioned – he seemed equally unsure about why Joe left school early. She was sure Bobby was upset in some way with Clive but resisted the temptation to question him directly. She was disappointed when he went straight to his room without talking.

At last, Jake shouted from the other room to say he was switching the machine off unless she wanted it. A quick check on the way lunch was cooking assured her that she still had half an hour to look up her once buried treasure and she was soon putting up search after search for a matching dish. After several disappointing attempts and as time was running short, Pamela went to antiquesreview.com – her favourite site – and emailed the editor:

Dear Sir,

I have in my possession a small, crudely painted, blue and white shallow dish. It looks Chinese, but the porcelain isn't the right texture. There are three little cannon balls in the pattern and trees with a pagoda and a hut on islands and on the left of one is a tiny fisherman, sitting fishing. Although it was covered in soil when found, it is in excellent condition. Can you please tell me what it is and if it is valuable?

She had written to the editor before so she was sure she would have a reply within hours and as always, while there, she browsed the site for new articles. When she saw one about Eastern weapons she made a quick note – Stella's father would be interested in it – Postie had a fine Kris displayed in his hallway behind the post office. He once said that if anyone chanced his arm at robbing the till he could slice it off at a stroke! A violent thought for such a quiet man, she had thought at the time.

Bobby had seemed extremely put out at being unable to talk to Sarah again before she left the village and Pamela wondered again, why he had formed such a strong bond with her, so quickly. She liked Sarah, but she was old enough to be his grandmother. What was it about her that made her such an important part of his life?

Bobby, upstairs in his room, was worrying about Monday. He knew he would not be able to contact Sarah from School – and, once there, how could he be sure that he would not have to walk home alone again? The more he thought about Joe's Uncle Clive, the more agitated he became. Yet when he tried to pin down exactly what he suspected, his thoughts would not take shape. He found it difficult to believe that someone he knew so well was evil enough to attack anybody, but several times he saw the hiker looking angry –

especially after they walked from the woods together. If only he could have heard what the ghost was saying! Sarah said he should pay heed to the thoughts that came to him when he saw dead people, because they might explain the message and there was now no doubt in his mind that, when standing at the gate holding the dish, watching the dead boy, the word echoing in his head was 'murderer'.

No way would he walk through the woodland to school again, with or without Joe, but what should he do? Somehow, he would have to hide until he could tell Sarah everything he suspected. She would know – his faith in her was absolute.

103 – Sarah & Clarrie

Sarah glanced up from the book she was reading and looked yet again towards the bed where Clarinda lay sleeping. It was likely that her daughter would soon be well enough actually to converse with her, and the knowledge came as a blessed relief. The few words that had passed between them so far were all to reassure each other that the worst was over and it would not be long before they were all back home together. The injury to her brain was not as terrible as first feared and Clarinda seemed to be thinking clearly, although she was slower in translating her thoughts into words. Most of the time, she slept. The doctors expected this stage to last for several days and urged that she was not yet strong enough to be questioned about the attack on her.

Among the many messages left at home, enquiring about Clarrie, was one from Maud, one of Sarah's oldest friends. Maud always treated Clarrie like the daughter she would have loved had she not been widowed when young, and childless. Maud was the only person Sarah contacted personally because it would have been heartless not to reveal that her Godchild was slowly recovering. Maud was coming to the hospital for an hour during the afternoon. She would understand that they could not talk much with Clarrie and Sarah was looking forward to seeing her.

As luck would have it, within seconds of Clarinda waking up Polly entered the ward bringing Maud with her. Being barely conscious as she tried to adjust to her surroundings again, Clarinda looked lost and worried, so, after patting her hand and dropping a kiss on her brow, Maud suggested that she and Polly would chat elsewhere and Sarah could join them later. For a while, Sarah thought that the opportunity to talk to Clarinda had been lost but then she heard her say, "Mother, what happened to me?"

What followed could hardly be termed conversation but the ever-present constable was able to report that the patient was coherent, although it was doubtful that she would be able to identify her attacker. He said there was a strange reference to open farmland being suddenly full of houses so perhaps they had been too hopeful about the victim's mental state – she was definitely confused on some points. He received instructions within minutes to take up his position outside the room. DCS Holmes was sure he could rely on Sarah to tell him if Clarrie said anything significant. Sarah was extremely relieved to see the young man go. Alone at last, the oppressive atmosphere seemed to lift and they smiled at each other.

Clarrie listened, wide-eyed, as her mother explained what had happened on the hillside and it was obvious that she was at a loss even to hazard a guess about who wanted to kill her. "What did I do," she whispered. She had no difficulty recalling everything she did prior to the attack and described her encounters with the few people she met in Lesser Peasey. Apart from a couple of young boys and the barmen at the pub, she said she only spoke with Postie Parker and Doris Lynch at the guesthouse, and Mr Lynch. In view of the picture having been stolen and the possible connection between the vision of the valley as it used to be, Sarah explained that someone saw her as a threat. Someone with a secret was anxious to protect his past from exposure.

There were many angles to the mystery and Sarah did not try to explain all they surmised or were planning – it would be too much for Clarinda, in her fragile state. She therefore confined herself, as with a child, to answering only the exact questions asked. When her daughter closed her eyes and her breathing became quieter and steadier, Sarah guessed she was sleeping again. Even so, she picked up her book again to read until she was sure. It was Bet's present to her, a tiny volume: 'The Book of Table Talk', published in 1847. The contents were fascinating, reflecting life one hundred and fifty years ago but, until she read the hand written dedication, she was mystified as to the reason for such a special gift. Written on the flyleaf in beautiful script, were the words, *To Sarah, from her affectionate sister on the occasion of her 18th birthday, July 8th 1850.*

The coincidence of both her name and her birthday – apart from the year – were too much for Bet to ignore! Whoever the original owner was, Sarah hoped that she had enjoyed her birthday present and her life. In spite of everything, existence in the soon-to-be-over 20th Century was definitely preferable to the mid-nineteenth. Psychometry was one of Sarah's strong points and she felt a fleeting empathy with the long-dead girl, but at this moment was disinclined to pursue such fancies. Maud was waiting. Putting the book aside, Sarah went to meet her friend.

104 – Edna

William and Edna, as planned, were walking to Frank's cottage rather than driving, enjoying the short stroll in the fresh air, having rested after lunch. It was exciting to think that they would soon meet at the Home where so many people lived who were old enough to recall the search for their son. They agreed not to be disappointed if nobody remembered speaking to him, but it was only natural that secretly they should hope.

On their arrival they found Frank backing his car out of the driveway – he had decided after all against walking because of the quantity of sheet music he wanted to take. Edna was not at all sorry. She could see that William was also a little out of breath. They were not as fit as they'd thought! As they drove to the residence Frank explained again, between pointing out places of interest, that although he hoped they would meet someone who remembered their son, they could help him a lot if they also asked about other people who perhaps disappeared unexpectedly at any time in the last sixty years. The police were looking into Anthony's case again very seriously and others might be connected but, of course, they were to be very discreet and not mention any official involvement.

Their arrival caused quite a stir. Everyone knew, via village gossip, why the Daniels were there with Frank and there was commiseration on all sides about their long-lost son. The posters and newspaper cuttings William handed round resulted in many comments; the search was remembered but nobody claimed to have spoken to Anthony. One of the most elderly said that she well knew how devastating it was to lose a son unexpectedly. "Just a couple of years after the war it was," she sighed, "and we'd been so relieved that it ended before he was called up, then we lost him anyway, in those dreadful floods."

Frank guessed that she was Mrs Cooper, Colin's mother. There was little point in dwelling on the fact that his body was never found, causing her more pain, but he was glad it gave him an excuse to guide the conversation towards other disappearances. "This area has been the scene of a good few tragedies, hasn't it? Like the foreigner who never turned up after getting the job of gardener at the local school." Nobody at all recalled the poor man, so Frank continued hastily. "Of course that was about 1940, when the war was still on, so anything could have happened to him. But," he improvised, "I think several other people have gone missing in the last thirty years or so."

This resulted in a lot of head shaking, blank looks and whispers of 'how dreadful', and he was disappointed until one of the nurses waved to attract his attention and repeated what she was hearing from a frail man in a wheelchair, whose quiet voice had not carried over the hubbub. The man's memory was clear about everything except the exact year, but it was either the winter before the war started or the first winter after and it was the worst tragedy he could remember. "The snow was deep all over England and even the Thames froze," he whispered. Several in the gathering nodded and all listened as he told his story. "Most country people are always prepared for anything the weather can throw at them," he said, "but my young neighbour had been ill for weeks and was still unfit when it set in, really badly.

"The man's wife was expecting any minute and they already had two infant sons, so imagine how upset he was when their fuel supply ran out and the telephone lines were dead. After we found his car abandoned and eventually got to her, she told us that he intended to come over to my place to borrow logs or paraffin but over two feet of snow fell and there were drifts of nine feet. He'd been trapped in one." He took out his handkerchief and even after such a long time, shed a tear. "The worst thing was that she'd been waiting for him to return for days, all alone, trying to keep the children warm and fed, worried out of her mind, knowing all the time that something terrible must have happened to her poor husband."

There was no happy ending to the story, because he was never found and she lost her baby. A few other people then recalled the tragedy and Frank tried to follow all the comments... It must have been dark when the car hit the drift and there were no clues as to which way he might have walked, or crawled away... he was probably disorientated, as he was ill, and headed towards Lesser Peasey, missing the nearest farm. Even after the snow melted his body was not found. Frank managed to swing conversation by saying that if the man had headed towards Lesser Peasey he would surely have arrived safely at the smallholding on the outskirts of the village. The general opinion was that having managed to get that far, he would most likely have opted to go on. It was obvious that in those days, everybody disliked the Gleaseys.

Frank had to be content with that because everyone was anxious to begin the afternoon entertainment; shouted requests for favourite songs reached him from all directions. In spite of protests from those still in good voice, tea was served eventually well after four-thirty and it was almost six-o-clock when he drove Edna and William back to their hotel. They assured Frank that they had enjoyed themselves immensely and complimented him on his playing – Edna wished she had kept up her own piano lessons. Later, as the evening drifted on, they discussed the various things they had seen, heard and done, but neither mentioned their disappointment at failing to find one single person who could add anything to their knowledge of Anthony's last few hours. Each was pinning all hope now on meeting the police team tomorrow, and having confirmation that officialdom had not forgotten him.

105 – Maud

Maud and Polly were obviously in a state of high excitement when Sarah joined them in the anteroom. "You're not going to believe this," laughed Polly, even before the door closed behind her. "Raymond Butler's father Cedric and Maud are old friends!"

"Yes," interjected Maud, "He's a dear man in spite of his terrible bridge. He never counts his high cards and makes the most ridiculous bids." Maud closed her eyes and shook her head indulgently. "Cedric's place is in Wroxton Regis, a good way from our usual haunts, so whenever he hosts the group he lays on lunch – so generous. Wine flows freely of course, so by the time we get round to playing everyone readily forgives him anything." They discovered that Maud met Cedric's fiancé there several times and found her, "Charming and so like my dear sister, God rest her soul."

Sarah and Polly exchanged wry glances, well remembering how relations between the two sisters had never been smooth. Her untimely death had evidently bestowed a saintly status on Norma. Maud also met Raymond several times apparently, and declared him to be 'very pleasant and well meaning, but a bit wet'. She was not acquainted with Sonja at all but Polly's account of their theories relating to the death of the Ward Sister and the attempted murder of Amy, fired Maud with righteous anger and she was now very keen to meet her. Polly immediately understood Sarah's warning glance. There was no way they could let Maud meet Sonja – her acerbic tongue would get them all into trouble.

"Now," said Maud, "What is our next move? This Sonja person is not aware of my connection with you, so I could bump into her, as if by accident, and ask her how dear Raymond is and if he is with her in England or I could ask if she's staying with Cedric. Should I ask her about the friend she is visiting, the young woman, Amy?" As they feared, it was going to be difficult to restrain Maud.

"There is really nothing we can be sure of until we have the lab report on the liquid she spilled on Amy's sheet," Sarah replied hastily. "I think we should keep your existence secret for now, in case we need your anonymity later. You might be a useful ace to have up our sleeves." The way Sarah phrased her idea, smacking as it did of intrigue, had the desired effect and satisfied Maud for the moment anyway. Even so, she promised to keep an ear to the ground next time she went to Wroxton Regis. She knew the staff there very well and might be able to quiz some of them – 'very discreetly, of course'. It was the best Sarah could hope for: at least she had averted immediate complications.

Maud said that Jack was unlikely to meet Cedric in Spain as he returned home only last week. Because Sonja also was here, Jack might have Raymond to himself. "If he confines the conversation to stamp collecting and wine, he'll have no problem, but Raymond is more interested in playing draughts than following football or politics. He is a lovely boy and was probably bullied at school because he's very shy." He did not sound like the type of man to whom Sonja would be attracted Polly commented, and they all found it difficult to understand why Raymond was tying the knot with Sonja. "He has been sensible enough to avoid a succession of gold-diggers," Maud said, adding shrewdly, "Perhaps she claimed to have plenty already!"

Knowing that Alec would come soon, to drive Sarah back to Lesser Peasey, Maud left, but promised to return later to sit with Polly and Clarrie for an hour or two. Much as she liked Maud, Sarah was glad of the chance to talk to Polly in private. There were so many little things to relate – things that puzzled Sarah and she missed having Polly on hand, asking questions and suggesting answers. She had not even told Polly about Bobby, still aware that he wanted to keep his gift secret and had not discussed her vision of the coffee being spilled; she still wondered what there was about it that troubled her. As soon as they were alone Sarah expressed her many nagging worries, and Polly pointed out immediately that most of them were connected to the house she was lodging in.

Sarah laughed and dismissed the idea but later, back in Lesser Peasey, as she lay in bed listening to sounds of conversation in the hall below and footsteps climbing the stairs and passing her room, she had the eeriest feeling; perhaps answers to all her problems really did lie close to home. Inside the house, she always attributed the constant waves of unease and foreboding to something she could deal with later – something troubling Doris – nothing to do with Clarinda. Every time she stepped outside it, her mood changed, but she felt no closer to finding the monster who attacked her daughter than she did when she first arrived. Perhaps she should keep her mind more open – deal with the imploring voices when they came through. If nothing else, it would clear the path and her conscience. Although Sarah hated letting people down she had continually ignored them, selfishly convinced that they could have no bearing on her own problem. Drowsily, she remembered hearing the voices on Alec's tape in the house, although they were completely inaudible to her on the hill. Close to sleep, she dismissed her last thought as silly – clarifying the sounds on the tape was clever technology, nothing else – but there was no doubt about it, she had never felt at ease in the Lynch household...

On the brink of drifting finally into unconsciousness, Sarah started worrying about the Mr Lynch Clarinda met. Who was he? Where was he now? Why had she not met him, or even heard of his existence? Tomorrow – it was something she would have to ask Doris.

106 – Clive

Clive's day had been frustrating. If he never saw another train in his life, he would be happy. Joe and Bobby obviously enjoyed themselves and stuck together like glue, but in any case, it was clear that the chance of pushing anyone under a train at the exhibition centre was slim. It was a stupid idea and he would have to put off his final solution yet again. In flashes of clear thinking, he wondered why he was so convinced that Bobby suspected him of the murderous attack but, whenever the boy looked at him these days, he felt that none of his secrets was safe. During the evening, relaxing and watching TV, he calmed down; his own adult logic could explain away anything Bobby could possibly do or say; Bobby was only a kid! By the time Clive went to bed, he was in a mellower mood. He would keep an even closer eye on the boy and plan accordingly. He was scared of being cornered – he alone knew how dangerous his blind rage could be.

107 – Edna

Edna went to bed happy after an unusually exciting day. She had thoroughly enjoyed her visit to the Rest Home, even though there were no revelations about Anthony. She went to sleep praying that he would contact her again and thinking too about the other tragic stories she had heard. Perhaps because she was in such a receptive state, it was easy to invade her thoughts. Everything in her dream was so clear and real to her that she had no problem describing it to William as soon as he woke up.

A wall calendar was open at *March 1947*.

A young man was staring out of his bedroom window and she seemed to be in his head, reading his mind. She knew it was Colin Cooper and relayed his thoughts.

...Colin had been staring out at the rain for over an hour, between stuffing things into his rucksack and listening to the radio, always anxious for the latest weather forecast. He should have gone for the job when he first heard of it last week.

If only he had known that the storm would turn so savage and rage for what seemed like ever, he would have given his mate's birthday bash a miss because he really needed the money.

His father said there was no point in going, there could be no work in flooded fields but Colin protested that if there were animals, it was likely that help would be needed more than ever.

Ever since first saying that he was applying for a farm labouring job his whole family had been against it. He had done well at school and his School Certificate was good enough to earn him a place at a teacher training college – but so what?

He had no desire to teach anyone anything. Training for a different career would be possible, but it was not worth fretting about the future – he needed to earn money now. None of his friends had to rely on pocket money from their parents. His were as generous as they could afford, but one round of drinks cleaned him out ...nothing left for a night out at the flicks; he couldn't afford to take himself let alone a girl!

The weather appeared no better and was likely to get worse so it was now or never. Shrugging his knapsack onto his back, he pulled a waterproof over his head and went downstairs.

He knew he would face another argument if anyone saw him, so he waited for a moment at the bend of the stairs to decide which way to go out. Voices coming from the kitchen indicated that it was safer to use the front door. Had his father been in the sitting room he would have seen him through the side window.

He always joked that from his armchair he was in command – he had a good view of both the entrance and the television – his pride and joy. Very few people had one and he even enjoyed watching Muffin the Mule on his afternoon off. As soon as the weather cleared, Colin thought, he would return and collect more clothes and make his peace for leaving without saying goodbye. They were sure to forgive him when they realised he had become independent and was no longer a drain on their income.

His feet floundered and squelched as he leaned into the wind, making his way to the main road; it was certainly no use trying the short cut across the fields. Sheets of rain clouded his vision and within ten minutes, for the first time, he doubted the wisdom of what he was doing.

Had it not been for a van that swished slowly near him he would not have known that he'd left the lane and was actually on the main highway and reluctantly, he decided to turn back. By then, he was so disorientated that he struggled on for over a mile before he recognised where he was and realised that he was heading the wrong way. At that moment a car stopped near him and the driver pointed rearwards and gave him a thumbs-up.

Colin saw that the car was towing an open trailer and, without a second thought, he waved his thanks and climbed into it.

Luckily, the car was heading for Lesser Peasey, so as soon as it was obvious that they were almost there, Colin leaned over and knocked on the car's rear window, whereupon the driver stopped and allowed him to alight.

With a cheery wave his rescuer drove away, leaving him to walk away from the village towards his destination, The rain lashed his face and the wind threatened to bowl him over but he was happy as he leaned into it, sure that he was doing the right thing. Even if there wasn't a job for him, they would surely not mind if he flopped in an outbuilding until the worst of the weather was over. They might even offer him a hot drink. Life was suddenly full of possibilities.

Edna had been describing her dream with her eyes shut and when she opened them, she saw William staring at her, open-mouthed.

He was astonished but because he knew Edna could not have made up such a tale, he truly believed that

Colin Cooper had conveyed his thoughts to her.

They talked it over and decided to find a way of telling his mother. The young man must want her to know he had meant well, otherwise he would not be using Edna.

108 - Bobby

Bobby woke up far too early on Monday morning still agitated and unable to get back to sleep. He was worried about how he was going to be able to hide until Sarah returned; she was the only person he could tell who would understand and believe him. He could not tell Joe what he suspected, about one of Joe's own family.

He wished that he'd taken Sarah's advice and let her explain to his parents that he wasn't a nut case.

Yesterday had been okay because there were lots of people about, but even Joe would not be around today. He'd come back from Didcot with a bad headache and feeling sick, so his mother was keeping him at home until they knew it wasn't catching.

He could think of no excuse for staying at home himself and feared that Clive might attack him if he walked to school on his own. His only hope was to hide somewhere until school was over. He could leave the house as usual then turn back before reaching the woods …after that, who knew?

Too tired to think beyond that, he fell slowly into a troubled sleep.

109 – Jack

It had been later than Jack hoped when they arrived in Gandia last night, but touring the valley, visiting bodegas in picturesque villages had been an interesting experience, especially in such enjoyable company. Even though they were too late to enjoy the Sunday paella lunch, George drove up to the Mazarof, a vineyard, where they owned vines ... twenty, in fact, from which they were allotted twenty bottles of wine annually for ten years. Apparently they had not been up to the Sierra Bernia for months, so had two boxes of wine to collect ... "Might as well kill two birds with one stone," said George, "and Peter, who owns the place might well know Raymond Butler, and in any case, he'll be glad to have his bottles back." Grace expressed amazement that George had actually remembered to put them in the boot and explained to Jack that the vineyard sometimes had a problem unless members returned their empties.

The excellent dinner they enjoyed last night, a good night's sleep and an English style breakfast had put them all in a good mood and they could hardly wait to start investigating. They decided to split up but remain in close contact as they progressed through the main thoroughfare, in case something promising cropped up. Jack was also glad that they would be within call if he needed a translator. One of the first three shops he went into sold newspapers and magazines in several languages, but it took him at least ten minutes to discover that they had no delivery system, so seemed not to know many of their customers' names. They did ask '¿Le gustaria reservar un periodico?', which encouraged Jack to ask if many English names were on their reserve list for collection. With a shrug, the **señora** turned her folder to let him check for himself; no worries about privacy here, he thought gratefully. Judging by the number of top-shelf publications that were on order, there were opportunities in plenty for embarrassing gossip, but no names familiar to him among the few English customers.

The young man serving drinks at the bar next-door spoke English and was eager to show off his conversational skill, so it was easy for Jack to be more open about obtaining information. Raymond and his wines were well known and 'the old man' dropped in for a drink sometimes. "Señor Cedric lady, she long time not come now, she very nice," the barman said. Jack decided it better not to say that the lady was dead – Cedric might have more than one friend. Instead, he asked if Señor Raymond lady came to drink with him sometimes. "Very much," was the reply, "she also very nice and very beautiful.

It was obviously ridiculous expecting the man to pinpoint Sonja's movements in and out of the country, especially when it might have been a lightning secret trip, months ago, but he did learn something. The barman's mother ran a Lavenderia and she collected laundry from the villa every other day. Hardly believing the luck that had brought him so quickly to a possible source of help, Jack jotted down the directions to the laundry and left happily. George and Grace were impressed, especially George, who had nothing to report. Grace however was clutching something she'd bought and refused to show it to them in the street.

The shops would be closing soon for the afternoon siesta, so they decided that the laundry should take priority and they would find it together – George's fluent Spanish would be an asset because Jack knew that the owner had no English. Afterwards, they would have lunch. It would be bad manners to visit the villa anyway without an appointment, especially before four-thirty.

110 – Sonja

Since the heart-stopping moment when she was interrupted and prevented from doing the job properly, Sonja could not stop her mind churning... for all she knew, the spilled liquid from the phial had landed on Amy's skin and she could be dead or dying! On the other hand, if it had soaked into the bedding would it leave a stain? If someone else handled the sheet while it was still wet, would they end up ill – or dead? It was a nightmare and she could not bring herself to visit the hospital to find out. Taking to her own bed at home seemed the best option; surely, someone would ring up soon, either to find out where she was or to give her the 'terrible news' about her dear friend! Fervently hoping that it would be the latter, Sonja turned over and tried to sleep.

lll – Polly

Polly was overjoyed to find Clarrie more and more responsive to everything that was happening around her. She didn't try to push conversation, being quite happy reading the daily newspaper or a magazine. On the side locker was her book about keeping fish, which she wanted to show Clarrie when next she woke. She would be sure to love the beautiful pictures.

Under police supervision, Clarrie was moved from Intensive Care to a ward in another wing so Polly was able to make it more comfortable for them both. She was glad to be rid of the lowest armchair she had ever had to struggle out of and consequently never used. Now she had a recliner, which was a Godsend at nights. Today, Sarah might hear the test results on Amy's sheet. Polly shuddered when she thought about what might have happened, had Sarah not been there. She had just spoken briefly to Grace Weston on the room phone and it seemed that since Friday afternoon Sonja had not visited Amy. They expected her on Saturday evening but apparently, she didn't show up. Grace expressed the hope that Sonja was on her way back to Spain. It had seemed a good idea to have her support, but nothing – no amount of talking to or at Amy – had so far been any use. Polly tried to convince Grace that she should not give up trying. Although she could not tell her, Polly believed that with Sarah now taking a hand, there was reason to hope for her recovery.

When Clarrie sighed and stirred, Polly watched her

anxiously until she opened her eyes, ready to speak. They had not told her anything about Amy and in fact, she should not have known about the poor girl's fall, or her current condition, so when the first thing Clarrie said was, "Oh, hello Polly – how is Amy?" it was a shock. Sarah had told her that Amy and Clarrie communicated in an amazing way while both were comatose – dead to the world – but although curious, she did not tire Clarrie by talking over things she would have to repeat for her mother. Polly merely said that Amy was still sleeping. Instead, she picked up, "Fish as Pets" and opened the book to a picture of an aquarium. Pointing it out, Polly asked if Clarrie had ever seen the one in the shopping precinct that was similar. Agreeing that they were very pretty and would be an attractive feature to have at home, Clarrie added that they were not like those in the cafe aquarium but she preferred tropical ones anyway.

At the time, Polly thought the remark odd so while Clarrie slept she read her notes to check what the woman had said about liking the gold ones better. She was ecstatic, realising that when Sonja claimed to have seen Angel Fish and Kissing Gouramis at Christmas, she had lied. She must have returned to England since the display changed, because the fish in December were cold-water fish. Jack planned to ask more questions at the Mall when he returned and establishing exactly when the restaurant changed the display must be high on his list of priorities.

112 – Jack

Jack left it to George to select a restaurant and he knew a good one nearby where the seating was in bays, which reduced noisy chatter from other diners. It would be easier to talk privately and there was a lot to talk about after their visit to the laundry. Their interest in one of her oldest and best clients puzzled Candida, who owned and managed it. Although reluctant to discuss them at first, she relaxed when Jack told her that her son was sure she could help to solve a mystery.

He struggled with his poor Spanish, but even George could not translate Jack's words exactly, so they gave up when Grace began to laugh uncontrollably, while shrugging her shoulders at Candida.

Eventually, both women were giggling together happily and exchanging scathing comments about husbands and sons.

Candida soon relaxed enough to accept that they had nothing against the family but were enquiring into the movements of his guest, Señora Sonja. They all noticed that Candida became more galvanised by this information.

After checking her workbook, she confirmed that there was no laundry for her to collect from Raymond's villa on two occasions in January and March and now, for more than two weeks, there was laundry only from the Señor. She added that on one occasion there had been very little from the Señora, and the date matched the one on which the hospital Sister died and Amy fell.

It might not be good enough for the law but the three sleuths were delighted.

At the restaurant, after placing their orders, Jack opened a new page in his notebook and recorded their latest findings. He underlined the coincidence of the dates, to emphasise the probable importance. Once in full swing, Candida enjoyed telling them all she knew about the family. It was all good; she especially liked Raymond. Señor Cedric's lady was very nice; she was trying to learn Spanish. Señor Raymond's lady was very pretty but spoke no Spanish, not even 'Ola'. The obvious disapproval in her tone said it all. They continued to discuss every aspect of the case throughout the meal and decided it might still be worthwhile trying to talk to Raymond before returning home. Jack especially was curious to know how Sonja had explained her brief absence to Raymond. Grace, looking extremely smug, surprised him by saying she could make a good guess.

Lifting onto her lap the shopping bag she had been carrying all morning, she still hid its contents while she explained. "It seemed to me, when we set out, that I might find out more about Sonja if I discovered which hair stylist she favoured. So I concentrated on hair salons only." Grace smiled, acknowledging the approving nods from the men. "Then," she said, "After four failures, I saw a display of wigs in the window of the fifth, and knew I'd hit the jackpot. So I went in and bought this one!" With a flourish, Grace lifted out a short-cut fringed wig of black hair. It certainly matched the hairstyle, of the girl going into the lift with Amy, as described by the witness.

"Fantastic," Jack exclaimed, "but do you really know where she said she was going for a couple of days?"

He was full of admiration for the way Grace had charmed the receptionist into boasting that she knew Sonja very well – she was a regular customer. Grace had begun by saying that her friend possessed a wig bought in Gandia... could it have been from here? She hoped so, because she wanted one exactly like it, but had forgotten the name on the label.

Grace had only to say that she could not imagine why Sonja would want a wig anyway as her own hair was so beautiful, and the receptionist said that Sonja was meeting some old school friends in Paris – she had not seen any of them since sixth form. For a joke, she wanted to make herself look as she had done when they knew her.

Apparently, the receptionist reported, she kept up the pretence until they met again for dinner in the evening and, when she arrived looking blonde and glamorous, they were stunned!

They had no doubt that the story was complete fiction and that Raymond would have been given the same explanation, so rather than waste time visiting him, and perhaps arousing Sonja's suspicions if he mentioned it to her – they were surely in touch by telephone – they decided to have a leisurely drive back to Jávea.

Instead of using the motorway they explored several small coastal villages and enjoyed leisurely drinks at bars that saw few tourists.

Jack's return flight was tomorrow, and he planned to drive back to spend the night in Alicante but he didn't have to book in at the airport until the afternoon. Grace and George therefore insisted that he should stay with them rather than in a lonely hotel room; there was still so much to talk over, they said he would be doing them a favour.

They made it difficult for Jack to refuse and as he was enjoying their company, he accepted.

He was glad they hadn't spent more time tramping around asking yet more questions; the answers he had already were more than enough to justify the trip. Now he was looking forward to seeing Polly's reaction to everything he had to tell.

113 – Bobby

Bobby, consumed by guilt, was hiding in the Parkers' garden shed behind the post office. It had seemed like a good idea, rather than walk alone to and from school. Nobody would think of looking for him among the old tools at the back and he'd know when school was out because he would hear the kids shouting on their way home along the track beyond the fence. He had a clear view of Clive's window and Mrs Lynch's back door but, of course, he usually left the house by the front door, and could be anywhere.

Mrs Biggs had waved to him from Joe's bedroom window when he left home and his own mother was at their front door, watching him, so he headed in the direction of school, his feet dragging. At the top of the hill he looked back to see his mother walk to the gate to stand talking to another neighbour, so he could not turn back. Looking down on the parkland, he saw police cars and vans and a few men kicking the ground as if testing for the easiest place to dig. Rumours were going around school that there was buried treasure there but Bobby suspected that whatever was down there, the boy with the yellow rucksack wanted them to find it. He was not tempted to join in the guessing game; silence about anything connected to his ghostly friends was second nature to him now.

Circling round to the side of the hill, towards the village, Bobby chose a quiet moment to cross the road and dodge between the houses to the allotments. There were several gates along the fence, which allowed access to the allotments from the public right of way. The gardens adjoining the other side of the footpath belonged to properties that fronted the main street and although fenced for privacy, all had gates. Bobby knew which gates were never locked, so had no problem entering one and pushing through a few hedges or climbing walls to reach the Parkers' shed. After an hour in hiding, he had a bad moment when Mrs Parker came down the garden, but it was only to pull up a few potatoes and she didn't even glance towards him.

Now, He was thoroughly bored and stiff, even though he had dragged together a few sacks for comfort. In spite of the dimness, he had read a comic he'd pushed into his satchel when his mother wasn't looking and even checked his homework again, but the sun still seemed bright outside. It was no good, he had to make a move... after all, even if he didn't manage to leave the village without being seen, it must be near enough to lunchtime for it not to matter; not all kids stayed in for school dinners.

Through a clean patch where he had rubbed the grime from the windowpane, he could see Sarah's room window, next door. She should have been back last night and he'd persuaded his mother to ring her but Mrs Lynch said Sarah had been delayed. How could she not be there when he really needed her? Through a crack in the boarding he saw, the last person in the world he expected looking out from Sarah's window; Joe's great-granddad was staring straight at him and he shuddered, imagining for a moment that it must be possible for anyone else to see him. Then he realised how silly he was being; ghosts were different from real people. He must be waiting for Sarah too – but why? Why didn't he just go to her, wherever she was? There was so much Bobby did not understand, about the dead people he saw. Where did they go when they disappeared? Could he ask one of them to sit with him when they had tests at school, to give him the answers? He immediately wiped that question from his thoughts; it would be cheating and he hated cheats.

His thoughts were interrupted. He heard kids shouting as they approached, along the footpath.... That meant school was out and he could leave the shed and mingle with them to escape from the area. Perhaps, by now, Sarah really was inside the house next door, but he couldn't risk going there to ask; he might run into the very person he most wanted to avoid. If only he knew where she would be later, he would go and wait for her. In the meantime, he'd try to stay out of everybody's sight.

ll4 - Sarah

When she woke up on Monday morning, Sarah was keen to ring Bobby, but her alarm clock showed that she had overslept – he would be at school. It was a shame, she wanted to talk things over with him, but most importantly, she needed to know what Clive knew more about than he should! It was so frustrating that Bobby, in such a hurry, had run away on Friday before she could ask, but for whatever reason, Clive was certainly not one of Bobby's favourite people now. Thinking about Clive, Sarah wondered why she had not paid more attention to him. She had heard Clive walk along the landing and he had already gone out; from her window, she could see him talking to Postie, who was putting a few news-racks outside the shop. They spent a fair amount of time together in The Wench's Arms, as one might expect, being cousins.

Clive did seem to be absent a lot when she was around; was he deliberately avoiding her? Doris was always so full of praise for him – in her eyes, he could do no wrong but that meant nothing... Sarah was beginning to think Doris's brother-in-law really did have something to hide.

When she went downstairs, Doris handed her a sealed envelope that Duffy had left for her. The message inside wiped out all other concerns from her head. He had met the parents of Anthony Daniels and was bringing them to the meeting this afternoon... "They are a great couple," he wrote, "even though a bit weird. They really think their dead son brought them here, and she even thinks she's seen his ghost, but please don't laugh. I wanted to prepare you, so that their feelings won't be hurt."

As if to confirm that the hiker with the yellow rucksack was their son, Sarah felt his presence very strongly. She was looking forward to meeting his parents and hearing, if she could do so privately, exactly what his mother had experienced. In what was left of the morning she intended to visit the park to see what was happening there – overall, it promised to be an extremely interesting day.

115 - Algy

DI Algy Green was pleased with the way his dig was going. There had been nothing of note found in the topsoil and for the first three feet down, but an empty wallet and pair of spectacles were uncovered together, a few inches deeper. A man's vest beneath them had disintegrated but a faded utility mark on the label, suggested that it was buried, or lost there, between 1939 and 1950. They were excavating an area thirty feet square and, by the time it lowered a couple of feet, they had assembled a large number of interesting objects. It was clear that the patch had never been an ordinary rubbish dump - the objects were not randomly scattered. Each group had probably belonged to only one person and it was easy to visualise them as being thrown in with individual burials.

The way the ground was harder to dig between the 'graves' convinced Algy that there would indeed be a body at the bottom of each hole. The location of each carefully labelled item was marked on a grid in the hope that bodies, if any were found, could be identified... a daunting prospect, as there might be at least five. Studying his original plan, Algy estimated that they could ignore at least a quarter of the taped area and should extend it on two sides. He was tempted to continue digging down where he was confident of finding something interesting, but decided instead to establish the extent of the assumed burial site. Everyone was too wound up to think about coffee breaks or lunch, but there was a refreshment tent on the site, so work continued throughout the day.

When Sarah arrived just before lunchtime, she found a young constable she recognised, asked him to find out if Detective Inspector Green could spare a minute to talk to her, and soon found herself conducted to the refreshment tent. Algy was delighted to see her and glad of an excuse to take a break. It was not a good place to hold a private conversation but they knew each other well enough to talk 'shorthand'. Algy's query – 'How is the patient today?' brought the response from Sarah – 'No change from when you last saw her, I'm afraid'. They both looked suitably solemn and several people within hearing shook their heads in sympathy. He then handed Sarah an envelope from DCS Holmes, asking her to open it in private, as the contents were for her eyes only. Apparently they might lead to an arrest but she would understand what it was about – he had no idea; too far down the chain to be in the Super's confidence, he added with a wide grin.

Algy assured Sarah that all her suspicions about there being something interesting under the drinking fountain were proving right and he promised to call on her when he finished for the day. She was quite satisfied with that and, on the point of leaving, asked if Adam had enjoyed his shopping trip. "Well, up to a point," Algy said, "but he was very upset about the fish – all his favourites have gone and been replaced with what he calls foreign ones!"

"What on earth does he mean?" Sarah started to ask, and then caught her breath. "Tell me... are they now tropical, like those in Polly's book, meaning that when you went there at Christmas they were not?"

"Exactly," said Algy, "it was a cold water fish tank then. He admits that the new ones are pretty but I have the feeling that he thinks he should have been consulted before the others were replaced. We had to let him ask the owner of the restaurant if they were happy in their new home." Algy laughed but said he had held his breath, hoping Adam would not ask if he could visit them. He then left Sarah to stay or go as she pleased, as he was anxious to get back to the dig to see if the newly taped section was down to the same level as the rest. If it was, he could now risk going deeper across the whole plot. Part of him dreaded the horror they might encounter, but the excitement and challenge of being on the trail of a mass murderer and bringing him to justice was what made his job worthwhile.

116 – Clive

Clive couldn't keep away from the hill. A small crowd had already gathered at the top, so he approached sideways through trees and kept out of sight. They had a better view than he did and he strained his ears to eavesdrop as they commented on what was happening below. The drinking fountain had been removed and a huge area was marked out inside the cordoned off parkland. There was a mechanical digger on hand but a gang of men took over when the top layer was removed and progress slowed down. Even so, a huge hole now existed which, as far as Clive could judge, might just miss the site where he had dug so often himself.

He held his breath as he stared down at the busy scene... yet again his luck might be holding. Deep down though, he could not really believe that his secret was safe. It was the closest he had been to despair for nearly thirty years. In spite of his initial trepidation, he and his wife settled happily near her family in Greater Peasey for the first few years of their marriage; he was accepted as what he claimed to be – someone who had lost his only relatives in a fire when he was an infant. His parents-in-law vaguely remembered the tragedy but, overall, had little interest in Lesser Peasey. Life was good until Mary's sister Doris and her husband moved next door to the post office in Lesser P and reported that the Postmaster must be his cousin! He was horrified and hardly had a good night's sleep until he learned that Albert knew very little about his father's family.

Albert was actually thrilled, happily accepting Clive as another cousin, the son of a previously unknown uncle. Albert explained that when he was little, his parents died in a car crash. His mother's parents, who brought him up, knew only that his Uncle, Aunt and Cousin Andy died years before in a fire. They believed that his father had been the last in his branch of the family. Scarcely able to believe his luck, Clive breathed again. Instead of being exposed, he became more secure. Albert's son, Dave, looked very much like Sammy, Clive's son, which made his relationship to the Parkers even more credible. Clive suddenly started to shake. He felt sick and weak, imagining how Sammy, Dorrie and Lizzie would react when they learned about their father's past. However he explained and defended his actions when a boy, he had finally become a murderer. They would be mortified and his only chance of escaping the consequences of his crime was to kill again.

The woman or the boy...

Which should he deal with first?

117 – Sarah

Sarah reached the police station just as White and Dee were leaving. Duffy looked happy as he trailed after John Dee who was hurrying to his car.

"Good to see you back, won't be long, Terry will explain," John called to Sarah as he climbed into the driving seat.

DS White smiled reassuringly as he took Sarah's arm. "I was just coming to find you," he said. "We need somewhere more comfortable to meet than the station, because we will be joined by a very special couple – and I need to explain something about them before they arrive. Unless you've had news already on your private line, you will be amazed!"

Sarah guessed that Duffy had warned them also, about the Daniels' so-called weirdness, but knew she would not hear more until they settled down at the Wench's Arms, where they had apparently booked a meeting room for a few hours, so she reported her good news about Clarinda. She should have realised that Algy, his DI, had already informed him, but by the time Terry said how relieved they all were, the hotel was in sight. It did not take long to make themselves comfortable and organise a selection of drinks for everyone, to avoid being disturbed later, and Sarah had to wait no longer for an explanation. First, Terry told her that John was collecting Mr and Mrs Daniels, an elderly couple, from Greater Peasey. Duffy had been their only contact so far, so they knew nothing about her or the attack on Clarrie.

Duffy and Dee would like to have talked to Sarah about the reason for the Daniels' presence, but Duffy especially wanted her to know why they were there, before meeting them, Terry explained. "He was so sure that you would think they were crazy, and didn't want to risk their feelings being hurt – he's a decent lad – youngsters these days are not all bad are they?" Sarah agreed and then listened with delight as Terry filled in the background story of the road trip. The ways of the Spirit World never ceased to amaze her and she was fascinated to learn that Edna was genuinely psychic. Of course, she would not be able to pursue the matter with Duffy present, but Terry said he would make sure that she was able to talk privately with Edna and William before they left.

Knowing that she would soon meet the parents of the missing boy was wonderful but daunting. She must not lose sight of the fact that their sole interest was in their son and her role was to comfort them as well as she could when they learned about the way he met his end.

118 – Bobby

After reaching what he felt was a safe distance from the village, and sure that he was not being followed, Bobby sat on the low wall that separated the cemetery from the lane. There was little traffic because there was now a wider, new road between Greater and Lesser Peasey and the Church lane had become little more than a service road for a couple of farms. It was a favourite route for those who enjoyed walking, and many took the opportunity to visit family graves with flowers. He and Joe often wandered around searching for interesting epitaphs. They made up stories about the people, imagining what their lives must have been like. Of course, Joe was unaware that Bobby sometimes saw spirit forms hovering nearby, which accounted for his tales being more elaborate.

There was one old grave that Bobby liked particularly, where, in fact, he never failed to see at least one ghost, and he went there now. There were never any fresh flowers on it and, in fact, the burial of the last occupant was in 1705. Sometimes there was quite a ghostly crowd near it – far more people than could actually have been buried in the grave. They all wore strange clothes, especially the men, and the ladies all wore long dresses. The lady with the big hat was the only one who ever looked at him; the others seemed not to know that he could see them. When he reached the grave only the lady was there... she smiled and spoke. Bobby was amazed. She had never tried to talk to him before and, of course, he could not hear her voice.

Remembering Sarah's advice, he relaxed and immediately thought of Joe. She must be wondering why he was alone so, after a quick look around to make sure nobody else was near, he spoke aloud, telling her that Joe was at school. She looked perplexed and her mouth moved again. This time, just staring at her mouth, Bobby's mind flashed back to Joe's great-granddad when he said, "He's not Andy", and the lady nodded. She began to walk away, but turned to make sure he was following her. They were moving away from the oldest part of the cemetery and, after a few minutes, she stopped, looked back once more, and then pointed at the headstone. The last name on it was Andrew Clive Parker.

As the significance began to sink in, the lady disappeared and a voice behind him whispered shyly, "Hello, my name is Andy and I'm nearly four."

Spinning round in alarm, Bobby saw the form of a child slowly materialising.

Apart from relief when he realised he was not being followed, he was heady with excitement...

The boy had spoken to him and he had actually *HEARD...*

He could hardly wait to tell Sarah. Surely, she must be back by now. Anyway, he should go home before he was missed.

He was glad he didn't have to worry about Joe arriving next door and asking questions about where he had been all day.

Hopefully Joe would be allowed to go to school tomorrow so he wouldn't be walking there alone. More sure than ever that his instincts about Clive were right, he must avoid him at all costs.

While pre-occupied with his thoughts the child had approached and held his hand. Bobby stared down into Andy's trusting face and was unsure what to do, until Andy said, "Can I stay with you please? I promise to be a good boy."

Together, they left the cemetery and Bobby was bewildered. He was only a kid himself – how could he look after a little boy, who didn't even seem to know he was dead! It was even more urgent that he find Sarah now.

119 – Sarah & Edna

On the way to the meeting, John Dee explained to the Daniels why, after so long, the police were reopening the investigation into the disappearance of their son. It was not easy, because he had to wrap Sarah's involvement in language that excluded any reference to the paranormal. If Edna really was psychic, it was Sarah's province. He therefore confined himself to the facts, as he knew them. Other men had disappeared before and after Anthony and suspicion pointed to the occupants of a small farm. The owners had died in the fire that destroyed the buildings but excavation of the area was in progress. It was likely that several bodies would be unearthed and with William's DNA available, they would soon know if one was their son.

His summary was enough to satisfy William and Edna, who sat holding hands quietly behind him, watched anxiously by Duffy, who continually twisted in his seat to smile and nod reassurance. Being similar in age to their son when he last saw them, he imagined how his own parents would feel if he disappeared now... and a feeling of empathy consumed him; he suddenly understood why his mother kept asking him to ring her more often and explain his every movement. He determined to make more effort and not feel resentful.

The meeting went well. It took less than an hour to cover the aspect of events concerning the Daniels and after a police medic had taken a DNA swab of William's saliva, they prepared to leave. With a nod to Terry, who kept Duffy occupied, Sarah walked to John's car with them. They had said that they would stay on in their hotel until there was definite information about the dig; one way or the other they had come too far to leave yet. They were obviously pleased when Sarah said she would like to meet them again and immediately invited her to dinner later. Knowing she had no transport, they insisted that they would call for her and drive out to a restaurant they wished to try. Sarah accepted and they parted, all looking forward to their evening together.

It was obvious that Duffy, being a newspaper reporter, was eager to see what was happening at the excavation so they let him go; there was nothing immediately he could do for the team. In addition to sending copy to his own editor, he told them, he intended to send a report to Boris Thwaites at the Peasey Reporter – with pictures if he could get near enough. Terry decided there was nothing more he could do either, until DI Green contacted him, which he probably would do after he saw Sarah. She told Terry her recent doubts about Clive Parker and suggested that they check his background. It would not be easy because although he had lived locally for over forty years, they needed to know where he was before he married. Terry said he would set the ball rolling immediately and Sarah decided that she might still have time to talk to Bobby if he was home from school, so they each left in an optimistic mood.

120 – Bobby

Imagining how upset his mother would be if he did not go home, Bobby had given up the idea of staying out all night. He was heading back but changed his route – it was either that or returning to the cemetery. He was more comfortable with friendly dead people than he was with the nasty live one, who, he was now convinced, had bashed the poor painter lady nearly to death. After crossing a field, he had an angled view of the other end of the village and, when halfway down the hill, he saw Sarah leaving the hotel with an old man and woman who climbed into the back of a car that drove off. He was ecstatic when he saw her go back inside with a policeman he recognised. They would probably be talking for ages before she came out, so there was a fair chance that he could waylay her without passing down the street where Clive lived. With luck, he might reach the main street unseen by anyone. Then, whether he saw Sarah or not, he could get home the back way before his parents realised he had not been to school. Explaining his predicament to them would be impossible.

At the edge of the field he climbed the gate to reach the lane and was amused when Andy tried to climb with him... surely a ghost could walk through it! Nevertheless, Bobby helped him and tried not to laugh as they continued to walk hand in hand. More and more houses began to edge the footpath, now paved, and within a few minutes, the child tugged Bobby trying, but of course failing, to make him stop. Andy looked frightened and wanted Bobby to turn back, which Bobby found disturbing; what was wrong? The hotel was only yards away and Sarah must still be there – he didn't want to miss her. He began walking away backwards as he kept his eye on Andy, wondering what he was supposed to do but determined to go on, whether the child came with him or not. Andy was so upset that his image kept fading and then abruptly vanished... and as Bobby shrugged and turned away, he felt firm hands on his shoulders. He knew before he looked that it was Clive, and realised that Andy had tried to warn him.

Before he could squirm out of Clive's grip, he was pushed through an open gate and they were inside the garden of a bungalow, which Clive must have been leaving. It was just bad luck that because of the high hedges, Bobby had not seen him in time to hide.

121 - Sarah

Sarah strolled back to her lodging, and when she reached the privacy of her room, she opened the envelope Alec had sent. As she suspected, it was a copy of the report on Amy's bed sheet. Sarah skipped immediately to Alec's note, which confirmed that, had the liquid contacted Amy's skin, it could have proved fatal. Being in a coma, it might have been undetected until her nervous system was destroyed, and too late to save her. It certainly pointed to the likelihood of Amy's fall being Sonja's first attempt on her life and Sarah hoped that Jack would return from Spain with more evidence to prove the case against her.

It was unlikely that Algy would come before six-o-clock so Sarah dialled Bobby's number; there was still time talk to him, with luck. It was disappointing when the 'phone was not answered, but in addition to seeing Algy she was out for dinner this evening so talking to Bobby would have to wait until tomorrow. It was also frustrating because Sarah still had to confirm that it was Clive who had known something he shouldn't.

As she sorted out what she would wear for her dinner date, Sarah wondered again about the mysterious Mr Lynch Clarinda mentioned, until she realised that Clarinda had assumed that Clive was the brother of Doris's husband, not the husband of her sister Mary! Even though Sarah distrusted Clive, it was difficult to see why he might have attacked Clarinda. It was not often that Sarah's intuitions about people were wrong and had her mind not been so full of fear for her daughter's life, her mistrust of the man might have crystallised earlier. Fleeting recollections from those dreadful days when she first arrived in Lesser Peasey, distracted her now. There had been so many jarring moments whenever she had been near Clive, she could hardly credit that she had totally ignored them.

It was perhaps forgivable that she had also ignored the clamouring spirits she sensed during her first hours in the house; she had assumed they were associated with Doris, but should have kept an open mind because they were definitely part of the mystery. Doris's voice calling from the foot of the stairs interrupted her thoughts and she realised that Algy had arrived... no time to worry more now. Sarah hastened down to hear what, if anything, had been unearthed at the dig.

l22 – Betty

When Albert and Betty closed the shop for the day, she insisted that he should sit down and talk for a few minutes before they had their evening meal. For days, she had been trying to show him the family albums and ask him how much he could remember about his childhood. When he saw what she had spread open for him to see, Albert was puzzled.

He hadn't given the albums a thought for many years. He had not remembered their existence until his grandmother handed them on to him when he left her home and married. Initially, he was thrilled to see photos of his parents and himself as a baby but, as he now reminded Betty, many of the people in them were not familiar.

"I do realise that," said Betty, "but look at this one – it says underneath it that it is your father's family, when he was about fifteen. Look – he is with his parents and his brother. So where is his other brother, Clive's father?" Albert shook his head and suggested that the missing one might have been ill, or away. Betty insisted that it was a formal family portrait; they would have postponed it until all the family members were available.

She then turned over the pages until she came to wedding pictures of the two brothers and eventually their children...

"So where is the third brother and his children?" she asked.

Betty also pointed out the fact that Clive was apparently given the same names as Andrew who died in the fire with his parents. To her, it was highly suspicious, but to her extreme annoyance and frustration, Albert refused to accept that there was a problem. He pointed out that Clive was a good bloke whether or not he was his cousin. Making it clear that the subject was of no interest to him, Albert asked how long supper would be, as he would be going to the pub for an hour, later. She was disappointed, but decided that as soon as he went out she would ask Doris to come round...

123 – Sarah & Edna

As soon as Algy left her, Sarah hastened to wash and change. She would have liked to try ringing Bobby again, but William and Edna would be picking her up within half an hour. Although she had expected the removal of earth from the area around the drinking fountain to reveal human remains, she was staggered to learn that the body count had already reached nine and expected to rise.

If Clive was involved, or knew anything about the poor people who had come to such a dreadful end, he must be frantic with fear. She had not seen him all day, and in fact was almost fearful of facing him in case her demeanour put him on his guard. The whirr of the doorbell put an end to her nagging worries – she was determined to enjoy herself tonight.

William was surprisingly sprightly for his age; he drove well, at a comfortably steady pace. Sarah commented on their undertaking such a long tour by car, although it was obvious that he enjoyed driving. It gave Edna an opportunity to explain that, in trying to follow the route their son had taken, they had hoped to bring memories of him closer and having an excuse to talk about him had been wonderful. They had hoped, but never really expected, to uncover the cause of his disappearance and were still a bit dazed by the way things were working out. Sarah was aware that Anthony was with them in spirit but now was not the right moment to reveal her own psychic ability.

From the instant they were ushered to their table, to the end of the meal, conversation was easy but impersonal. They all got on well together and were amazed when they realised that they had been sitting at the table for three hours. William suggested that they have coffee and liqueurs in the hotel lounge – he needed a change of seat, he said with a grin. Sarah was glad that the more intimate atmosphere resulted in a change of topic.

Edna settled back into her armchair with a sigh and said, "It has been a real pleasure meeting you Sarah, but I'm still not quite clear how the awful attack on your daughter has anything to do with the farm where the police now think our son's life could have ended."

It was not quite a question, but Sarah, happy to interpret it as such, watched Edna's eyes widen in astonishment as she explained that Clarinda was psychic, and had seen the valley as it used to be until thirty years ago. Being inexperienced and still not appreciating her own powers, she had not questioned what she could see. She painted exactly what she saw and was very puzzled about the stir it caused in the village. Everyone was fascinated. "Unfortunately," Sarah said, "someone interpreted what she painted as a threat – a hint that she knew about his past and was paving the way to blackmailing him."

Edna was thrilled to realise that Sarah would be unlikely to scoff if she mentioned her own experiences and her conviction that Anthony had guided them here. When Sarah nodded and glanced beyond her, Edna turned and saw nothing, but Sarah told her that Anthony had been with them all evening. The fact that Sarah might also be psychic was just too much for William to believe and he suddenly seemed to withdraw into himself. He was still not totally convinced about

Edna's revelations. To him they could be mere wishful thinking and intelligent guesswork.

Edna too looked taken aback and Sarah could understand their scepticism. Under normal circumstances, she would not have discussed her own experiences but to be any help or comfort to them in the coming days, they had to have confidence in her so, after a brief reference to her connection with the police, Sarah mentally asked Anthony for guidance.

Almost immediately, she knew what to say. "Anthony wants you to know how sorry he is that he could not return to celebrate his birthday that year. He would have loved the birthday present you were planning to buy for him. He tells me it was a car... no, a van... and says he would have loved it – especially as it was green, his favourite colour."

After Sarah had described highlights of their trip, which she could not have known, William and Edna had no lingering doubts. They were both eager to ask questions. It is often difficult for people to understand why, if the dead can communicate trivial things, they hardly ever volunteer more important information about, for instance, their own death. Sarah could have explained that, in their son's case, he'd been the key to unveiling several murders and pointing them in the right direction, but really there was no answer. Her own perception was that if the stark truth were given without preamble it would be more difficult to accept. Being nudged in the right direction allowed time to seek proof, and have confidence in the result.

In her experience, most people who met a sad end were more concerned that their loved ones should not continue to grieve for them. Seeking vengeance was rarely their main aim but the combined emotions of the many victims at the farm were strong.

l24 – Sarah

Polly, knowing that Sarah might not be back in her room until late, waited until after llpm to ring up and, when her call came, Sarah was puzzling over a note from Doris. Apparently, when Doris came home from wherever she'd been, there was a message for Sarah on the answer machine – from Bobby's mother.

Sarah guessed it would be about seeing him tomorrow, so decided she need not go down to check it until the morning.

Polly was so excited about Clarinda's continued progress and Jack's impending return from Spain that all else was driven from Sarah's mind.

Afterwards, she was so exhausted that she was soon in bed. She had a hazy vision of a small child wandering, looking lost and unhappy, but it meant nothing to her and it faded before she fell asleep.

When she woke up on Tuesday morning, the first thought in her head was the distracting incident at the supper table soon after she arrived in the house. Sarah suddenly realised... it was when Clive had reached across the table for something and she now knew exactly why it had disturbed her.

She should have recognised his arm instantly, as the one she saw in the flashing vision of the liquid spilling onto Joe's drawing. Clive's fingers were unusually short and the little one stuck out oddly – it was now beyond doubt – Clive was deeply involved with the macabre discoveries at the dig.

125 – Jack

Because Jack's flight from Alicante was not until late afternoon, George suggested that they should all lunch together in Jávea before he left. He had to pick up new business cards and some flyers for his gardening club from the Sign Shop and thought Jack might like to do a bit of shopping in the Arenal – for the girls, he winked. Jack leapt at the offer, because he had not even given a thought to taking any mementos back! He would probably have remembered to buy them chocolates at the airport, he mentally excused himself, and after all, he had been preoccupied with other things...

It was a beautifully sunny day and with two hours to enjoy before lunch, Jack was happy. The sandy beach was not overcrowded and coffee had never tasted so good. As he watched the palms waving and the boats at anchor offshore, he decided that Grace and George could not have chosen a more pleasant place for their retirement – he might even do the same one day. A voice boomed suddenly behind him. "Enjoying the sunshine eh? ...So what did you buy for the girls?" It was George, of course, and Jack had to admit that he would probably take them chocolates. To his surprise, George dumped a carrier bag on his lap. "Here, take them these. When I picked up my stuff, I spotted these T-shirts. Corinne printed them with Jávea slogans."

They were perfect gifts – three in different colours with the same logo. Jack was delighted and he spoke his thoughts aloud, hoping that he would soon see

Clarrie fit enough to be up and able to wear hers. They met Grace for tapas at a bar nearby and the time for Jack's departure came all too soon. He had driven his own hire car from the villa so he left them alone, enjoying coffee, promising to ring them with the latest news, as soon as he had seen Polly at the hospital. Now that he was on his way home he began to feel quite excited to see how Polly and Sarah reacted to all he had to tell them.

126 - Doris

Doris's thought were in a whirl. Betty's suspicions about Clive, backed up by the photographs - or rather the absence of some - were compelling. Now that she thought about it, she had to admit that he had never talked about his childhood. She couldn't remember even what he did for a living when he married Mary. She thought it might have been in a shop, or warehouse; he was managing something, but she could not think what. She didn't really think it mattered, unless he had done something criminal; if Betty was right, he had adopted Andy's name, so who was he really? Did she dare raise the subject and ask Clive outright? If he had kept something secret for so long - did she really want to know? Perhaps she shouldn't risk antagonising him. Her worries increased when she could not find Clive. Last night, after seeing Betty, she assumed he was in bed, but he might not have been because his room was empty now and she had not heard him go out.

Loud voices and shouting in the street outside suddenly distracted her. She had been tired and only half-listened to the message on the answer machine last night but the gist of it came back to her when she went to the window and looked out. All the neighbours seemed to be gathering, talking excitedly, looking worried, and someone with a loud hailer was organising people into groups. The message on the answer-phone, was from Pamela Goswell, Bobby's mother, wanting to know if Sarah had seen him. Now, search parties were going out looking for him. Doris was devastated – she should have made sure Sarah listened to the call last night. She still couldn't see Clive anywhere, but seized the thought that he might already be out helping to search for Bobby... he must have had a good reason for leaving the house so early without letting her know why.

127 - Algy

The excavation of the farm site was well advanced before the local police withdrew full support of the dig and DCI Algy Green was profoundly glad that the inhabitants of the Peaseys - Greater, Lesser and New were - for the most part - law-abiding; they were unlikely to breach Police cordons. He wondered if Sarah knew that her young friend Bobby Goswell was missing. In spite of his concern, he had to get on with his own job and he could foresee that unless the area of exploration was widened, they might never know how many victims there had been. It might be impossible to identify them all. Preliminary findings were that at least five bodies had been buried for over sixty years; among the remains was a battledress from World War l.

He would have relished the challenge of tracking down the mass murderer but, if still alive, he must be at least in his eighties and in all probability, he and his family died when fire destroyed the farmhouse. In view of what Sarah surmised about Clarrie's attacker however, someone local must have been party to the crimes, so there was a good chance that he would be caught. The reasons for his fear of Clarrie, a stranger to him, could only have arisen when he saw her painting a scene from the past, forgotten by all but him - or so he thought.

Now that there was hard evidence that it was a crime scene, Algy would soon be under pressure to hand everything over to the local force, at least until they decided how they wished to proceed with the investigation. He didn't mind; he had already set the wheels in motion with forensics and was eager to get on with some real detective work. As soon as he could get away he was anxious to talk to Sarah again, but her immediate concern would be Bobby and he wanted to help her to find him.

128 - Clarrie

Clarrie was feeling strong enough to stay awake longer and even walk around her room a little, by the time Jack arrived in the early evening.

Polly had explained Amy's predicament to her and little by little, every day, Clarrie recalled the dreams she had had.

She remembered Amy calling to her and how frightened the young woman was. Clarrie was at a loss to know how she could help and Polly suggested that, when she felt up to it, they could go and sit with Amy for a while, when she had no visitors.

Now that she understood how anxious Sonja was to get rid of Amy, Clarrie began to forget the danger she might be in herself and was, instead, filled with anger about Amy's suffering. T

hey both were targeted because they were considered a threat. It was so unfair.

When Jack arrived at the hospital he rang Clarrie's room and asked if she was able to receive visitors. Polly was delighted to say that she could and they were soon together, exchanging news.

They were surprised and pleased with the T-shirts and Jack said that George had told him to bill him for the biggest bunch of flowers he could find, for Clarrie but, knowing that the hospital was probably running short of vases, her room was always so well-blessed, Jack said he was holding them back until she returned home.

Clarrie listened, fascinated to hear about all the evidence Jack had collected and laughed aloud when Polly tried on the black wig. It was evident though that she was becoming tired, so Jack and Polly left, to continue their catching up in an anteroom. Clarrie was not sorry to see them go although she had been pleased to hear news of Grace and George.

Now in full possession of the facts, she wanted to think quietly and decide how she could help.

It would be late when Jack left but if she slept for an hour or so now, perhaps she and Polly could visit Amy tonight. The nurse was bound to agree because Amy was still in a coma, so if anything did disturb her, it would be a welcome development.

In this positive frame of mind, Clarrie fell asleep.

Not thinking, not dreaming, drifting through occasional shafts of sunshine and misty shifting fog, her world grew darker...

She did not feel fear because she floated effortlessly at the end of a strong silvery thread.

As her mind started to marvel and thoughts formed, she was relieved to see that her lifeline anchored her safely to where she lay safely in her bed. She wished she could see her mother or Del ... she felt happy, remembering that she had been able to speak to him, reassuring him that she was getting better and knowing he would be home soon.

Her wishes made no difference; instead, she was with Amy, who lay still and pale, unmoving and unaware.

Gently, Clarrie laid a hand on her forehead and whispered. "Amy, you have slept long enough. Wake up now, come back to your family."

Clarrie spoke of the day Amy visited the hospital to see her boyfriend before his operation and afterwards met her old school friend, and how they had gone together to the restaurant to talk.

She spoke endlessly about that day, reminding Amy repeatedly of everything except how the meeting ended.

At last, when her own resolve was beginning to weaken and she was unable to resist the force that was pulling her away, Amy appeared and slipped quietly back into the shell she had abandoned...

129 - Pamela & Jake

Duffy was trying to follow developments in the search for Bobby from all angles. Implications that there might be a link between the little boy's disappearance and the attack on Sarah's daughter puzzled him. He had been unaware that Bobby might have fallen foul of the attacker until he half-heard exchanges between White and Dee. Before he wrote anything for the two papers he now represented he would have to tackle Sarah, who was now too distressed. Frank Brown had been organising volunteers into search parties before the police arrived on the scene because he had been with Bobby's father half the night. Jake Goswell was with Frank in the local pub when his wife, Pamela, rang him at around 8pm., to ask if he knew where Bobby was. Jake went home immediately, promising to let Frank know what was happening. At ten-thirty, as Jake had still not telephoned, Frank went to their house to offer his help.

None of Bobby's friends had seen him since yesterday; apparently, he had not been to school at all. It followed that he might have met with an accident or even been abducted on his way there. Pamela, in tears, said that she had watched him walk up the hill.

Frank immediately took a lantern and followed Bobby's route to school through the woodland in case he was lying helpless somewhere and, as soon as it was light enough, he had walked the route again with several helpers. Before ten o clock, dozens of gardens and outhouses were searched but no trace of Bobby was found.

Sarah was devastated. As always when she was personally involved, her psychic power seemed to desert her. She blamed herself for allowing Bobby to become involved even on the periphery of her enquiries, although she had warned him not to discuss his feelings or Joe's drawing with anyone. She knew he suspected Clive of something bad and might well have been unable to conceal his distrust of the man. If Clive was responsible for the murderous attack on Clarinda, he could be responsible for Bobby being missing. She prayed to God that he had not harmed the child but if he had abducted Bobby how could he risk setting him free. It was a nightmare and, as usual, when she couldn't cope, she rang DCI Holmes – Alec would know what to do.

After telephoning to inform Polly she went to be with Bobby's mother. She determined to be calm and pray for guidance. The police had advised Pamela to stay at home and Sarah hoped that being with her would make her own mind more receptive to anything that might come into it.

Pamela told her that the house was empty when she returned home just after six-thirty last night and she thought that when Bobby came back after school, he must have played back Sarah's message and gone off to find her.

It was only when he was still absent at eight-o-clock that she started to worry. There was no answer when she rang Doris's number – she knew now that everyone was out. Sarah apologised for not going downstairs again to re-play the message when she read Doris's note. She had assumed it was about arranging a meeting with Bobby.

As they talked, Sarah kept catching glimpses of Joe's great-grandfather holding a child in his arms and it was maddening that she could not grasp whatever message he was trying to convey; the only thoughts in her head were about fish and fish tanks! The last thing she needed now was a reminder of Amy's last few hours before she fell. Doing her best to banish the fish resulted in the vision also vanishing. Rather like an afterthought, she recalled the old man's earlier message, the warning to Bobby – *he is not Andy* – and immediately realised that he was introducing Andy to her... his little grandson who had died with his parents in the house fire – not a good moment to pick, Sarah thought wryly. Fleetingly, she wondered who the 'he' could be, who was pretending to be Andy, but she had problems on her mind that were more pressing than solving riddles! In spite of not knowing where Bobby was, Sarah could not sense any trace of him in the world of spirit and this gave her the strength to comfort Pamela, keeping her optimistic about her son's safe return.

130 - Polly & Maud

Polly had been surprised to get a call from Sarah during the morning. The reason for it, Bobby's disappearance, was shocking. She would have liked to tell Sarah about Jack's return and latest news. She also wanted to tell Sarah that she and Clarrie sat for two hours last night at Amy's bedside, but it was not the right moment.

It had been thrilling. Clarrie held Amy's hand and talked to her, much as she had in her dream. Polly almost fell asleep, lulled by Clarrie's calm, clear voice, until she heard a change in Amy's breathing. Within seconds, the nurse came in and sent them out of the ward.

They went back to Clarrie's room, wondering what was happening and about twenty minutes later, the nurse came in, smiling, to tell them that the doctor had been and confirmed that, miraculously, Amy was breathing on her own. Her eventual recovery was now a possibility.

Before lunch, Maud arrived to visit Clarrie, weighed down with books, magazines fruit and chocolate. "I didn't bring flowers – I know the nurses don't really like them: difficult to look after in hospital, and too depressing watching them die." She said she would not stay long but wanted to know how Jack had fared in Spain. Polly wondered how much they should tell her because in an unguarded moment she might let slip something that would get back to Sonja and put her on her guard. In fact, she need not have worried; Maud accepted that Jack was sure Sonja was not in Spain when Amy fell, so could well have been in England. Maud was now satisfied that beyond doubt, Sonja was a murderess whose fate was sealed and became more keen to talk about the attack on Clarrie.

Her questions ranged from what the room and food were like in the guesthouse, how old Doris was and what the first thought in Clarrie's head was when she woke up. "Poor Sarah must be so upset, not being able to be with you, but I see that it is important for her to keep up the pretence that you are still comatose. We must not allow the killer to know that you could identify him at any time... Oh – alright, I know you can't, but he doesn't, does he!"

She suddenly saw that Clarrie was tiring and before Polly could intervene, Maud stood and announced that she must go. Her parting shot, which she delivered from the open door, was that she would go to join Sarah in Lesser Peasey, "To cheer her up poor dear, and give her moral support. Together, we'll get to the bottom of this, don't worry!"

There was no time to worry about what Maud would do next because the nurse came in before the door closed. She said that Amy was breathing on her own. She had been taken off the life-support machine and her sister was with her, talking at her with renewed enthusiasm.

There had been no visit from the patient's friend, Miss Norris, for a day or two, so the family wondered if Sonja had returned to Spain.

Polly was immediately worried that wind of their investigation had reached the woman and decided the time had come to take advantage of Algy's offer of advice.

She tried to reach him at his office but every time she tried to telephone, throughout the afternoon, his number was busy. Finally, she rang his home number and left a message with Bet.

131 - Edna

William and Edna, having told Sarah about Edna's dream, followed her advice on Tuesday morning. They contacted the home where they had enjoyed the Sing-Song with George and asked if they could call and see Mrs Cooper. They only learned about the hunt for Bobby when they arrived and found people searching the grounds. Every room, attic and cellar had been scrutinised and everyone was uncomfortably restless. Their privacy was usually respected but, although upset, everybody understood and prayed that the child would be found unharmed.

It was a perfect opening for Edna and taking a leaf out of Sarah's book she started by describing the bedroom she had seen in her dream.

By the time she had described the young man she saw and the clothes he was wearing, Colin's mother had no doubt that her dream was a vision of her son's last day.

Mrs Cooper had heard about the excavation of the farm and now, sensing a conclusion to her years of anguish, wondered if her son's body would be among those discovered.

She and Edna wept together while William looked on, moist eyed.

Funnily enough, he and Edna agreed later, there was a minute crumb of comfort in the thought that Anthony had not been alone... but they immediately squashed the thought.

The two boys had shared a horrible fate; nothing could mitigate their individual suffering. With the matron's approval, Mrs Cooper joined them to drive over to see the farm site for themselves.

Being together gave them all strength – nobody else could really understand what the place meant to them.

132 - Clive

Clive had been eavesdropping when Betty invited Doris round to see the albums and it was not difficult to work out why. He had managed to sneak back into the house after dealing with Bobby, needing to calm down and get his thoughts together before he came face to face with anyone else. With Betty questioning his origin and the immediate likelihood of Bobby being missed, how long could he expect to carry on as normal? His original plan to join the inevitable searches until the end of the week lost its appeal, although he would volunteer tomorrow; he needed to appear concerned. His recurring visions of the painting and the young woman who had been planning to blackmail him were making his head ache. With Bobby out of the way, the only loose end was the woman... He had put the moment off long enough.

Having made up his mind, he left the house as stealthily as he had entered only an hour earlier, through the back garden and over the allotments. His car was parked well away from the house but within ten minutes, he was driving away from the village towards the hospital. Finding a patient they were trying to hide would not be easy. It might take more than one visit.

133 - Clarrie

The constable on duty was PC Penny again. On his last stint he had allowed the patient he was guarding to leave her room to visit another. Although the nurse assured him that she would be safe, he had been very careful to make sure that the corridor was clear before Clarrie walked out – it was always very quiet after eleven at night but he insisted that she wore Polly's raincoat rather than a hospital gown. He had just heard that a boy was missing in Lesser Peasey and glad that Clarrie was safely asleep in her room tonight and not wandering about again, although she must feel a bit lonely now that her friend wasn't staying every night.

An unofficial warning had also reached him from no less a person that DCS Holmes about someone called Parker. The Super told him to be on his guard in case said person tried to get by him. Clive Parker was a local in Lesser Peasey and under suspicion; he might even be the villain who attacked Mrs Hunter in the first place. Penny was determined to be ready for him if he dared come anywhere near... but surely, he wouldn't have the nerve!

134 – Clive

Clive drove steadily at first but couldn't shake off the feeling that he was being pursued. He drove faster and faster until he suddenly realised how reckless he was being and pulled into a lay-by. Wiping the sweat from his face and neck he decided it was the best thing he could do – sit where he was until he was convinced that nobody was following him. While he waited, shadowy figures seemed to creep towards him from the woods and even though they never formed, he was reminded of the old days when he first became aware of the hidden graves.

He had always felt insecure and knew that if they decided he couldn't be trusted Art and Glenda would bury him too, without a doubt. He knew he must have been loved once because it was what he missed most in his new home, but he had grown to accept his lot because things could be worse. When he did finally realise just how bad his position was, he had foolishly thought it was too late. Now, of course, he knew how stupid he had been.

His presence at the farm had created an air of normality for the victims. He was encouraged by Art to befriend the casual labourers, discovering if they were in touch with friends or family. Sometimes Art took on men without papers, making them believe he was doing them a favour. Such men were anxious to keep a low profile – not leaving the farm to make friends in the local pubs. They were men who never banked their money; some tucked wads into their wellingtons but others even allowed Art to look after it for them. They were the men who always disappeared quietly, and were soon forgotten by the other workers, who accepted that they had moved on to better paid work or decided to head back to their families.

The mist from the river nearby rose eerily through the trees and triggered an unwelcome memory of a boy, then several years older than he was himself, who had pushed his way into the barn for shelter from a howling gale. He had seen that Art was stripping a dead body of strong boots and clothes too good to bury. The boy turned to run but Glenda had slammed the door.

Two bodies went into one grave that night, but he was sent out into the raging storm to throw the boy's belongings – all he was carrying – into the river, a mile away, along with his coat. Clive sighed as he remembered the coat – he had wanted to keep it.

Far from calming him, Clive's break had made him jittery... he felt sick with apprehension. A nauseating smell of decay seemed to have seeped into the car. He forced himself to stop thinking about the past and tried to plan his next move. When the hospital came in sight, he was still unsure how even to find the room where his quarry lay. He certainly couldn't ask at the information desk! The obvious move was to pick up a white coat from one of the staff rooms, which wouldn't be easy but should be possible. Then he would have to visit every floor and corridor until he saw someone sitting outside a ward door, obviously on guard.

He wasn't stupid – he knew the police would be anxious to protect the woman in case she could identify her attacker. Once he had found the right room, he mused as he parked the car he would get to her somehow, even if he had to kill the guard.

135 – Algy

When Algy arrived home and Bet gave him Polly's message, he didn't know whether to be glad or sorry that the case against Sonja Norris was building up rapidly. Too much was happening suddenly but he couldn't divert his attention from the most urgent situation – they had to find Bobby. He had only returned to shower and get into a change of clothing, before returning to Lesser Peasey, in case he could do something to help. Bet understood and packed him a cold meal to take with him.

On arrival, when he was satisfied that the local force had everything well covered and there really didn't seem to be anything for him to do, Algy looked for and found Sarah. Terry White had discussed the outcome of the meeting they had had with William and Edna Daniels and reported to him Sarah's suspicions of Clive Parker. He said that he had set the ball rolling before he left home this morning and had already heard that there could well be something worth investigating in Clive Parker's past; several years before his marriage he had applied and been issued with a copy of his birth certificate. So far, they had found nothing on record about him before that event. Within a day or two, Algy expected to have a copy of the certificate to show Sarah.

Algy discovered to his amusement that he was currently more up to date than Sarah with Polly's investigation of Sonja. He was pleased to report that

Sonja Norris was likely to be arrested soon on suspicion of attempted murder... it would take only about a week to assemble all the evidence, thanks to Jack Heywood Hall.

136 - Joe

Joe had been thoroughly upset all day. He was aware that the village was in turmoil - everyone was searching for Bobby. Nobody knew Bobby as well as he did and yet he wasn't being allowed to help. Both his parents were out helping, while he was locked in, baby-sitting his brother. He had been instructed not to open or answer the door to anyone, but he really needed to know what was going on. Fear knotted his insides when he imagined that his friend might be in real danger, or even dead. He had hardly left the window and knew that Bobby's mother was at home - just the thickness of a wall away, and he hadn't seen the old lady leave; she had been there for hours. Bobby called her Sarah... and she didn't seem to mind although she hadn't known him all that long. Joe thought it was funny when Bobby told him she was his second-best friend.

It suddenly dawned on him that he had not been ordered to stay off the phone, so there was something he could do... he could ring next door. Without really planning what he wanted to say, he dialled. Mrs Goswell picked up the phone immediately, which caught Joe by surprise and immediately made him feel guilty; she would be disappointed that it wasn't anyone important, saying Bobby was found. "I, I... I, it's only me, Joe," he stuttered. "I'm sorry. I want to help and I wondered if anyone looked for Bobby in the cemetery?"

Unable even to think about Bobby and any

connection with the cemetery, and distressed that the caller was not giving her good news, Pamela handed the phone to Sarah. As well as she could, Sarah calmed Joe and said she would come round to talk to him. "It will have to be through the window," Joe said, "I'm not allowed to let anyone in." Sarah quite understood and walked outside, assuring Pamela that she would be only a few minutes. During the afternoon, she had tried to open her mind more but was haunted, quite literally, by Joe's great-grandfather and the child, who continually babbled about fish. The possibility that Joe might give her a new lead was too good to ignore. She still felt that Bobby was alive but knew that she was just as likely to be misled by wishful thinking as anyone else.

Joe had been unable to open the high dormer window (presumably a lower one would have been wide enough for her to climb in) and pointed in the direction of the front door. They ended up shouting at each other through the letterbox. Joe asked if they had searched the cemetery and admitted that he didn't really know anything but couldn't get the thought out of his head, so he needed to tell somebody because if Bobby had been kidnapped and was being murdered up there, Joe would never forgive himself for not telling anybody! Sarah assured him that he had done the right thing and said she would tell the police straight away. She gave him Terry White's mobile number so that he could pass on any other thoughts straight away. Sarah knew Terry would understand. It was better for Joe to feel that he was part of the search and doing all he could to find his friend.

When Sarah telephoned him, as soon as she returned to the Goswell house, Terry confirmed that she had done the right thing. He said that nobody had been out as far as the church on the hill – although the whole county was on the alert. He said that cemeteries were more in Sarah's line and he would take her up there himself. He was insisting that Bobby's father should take a rest and would be bringing him home within half an hour. Mrs Goswell would then not be alone and they could go up there straight away. As she put the phone down, Sarah again saw the child, and felt a surge of hope when she saw that he was laughing.

137 - Maud

When Maud arrived in Lesser Peasey and found that Sarah was not at home she was obviously disappointed. Doris could have told her where Sarah was likely to be, but chose not to. Instead, she invited Maud inside and put the kettle on. Over a cup of tea, she hoped to discover more about Sarah and her daughter... neither had been very forthcoming about themselves and Doris was eager for a good gossip. It was not until Maud left, two hours later, that Doris realised she was very little wiser about her two houseguests. On the other hand, she had babbled on about herself, pouring out her family history and all her recent worries and now felt surprisingly comforted by Maud's many wise comments. With little encouragement, Doris had even admitted how worried she was that her brother-in-law might not be all he had claimed to be. He had a secret past, she was sure, and she could only pray it was not criminal.

Knowing that anything she could learn about Clive might be of use, if Sarah's suspicions were justified, Maud assured Doris that nothing Clive did, or had done, would cause anyone to think less of her. She followed this by asking innocent questions about Clive's hobbies or changes in his recent activities. If his behaviour or pattern of his activities had not changed recently, Doris was probably worrying for no reason. By the time Maud left, she was happy that she knew everything Clive had done since his wife, Mary, died and he moved in to run the guesthouse with Doris, particularly what he was supposed to have been doing during the last couple of weeks. It was obvious that nothing much escaped Doris, so it was no wonder that his unannounced absence now, was worrying her so much

The cottage where Maud was staying with her friend was on the edge of the village – it would not take long to walk back if Sarah returned early enough to see her, so Maud gave her friend's telephone number to Doris. Within minutes of Maud's arrival at the cottage, her friend's two sons walked in, dusty and dishevelled; they had been out all day looking for Bobby and reported that there was no sign of him. At least he could still be alive somewhere and they would carry on searching until all hope faded.

138 - Algy

On the way to the cemetery, Algy discussed the macabre discoveries at the old farm site. Early ordnance survey maps were lost when an incendiary bomb destroyed the record office and library in 1942 so, until they could get copies from the archives in London, Joe's drawing was the only indication they had that buildings were ever on the parkland. If the drawing was anything like accurate, they were now exposing the cellar of the house. They had come across remnants of what appeared to be a small cubicle, netted with rusty wire, giving rise to the suspicion that some unfortunate victims did not die without first suffering imprisonment. There was no way of proving that this had happened and little point, half a century after the murders were committed, but he did intend to allow digging to continue lower than the cellar. The team would be working the site for at least another few days to make sure no more human remains were there.

Sarah was intrigued but more anxious to know if they had located Clive. Since talking to Joe, she had become convinced that Bobby, alive, or God forbid, dead, was not far away. It seemed impossible in view of the fact that the search for him had been going on unsuccessfully for almost twenty-four hours. There was still an hour of daylight left when they parked at the church and Sarah immediately walked to the front porch. There, she turned to face towards the village and identified the first landmark Joe had given her. His directions were very clear and they were soon standing in front of what he described as Bobby's favourite place. Joe said that if Bobby wanted to hide away, it would be where he would start.

Algy gazed around gloomily. Except by crouching behind a gravestone, there was actually nowhere to hide. He almost spoke his thoughts aloud, but could see that Sarah was deep in thought. She nodded, started to move away quickly and stopped again soon in front of another grave. On it, he read the names of the occupants and the last one was Andrew Clive Parker. Suddenly, pieces fell into place and he jotted the details down in his notebook... Father, mother and child – all the details of birth and death one would need when applying for a birth certificate! He had no doubt at all that Clive's birth certificate would tally with it.

It was exciting because it indicated that whoever he was before he adopted his new identity, he was local. By leaving the area, he had been able to take up another life, leaving any problems behind. Algy could guess that the man's problem now was most likely to be associated with the discovery of the bodies on the site of the old farm. The Gleaseys had an adopted son who was supposed to have died with them when it burned down. If Ben Gleasey had lived and become Clive Parker, then maybe the third body found after the fire was – as Sarah suspected – that of the missing Anthony Daniels. Perhaps the sightings of the hiker after the fire were a false trail laid by his murderer. Finding Parker had suddenly become top priority, especially as it now seemed that he would lead them to Bobby.

Algy drove Sarah back to her lodging and promised to let her know if anything happened but advised her to get some rest. The local police were still on the job and knew that she would expect to be told about developments, even in the small hours, so she should try to relax. She might need her strength even more tomorrow and there was nothing useful they could do tonight...

Sarah was somewhat taken aback when greeted by Doris with the news that Maud was staying nearby with a friend. She was extremely fond of Maud, but knew her to be very impulsive and unpredictable. With the best of intentions, Maud was quite likely to let slip a hint that Sarah was psychic which, at this time, would be most unfortunate. According to Doris, they had had a lovely long chat! If Sarah hoped to be able to sleep at all, she would have to talk to Maud straight away.

139 – Sarah

On Wednesday morning, no clue to Bobby's whereabouts having been found and still not knowing if he was being held somewhere against his will, Lesser Peasey was still bustling with activity. Sarah had slept badly even though her chat with Maud proved reassuring. They would be meeting soon because Maud wanted to go over the entire conversation she had had with Doris. Sarah was slightly disturbed, not to have had a phone call from Polly, but people say no news is good news, so Sarah went out to meet Maud. It was Maud's idea that they should have breakfast together somewhere, so Doris was not expecting Sarah to pop into the kitchen but Sarah was curious to know if Clive had turned up. Doris said he had not and it was obvious that she was worried. Sarah could only promise to ring her if she heard news of him and she was glad she had an excuse to go out.

Sarah was reluctant to discuss Clive with Doris because Algy had revealed that one thing of great significance been found at the bottom of Doris's garden. It was a burned fragment of artist canvas. The rest was among the ashes in the incinerator. It was undoubtedly part of Clarrie's painting; it was an unfinished sketch of a hiker with a yellow knapsack on his back and there was enough of it to see that it matched Joe's drawing. It was possible that Clive, who she was now sure was the man who attacked Clarinda, would try to injure her again, but Sarah's faith in the police did not waver. She was quite sure they would be on their guard while Clive was still on the loose.

On her way to the restaurant, Sarah called at the police station but there was still no news of Bobby and, as usual, whenever she tried to concentrate, the child appeared to her, still talking about fish. He was a dear little thing – she couldn't be angry – but he wasn't helping. Maud was waiting anyway, so indulging in quiet thought was impossible. During breakfast, Sarah listened closely to all Maud had discovered about Clive's past and present. It was amazing how much Maud had extracted from her hour or two with Doris. Much of it was known to Sarah already but hearing it all in context was interesting. Betty's suspicions of Clive especially, were worth passing on to Algy and the team. His absence from the Parker family albums was significant, and supported the theory that Clive had abandoned his own identity and assumed another.

Sarah was so lost in thought that she almost missed hearing what Clive did on Monday, the day Bobby disappeared. Maud patiently repeated it for her... "He collected supplies for the house in the morning and tackled the business accounts in the afternoon – then he went out to check on a friend's house and feed his fish."

"Fish – you did say fish didn't you?" Sarah was stunned. How could she have been so dismissive of the child? Maud was puzzled by Sarah's reaction, but said again, "His drinking buddy is away for a month. The entire family is on holiday. Clive goes round there a couple of times a week to feed the fish and make sure the tank is clean and the heating working – they are tropical."

"Where is the house," Sarah asked breathlessly, and to her relief it was yet one more detail Maud had elicited. She insisted on leaving immediately and dragged Maud to the police station, which was only a short distance along the street.

As soon as Algy Green was informed that Sarah was at the station, with information worth following up, he left his excavation, where a special team from Greater Peasey was taking control, and met Sarah outside a bungalow on the outskirts of the village. There was no sign of life inside and the two constables who were with her said that the garden, and all the others on the road had been searched and they had spoken to the residents, but neighbours informed them that the occupants of this one were on holiday. Nobody knew the name of the man with the key, but he was unlikely to come again until the weekend. An inquisitive teenager was passing at an extremely slow crawling pace and heard the exchange. He hesitated, still walking away, but then turned back and said, "I don't know his name, but he lives next to the Post Office."

This information made a forced entry permissible unless he had left the key with Doris Lynch, so Algy keyed the number on his mobile and handed it to Sarah, saying that Mrs Lynch might be alarmed if asked by the police. Sarah understood and told Doris that there might be a problem inside the house of Clive's friend. Could someone call to collect the key please? Doris was sorry, but said Clive had it on his key ring. She sounded cross when she added that she had no idea where he was. She thought he had slept there last night but had gone out again. She didn't see or hear him and he had not left a note, so she was now angry as well as worried!

When they decided which way in would do the least damage – through a small conservatory at the back – one of the constables broke a window and climbed in.

By removing a large pane of glass from the French window, entering the living room was easy. Sarah waited outside and heard Algy calling for silence, inside. She hardly dared breathe; she was so pent-up with dread... Bobby was in there, of that she was sure, but in what state would they find him? Sarah fervently hoped that Clive was not there too and suddenly knew that he wasn't... he had gone to find Clarinda.

140 – Clive

Clive had spent the day shopping, many miles away, equipping himself with a weapon he could conceal in the sheath on his belt, and he arrived at the hospital in time to mingle with the last of the evening visitors. He had no trouble locating the intensive care unit, but it was impossible to move about as freely as in the other wings of the hospital. He risked going into an empty office but could find no information in any of the three filing cabinets about the patients under treatment there. Once the corridors emptied of visitors, it would have been impossible without his white coat. It had a name label on it which he concealed by clutching against it a folder he had picked up.

As time wore on Clive began to fret; he should have spent yesterday exploring the hospital, but it had seemed strategic to join the search party, and actually quite amusing. After dealing with the woman, he would still have to dispose of the boy's body – although there was no need to do that until tomorrow night, or even the end of the week when things might be quieter. Eventually, well into the small hours of the morning, he knew that wherever the woman was, she was probably no longer in a coma. She must be getting better but it was unlikely that she had pointed a finger at him yet, otherwise he would have had the police on his doorstep by now.

This thought quelled his panic. Assuming that she remembered her intention to blackmail him, she would not have admitted it. She would be more likely to wait until she was completely well and out of hospital... but he had no intention of waiting for her to renew her threats. He would still like to know who had informed her about him and the Gleaseys, but he dared not risk any noise when he ended her life. He would just live on happily, in ignorance! Of course, even if he could get into her room, approaching her to slip his knife between her ribs would be more difficult than if she had been in a coma but he had a dampened chunk of thick wadding in his pocket; with that clamped over her nose and mouth, she would not be able to make a sound.

First, he had to find the guarded room – he was sure it would have a police officer on the door. Clive hoped the man would be asleep; he didn't relish the thought of killing an innocent bystander, but he had come too far to back down now. It was several hours later that he found what he sought. At the point of giving up, halfway down the end corridor in the last wing he was checking, he saw a solitary figure, sitting upright, engrossed in a magazine. Clive dodged back quickly and assessed his situation. He might get away with walking casually towards the seated figure and going into the cloakroom, which was immediately opposite. From there he could take the guard by surprise. He might risk exchanging a word with the man, who must be a police officer, even though he was in plain clothes. Undecided, he risked peeping out occasionally but minutes were passing and there was no hint of tiredness in the guard's posture.

Desperation was beginning to grip Clive. He had come too far and had too much to lose now to give up... and then, just as he was about to risk walking out, showing himself, he heard the chair scrape gently and the flapping sound of the journal being thrown onto the chair. He looked out just in time to see the guard disappearing into the cloakroom.

He would never get another chance like this and Clive grasped it. He ran down the corridor and, within seconds, was inside the room. It was dimly lit but he could see his quarry clearly enough; holding his breath, grasping the cloth in one hand and his knife in the other, Clive edged nearer to the bed. Outside the room, the guard emerged from the cloakroom, checked the door and returned to his seat... happy that all was well.

141 – Pamela

Casting her mind back to Monday, Pamela felt angry with herself. Why had she not started worrying earlier about where Bobby was? She knew the answer of course – it was because as soon as she could, after preparing the evening meal, she rushed to the computer, eager to go on the internet before Jake wanted the machine. She keyed in the address, antiquesreview.com and was pleased to see that the editor had answered her question...

Dear Pamela,

Please, hold the bowl up to a strong light. Does the porcelain look slightly greenish with the light behind it? If it does, you may have a very rare pattern on what sounds like an early Worcester saucer. The presence of the fisherman adds a great deal of rarity to the cannonball pattern. I will put my full report up on the website for you once I have had your reply, but I think it safe to tell you that there is a possibility your piece is worth at least £250, possibly a lot more. Whatever you do with the saucer, please make sure that you send photos of it to the Dyson Perrins Museum. They might make you an offer but, at the very least, they will be able to authenticate it for you.

All the best,

The Editor

The thought that the dish might have monetary value thrilled Pamela – she anticipated Bobby's pleasure.

He had brought it home to give to her because it was pretty and was a little embarrassed when she made a place for it in the display cabinet. When he heard that it had more than sentimental value, he would be proud of his find. She was imagining how delighted he would be and looking forward to telling him, when she noticed how late it was. She then looked at the little dish with something akin to loathing... Pamela knew it was silly, but if she had not been so absorbed, she would have kept a much closer eye on the time.

Never mind, now that Bobby was back, safe in his bed upstairs, Pamela could stop castigating herself. Jake was also in bed, sound asleep. After over thirty-six hours on his feet, searching even when others stopped, he was exhausted. When the phone call had come, saying Bobby was on his way to hospital in an ambulance, thankfulness and fear vied for first place in her stomach. Jake had just arrived home so they were able to go together to be with him.

By the time the ambulance reached the emergency ward, Bobby was beginning to come round from what appeared to be a heavily drugged sleep. He hardly spoke for a couple of hours and until he was able to focus, and converse sensibly, the doctor would not allow him to be questioned. Finally, as evening approached, Bobby was allowed visitors, and asked to see Sarah Grey. She was staying at the hospital with her friend Polly and looked ill herself, but she was eager to ensure that Bobby was recovering.

Their conversation was strange and Pamela suspected that Bobby was rambling... at one point he said that when he realised he was falling asleep he sent Andy to tell her; he followed this by saying he was looking after Andy and asking Sarah if that was allowed. Sarah, aware that Bobby didn't want his parents to know that he saw ghosts, agreed with Pamela that he would be much more himself after a good night's sleep. He would be returning home in the morning, so the doctor must be happy with his condition.

Sarah hurried away before Pamela had thought to ask after her daughter... it must be about three weeks since she was beaten, nearly to death. Pamela thanked God for Bobby's safe return. It must be terrible for Sarah, her daughter being in a coma and not knowing how long it would be before she woke up... if ever.

Morning eventually came, after a very disturbed night. Had she not been frightened to leave Bobby's bedside during the night, Pamela would have ventured out to see what the commotion was but, even now, half the local police force seemed to be wandering about and she overheard two nurses talking about murder. She just hoped it would not distract them from finding Clive. They needed to find him soon, before Jake did! Until Joe's uncle was locked up, they would not let Bobby out of their sight.

142 – Grace

Amy Weston's sister Grace and Gordon, their brother, together with their parents, were meeting the administrator in his office. Algy Green was also there in his official capacity intent on making sure they understood that Amy must not be left alone. They had already been informed that Sonja Norris was suspected of murdering the ward sister and being responsible for trying to kill Amy at least once.

He stressed that they should not discuss this with anyone else, as Miss Norris's current whereabouts were unknown. She was unlikely to know that they were building a case against her and might show up at the hospital at any time.

Gordon asked if Amy could have a guard on her door, just like Clarrie Hunter did, but Algy said that his presence would alert Sonja Norris to the fact that the police were taking an interest in the case again. The administrator said that his staff were already looking out for Miss Norris and would inform him if she attempted to visit Amy again. A constable in plain clothes would be on the premises twenty-four hours a day from now on, and they would all have his number to call, in emergency.

Grace spoke to Algy after the meeting. "Surely," she asked, "the ban on talking about Sonja doesn't apply to Polly Bailey and her friend Jack? If they hadn't helped, I think Sonja might have succeeded in murdering my poor sister."

Algy assured her that it was safe to talk to them and also to Sarah and Clarrie – but nobody else, not even the hospital staff. He hadn't missed the inference that the police had as good as given up investigating Amy's accident, and he really couldn't blame the family for feeling let down. Thus reassured, Grace rejoined her family in the visitors' lounge, where they set to work on a roster to make sure Amy was never alone. Being unmarried, she volunteered for night duty and went home to sleep for a few hours. All her early suspicions of Sonja had been well-founded and until the wretched woman was arrested, she would not rest easy anyway, so staying by Amy's bedside was no hardship.

She hadn't seen Polly or Clarrie for a couple of days and now wished that she had asked DI Green how they were. There had been some kind of disturbance in the small hours but she didn't think it was likely to have had anything to do with them. If she returned to the hospital a little earlier than planned, she could go and thank Polly for all she had done. It was amazing that Amy had started to recover on the night Polly and Clarrie sat with her... although, of course, that could only be coincidence.

143 - Sonja

Her parents could not understand why Sonja suddenly decided to leave. They had been surprised when she returned specifically to help Amy Weston's family by sitting for hours at the girl's bedside, because they hadn't realised Sonja was so fond of her old school friend. Now, although she was still not better, Sonja had left. After several days in bed, worrying her mother that she might have 'picked something up' in the hospital, Sonja had come downstairs with her suitcase packed and driven off without breakfast or even sharing a coffee. Mrs Norris was hurt and confused.

After two police officers came, later in the day, asking to see Sonja, Mrs Norris was frantic with worry. They had been pleasant enough, especially the woman, but would not say why they wanted to speak to her daughter. All she could do was give them her Spanish address and phone number, adding that Sonja must be on her way there.

It was all very worrying.

144 – Joe

Bobby was feeling well enough to be out of bed and although he was to be kept home from school for the rest of the week, he was allowed to have Joe round for a few hours. By now, it was common knowledge that Joe's uncle Clive was the one who tried to kill the artist – local gossips accepted this as fact; they needed no jury trial to prove it! Fortunately, it was also 'known' locally that Clive was not really a member of the Parker family, but Joe's parents, Stella and Seth, felt it wise to keep him also away from school until things quietened down.

Their game machines were idle. The boys were trying to come to terms with what had happened and more anxious to talk everything through. Joe was mystified and asked where Bobby had been on the day Joe himself was home sick and why he was so sure that Clive meant to harm him. Bobby tried to hedge around the last question but admitted that one thing that made him suspicious was that Clive knew exactly which way the mugger had gone. "There were heaps of openings in the trees, where someone could have run away," he said, "but surely you remember when we were scouting, he was being mean to me and he asked how I could be sure the man ran *that* way – and he pointed down the right path. It was a secret – I didn't even tell you, did I?"

"I remember," said Joe, "but really, that's a bit thin –

there must have been something else!"

Bobby suddenly felt weary. Joe had been his true friend forever – it felt horribly sneaky that he should be keeping secrets from him. Before he met Sarah, Bobby had worried about being thought raving mad and locked up, but now he was confident that there was nothing wrong with his brain and being psychic was natural to some people. He was still cautious enough to swear Joe to secrecy. "If I tell you something about me that you mustn't, ever, tell anyone, not even your mother and father, could you promise, cross your heart and hope to die?"

Obviously mystified, Joe immediately promised. Whatever Bobby's secret was, he was confident that it would not be something really wicked that he would be burdened with for the rest of his life. His jaw dropped when Bobby began by describing how his own grandfather continued to sit with him at night, even though he died when Bobby was still at infant school. Bobby remembered asking his father why granddad didn't speak to him anymore. "He laughed at me... You should have seen his face! He said granddad couldn't visit us because he was in heaven, so I tried to tell him he was wrong – he was still in the house. He kept giving me weird looks, so I never mentioned granddad again. I felt as if I was being bad, not believing that he was in heaven. Later, I thought I was probably crazy."

"So when did you decide you weren't?" Joe asked. Bobby quite rightly decided not to tell Joe about Sarah and, instead, said he had met a grown-up who was psychic, so now he knew it was okay to see dead people. By the time his story reached the point where Andy appeared in the cemetery, Joe was completely hooked. He was proud to be trusted with such a big thing but now wanted to know how Clive had grabbed him and what happened at the house.

"I didn't see Clive come out of the gate," Bobby explained, "because I'd turned round to watch Andy, who kept trying to drag me back. I didn't want to stop because I wanted to see Sa... err... somebody in the village. He caught me and pulled me straight into the house. The front door was open and he never stopped talking – telling me how he had seen me coming down the hill and wanted to show me something. He sounded very friendly, telling me about this boy's pet fish and how he was looking after them."

It was difficult for Joe to understand why Bobby had not run away, but he could see why it might have appeared to be rude, when Clive was being so pleasant. Bobby went on to explain how Clive said he was in a hurry to get away – he was late for a meeting – and would be glad of Bobby's help. He handed Bobby a stick with a razor blade soldered to the end and showed him how to scrape the glass on the inside of the tank to remove the dirt. "It settles on the bottom and those little black sucker-fish will eat up all the mess," Clive said, and while you are doing that, I'll fetch their live worms; you'll enjoy watching the way the fish gobble them up."

When Clive returned, he also brought with him glasses of orange juice, which they both drank while they watched the feeding-frenzy in the tank. Bobby said that was all he could remember except for being carried into darkness and hearing a door slam shut. He didn't tell Joe that his last thought was the hope that Andy would tell Sarah.

Satisfied at last that he had the full story, Joe turned his mind to the amazing fact that his best friend had, for years, been able to see ghosts without mentioning it. He was surprised and a little disappointed that he had not been trusted with the secret before, but could understand really that when he was little he might have blabbed to other people about it. Telling him at last was really a sign that they were growing up. He could be trusted now and would help Bobby in any way he could.

145 - Betty

Albert was still stunned. Nothing Betty said made him feel any less a fool for being conned by Clive into thinking they were cousins. She eventually gave up trying and went round to see Doris, who was devastated. She had more reason than Albert to feel bad because her sister Mary had married Clive and their three children would have to live the rest of their lives with the stigma of his deeds, whatever excuse he had. Betty refused to let Doris feel guilty about trusting Clive. "We all believed he was one of the family," she said, "and it was only when I saw the headstone in the cemetery that I started wondering. The child with the same birthday as Clive, was given the same name... both must have been my Albert's cousins yet he had only ever heard about one, until you moved in next door and told us about your sister marrying a Parker from Lesser Peasey."

"I remember Mary saying how astonished Clive was to learn that he had a cousin Albert," Doris suddenly started to laugh hysterically. "My God, he must have been in a state of shock! He didn't come to visit us until I told Mary that Albert knew nothing of his father's family and was looking forward to meeting his cousin." Doris's laughter changed to sobs and Betty just held her hand tightly, until at last Doris pulled away and said, "Right - that's enough misery, let's have a glass of sherry, I'm awash with tea. I now have to think about my real family. Mary's kids are going to need a lot of support." Betty was sure she was speaking for the whole village when she said that nobody would hold their father's deeds against them and she and Albert would help in any way they could.

Feeling a little less dispirited than she had been all day, Doris prepared for bed. Someone called Polly had telephoned during the morning, asking that Sarah's room should be kept available as she would be back at the weekend so, being on her own with no guests, Doris decided not to set her alarm clock... she would have a lie in. There was still a little sherry in the bottle when Betty left and Doris changed her mind about putting it back on the shelf. Instead, she poured it into a glass of hot milk and took it to enjoy in bed.

146 – DCS Holmes

The police in Spain had been keen to cooperate and confirmed that Senorita Norris was not at the address supplied and not expected. They volunteered to check again, every few days, until he told them the information was not needed. They were more helpful than he had expected or dared hope and he promised to keep them informed.

Thanks to Jack, they could build a solid case against Sonja. His witness picked her picture – with the black wig photo-shopped onto it – out of a batch of ten different girls wearing the same wig. A maid at the hotel, where she stayed overnight, stated that in the absence of a 'Do not disturb' notice, she had entered her room, thinking it was unoccupied. Through the open bathroom door, she saw the guest putting on her black wig and retreated quickly. She only talked about the incident because the woman had beautiful blonde hair and it seemed a shame to cover it up.

There was evidence that Sonja had lied about her last visit to the Mall being at Christmas. The fish then in the tank were not tropical. A waitress at the restaurant, when shown the photographs, had also picked out Sonja as being the dark haired woman who was there with the one who fell. They had been sitting near the fish tank and the waitress thought the fair one was drunk when they left, although she didn't see her close up because they left money on the table. It sounded as if Amy was drugged – probably with sleeping pills, which would account for her helplessness when she was pushed over the wall of the car park.

The connection between Sonja Norris and the ward sister who died had been verified, so the motive for killing her, if she had, was obvious. More easy to prove was the attempt to harm Amy by poisoning. Sarah was a reliable witness to that and had had the sense to preserve the wet sheet immediately, as evidence. They certainly had enough to arrest Sonja Norris on suspicion of attempted murder – if they could find her.

Of more urgent importance was the multiple murder discovery in Peasey, where digging had now ceased. The local force took the case over, but he still had to file a report making clear, among other things, why he had authorised the excavation in the first place! Explanations, whichever way expressed, sounded lame owing to the fact that he could not reveal that Sarah and Clarrie were psychic. The fact that the original painting showed the valley as it used to be, and was stolen, did certainly arouse his suspicions. If he took that line, he could elaborate on it with confidence, because the digging had been justified by the discovery of eleven, hopefully identifiable bodies.

The man known as Clive Parker – who was now thought to be Ben Gleasey, had also attempted to murder Clarrie; remnants of burnt canvas near his incinerator were from the stolen painting and proved that it had been in Parker's possession. Clive Parker had also kidnapped Bobby Goswell. According to the Doctor, left undiscovered, the boy would have certainly have died.

Without the drug, it would have been even more horrible: locked alone and starving in the darkness of an empty house.

There was a massive amount of paperwork to read through and more to write, but before Alec felt able to tackle it, he had an interview lined up with PC Penny, who had been on night duty when Parker, armed with a knife, entered the ward he was guarding. It was going to be an interesting meeting to say the least and as he glanced at his watch, his buzzer sounded – Constable Penny had arrived.

147 – Clive

Clive's thoughts drifted between past and present; memories long forgotten came to him clearly.

He could only have been two years old when his foster mother placed him in the arms of Glenda Gleasey, yet he could see her tear-stained face and feel his own fear. Then he saw her smiling …

Images of Art Gleasey dragging his unfortunate victims to their newly dug graves dissolved into the painting of the valley, which he had burned. It suddenly became clear to him, why Bobby started to distrust him… but he still failed to understand how the boy knew the direction he'd taken when escaping.

For that matter, Clive still didn't know how the woman knew enough about him and the farm to illustrate the exact moment the hiker arrived… although he was less confident about her reason for doing so.

He was aware that Bobby had not died and was glad now.

He had attached too much importance to whatever the boy could have said against him. He would be held to account for his own stupid actions. As he had suspected, Sarah Grey's daughter had come out of her coma too, long before the night he went to find her: no longer a sleeping victim, but it hardly seemed to matter to Clive now.

Nothing mattered.

He was tired of worrying and scheming. Keeping up

appearances was exhausting and he was glad his ordeal had ended.

What would happen to him now, he wondered, as he eventually let himself drift to sleep.

148 - Duffy

For two days, Duffy had roamed the hospital corridors trying to piece together the events that had caused such a commotion in the early hours of Thursday morning. He had followed the ambulance that took Bobby into Emergency on Wednesday and stayed to make sure he would be okay. Later, after eating in Oxford, he returned to the hospital hoping to talk to Sarah and be able to add to the piece he was writing about the kidnapping. He had promised copy to his own paper and to Boris Thwaites for the local paper and it needed personal input from someone. He had noticed how close to the Goswell family Sarah had become, so was keen to interview her.

It proved to be a mission impossible because all his enquiries were rebuffed. Sarah and her daughter might have been on another planet - nobody would give information. He recognised several police officers in plain clothes and sensed that they must be expecting trouble of some kind. He didn't think there was any connection to Clarrie Hunter, unless they believed that Clive Parker was the one who attacked her. He knew that Sarah had asked them to check Parker's background, so he decided to stick around in case something interesting happened.

It had been well worthwhile. At around eight-o-clock, the staff rooms and corridors were buzzing with the news that Amy Weston, the young woman who had been in a coma for months, had woken up at last and was even speaking quite coherently about the fall that nearly killed her. As if this were not exciting enough, there was a commotion near the main entrance when a woman on her way out was arrested after a chase through the grounds... somebody called Sonja Norris. Reading between the lines and from bits of gossip he'd picked up, it sounded as if the woman in custody had intended to visit Amy Weston, but changed her mind when she heard of her recovery from a chatty nurse.

The police must obviously have suspected her and been on the lookout. The intriguing fact that made Duffy stay on in the hospital was that the police officers he recognised were not part of the chase and were still hanging about. Duffy knew that a few of them recognised him too and was careful to ignore them completely. After judging where their centre of interest probably lay, Duffy kept out of their sight as much as possible. After midnight, he lay stretched across several seats in one of the visitor lounges, and, although he had not intended to do so, he fell asleep.

The voices in the corridor, which woke him a few hours later, were not loud and he almost went back to sleep, but his instinct told him it was not normal conversation and groups of people rarely gathered near convalescing patients in the small hours of the night. Two were uniformed policemen and the other two seemed to be in charge. He followed them and saw them approach the constable who had earlier been sitting outside one of the wards. To his astonishment, he realised that the men in plain clothes were armed and, as he watched, the guard leaned sideways to unlock the ward door at which both guns were aimed.

One of the constables caught sight of him and immediately ordered him to stand round the corner. From what he heard and hasty peeps, Duffy gathered that either someone was arrested or someone was dead – or both. Teams of strangely garbed officials went in and out until lunchtime on Thursday and finally Duffy saw a draped body removed on a trolley.

In the distance he saw Sarah looking worried and as white as a sheet, but there was no way he could reach her. In spite of all the frustration, he was able to put together an article that pleased both newspaper editors, and he intended to stay on until he had a good follow-up story. Together with the snaps he had already managed to take, he was sure it would be time well spent. He had seen Bobby leave with his mother, who promised that he would be well enough to be interviewed at the weekend, so as far as Duffy was concerned it had been a great and profitable few days.

149 – Polly

After the disturbing and dreadful events over the last few days, Sarah had gone back alone to Lesser Peasey, to pack up her own and Clarinda's personal things. Alec promised to collect her there on Sunday evening. After the best part of two days she would have been able to talk to the people who had become her friends during the past few weeks, and one night was as much as she felt able to face in that house. It now held too many bad memories.

Polly and Jack were able to visit Amy and although a little embarrassed by the amount of praise heaped upon them for the way they had proved Sonja's guilt, they were thrilled that Amy could talk to them. She said that in the restaurant, she became dizzy and, watching the fish in the tank nearby, she felt as if she was inside it with them – her head was swimming. She accepted Sonja's help thinking they were going for medical help but must have passed out completely after reaching the car park – she remembered odd snatches of Sonja's conversation when they were in the lift. "She was explaining why she had to stop me doing something... I had no idea what, but finally understood that she was threatening me and kept thinking she wouldn't dare hurt me. I felt as if I was shouting it, but probably wasn't – then I blacked out".

As they walked away afterwards, Jack commented on the way Amy talked about Clarrie... "You would think they know each other well and had been friends for years."

Polly could only remind him that, "**There are more things in heaven and earth**, *Horatio, than are dreamt of in your philosophy.* There – you never thought I'd be quoting Shakespeare to you, did you!"

Linking arms, laughing companionably, they went off to enjoy supper. It would be their last in Oxford for a while, because Polly was returning home on Sunday morning to prepare for Sarah's arrival. There would probably be little to do as her niece had been looking after the place in their absence, so Polly felt confident about inviting Jack to visit them during the coming week. It would be some time before things were back to normal and the presence of trusted, close friends was going to be a tremendous help.

150 – Sarah

While waiting for Alec to collect her on Sunday evening, Sarah reflected on what she had achieved since arriving and hoped she had not forgotten anything. Yesterday, after visiting the Day Centre and the Rest Home, to thank the many local people who had supported her and the police after the attack on Clarinda, she had entertained a few local people for lunch. She was overjoyed to be able to tell them all that Clarinda was doing well and expected to make a full recovery.

In the afternoon, she spent an hour with Bobby. He was anxious to tell her that he had let Joe into his secret and hastened to add, "I didn't say anything about you, Sarah, or your daughter, I promise." Once assured that he had done the right thing, Sarah suggested that he could, and should, tell his parents about her, and his own psychic gift. To her surprise, he said that he wanted to tell them straight away, while Sarah was with him. They were both at home and it was a good time to talk.

Bobby was as astonished as Sarah when his father said he was not surprised and always suspected that he was clairvoyant, because there had been at least two in his family.

It was a great relief to be able to leave the village, knowing that Bobby had come to terms with his situation and could talk openly about it. He would also keep in touch with Sarah, who promised that he could come to visit her and bring Joe, to meet her daughter properly.

Doris was coming to terms with Clive's deceit and Sarah advised her to reflect on what had made him act as he did. He had an unfortunate childhood and for the best part of forty years was held in esteem by everyone who knew him. Something in him must have snapped when he thought he was going to lose everything – which showed, at least, that he had loved his family.

The Daniels went home, able to get on with their life after recovering, in a sense, their son, and Edna noted Sarah's telephone number as she looked forward to talking to her again. Duffy left the village as soon as the dig was over but was anxious to meet Del, so Sarah would see him again soon. It had been difficult to dissuade Del from flying back to see Clarinda as soon as he heard she had woken from her coma, but he realised that it was important for her to rest without excitement until she was well enough to leave hospital. He immediately started winding up his job commitments and when he returned it would be for good, not just a holiday. His daily phone calls cheered them all up and Sarah knew it would not be long before Del became her son-in-law.

Sarah phoned Maud who, now back at home, was anxious to be brought up to date on what had happened. It was a long call and would have been longer if Alec had not arrived. He busied himself carrying painting equipment and cases to the car, while Sarah desperately tried to say goodbye. Eventually, by promising to ring from home, Sarah ended the conversation. Doris waived away an attempt to pay for the call, declaring that she had met Maud – an amazing woman – and she hoped to see her again when she visited Lesser Peasey to stay with her friend.

Sarah sat back to enjoy the trip home, knowing that tomorrow, she and Polly would be driving back to the hospital to collect Clarinda. The past few weeks had been traumatic but, thank God, life should soon be back to normal.

151 – Ben

After a few weeks of being pampered and fussed over at home, and even having Del back to spoil her, Clarrie was eager to get back to work. Her mother knew it was pointless trying to dissuade her and, in fact, recognised that it was a good sign. There was no need to warn her about setting up to paint off beaten tracks...!

The wedding date was fixed. She and Del had decided on an August wedding – mainly because his parents would be glad to get away from roasting in Spain and while they were away, their villa would be a good place to start the honeymoon! Del was keen to show Clarrie the Far East – at least the Singapore, Borneo bit, so they would be away for two months. Owing to the fact that she was still supposed to be taking life easy, the wedding would be a quiet one but nobody said that they could not have an engagement party, and that is exactly what was happening tonight.

As she held Del's hand and gazed around at all her family and close friends, another figure caught her eye and held her whole attention.

He was looking straight at her as if hypnotised and she was aware that her mother was also watching him.

An eerie stillness crept over all who were there ...they sensed that something unearthly was happening and waited patiently. Comparing notes afterwards, Sarah and Clarrie both understood the spirit's bewilderment and re-lived with him his last moments on earth.

Clive Parker remembered approaching the hospital bed and drawing his knife but in the split second before he thrust it into what he thought was the sleeping figure, he heard the key turn in the ward door. He swept the heaped bedding to the floor, knew he had been tricked and had no way of escaping. It was over – his life was a wreck – even his children would hate him. Convinced that taking his own life would shorten their ordeal, Clive had turned his weapon on himself and plunged it into his own stomach.

Clive was barely alive when the door finally opened and all attempts to save his life failed. His sudden passing from the land of the living to the world of the dead left him dizzy and bemused. In the world of spirit, his days and minutes blurred; he was lost, not quite understanding where he was, or where he should go.

He stared pleadingly, not just into their eyes but into the minds of Clarrie and Sarah. They knew that Clive was confused and allowed him to see, through them, how he had been foiled in his attempt to commit murder. Slowly, full understanding came and he saw that although the room was full of people, they alone could see him. They knew everything and now finally, he too knew the truth. Clarrie Hunter had had no knowledge of him or his past. Shaking his head, as if apologising, he hovered in the background uncertainly, while mother and daughter stared silently at each other. How galling it must be for him to discover how simply he had been tricked by PC Penny!

The constable had moved his chair, ostensibly to guard the door of the room next to Clarrie's. From there, he was able to keep watch on both. He had been warned that a suspicious character was roaming the hospital corridors and also that Clive was likely to try reaching Clarrie, so was determined to trap him.

Penny, who had excellent peripheral vision, saw Clive peeping round the corner and timed his visit to the cloakroom perfectly. As soon as Clive entered the empty ward, Penny moved quickly to turn the key in the lock and immediately called for assistance. Quite rightly, he had been commended for his initiative.

The demeanour of their ghostly visitor was changing. At last, in increasing moments of clarity, he abandoned his claim to the identity of an innocent child and accepted his own birthright. He acknowledged with deep regret all his wrongdoing, and was clearly even more appalled by what he had tried to do. Sarah and Clarrie did not doubt that it was as Ben Gleasey that he gradually faded away.

Turning their attention back to their guests, Sarah merely commented on the fact that they had shared a vision, which was unusual, but all was well – there was nothing to worry anyone. Everyone happily accepted that when they were around Sarah anything could happen and, as always, they took things in their stride, doing their best to live normally.

Being able to relax with such good friends was the best tonic in the world, Sarah thought, as she joined in a toast to the future of Clarinda and Del.

The Ghostly Echoes Series

If you enjoyed reading "Haunting Echoes" and the rest of the "Ghostly Echoes" series then please look out for the final book Restless Echoes

Ghostly Echoes

Sarah sees and hears ghosts. For her it is a normal and mostly ignored part of her daily life. She doesn't like to talk about it. Only a few close friends know. Sarah hates publicity and won't hold séances. Her ability is private and personal ...but the police know and so do the spirits who seek her help (and some ghosts, especially children, are very hard to ignore). All Sarah wants to do is to live quietly with her daughter Clarrie. However, a quiet life is difficult to achieve when the recently dead keep intruding. Worse, her daughter might also be psychic and, without realising it, is walking into danger ...so a missing woman and child may soon be the least of all their worries! Originally published as Deadly Shades of Grey,

A Poisonous Echo

Joyce is angry that her boss won't leave his wife, so his wife will have to be removed... one way or another!

A poisoning is planned and Joyce sets out to leave a lasting impression... then Joyce goes missing... A malevolent ghost and psychic detectives form the core of this enjoyable stand-alone sequel to Mai Griffin's *Ghostly Echoes*. Originally published as *A Poisonous Shade of Grey*,

Dangerous Echoes

A young medium arrives in the village and is soon the object of much interest. So much so that she is welcomed into the household of an elderly relative of Dan's wife Elaine. Concerned, they need to enlist help to discover if the medium is as genuine as she seems and his Aunt Polly decides to investigate. Clarrie and Sarah are too involved in their own crises to realise the risks Polly is taking and Polly is so enjoying the thrill of immersing herself in old friendships and researching past romances that she is unaware of the dangerous path she may be treading...

Restless Echoes

A ghostly dog, a strange lady and the confused memories of a young girl are about to complicate Polly, Sarah and Clarrie's lives. Unravelling the different mysteries is going to need all of them working together and it is likely to put the family and their circle of friends at risk. Not only must they unravel two horrific crimes, they need to find a murderer before he strikes again.

Also by Mai Griffin 'Somebody Came'

The Background to 'Ghostly Echoes'

Sarah

As the wife of a successful artist, achieving normality for Sarah Grey was never going to be as simple as it is for most of us. But with the added impact of her extra sense, giving her the ability to see and hear the dead and the strongly telepathic living, 'normal' has always been a difficult concept.

After her husband died, her loneliness was almost overwhelming as she felt surrounded only by the dead, but in the background, there was always Polly, the Grey family housekeeper for many years, to keep her company.

Soldiering on alone, as so many other widows have done, eventually allows her to assume a calm façade and a gradual acceptance of death when it comes so close to home.

Selling the old house and moving to a small apartment seems a good idea until her daughter is also widowed but her instincts are to go and live with her to help out.

She has long suspected that Clarrie might have latent psychic powers and is concerned about what could happen if Clarrie tries to cope on her own. Once the grief has softened a little, she looks forward to having laughter back in the house...

Clarrie

As an artist's daughter it is, perhaps, not surprising that Clarrie grew up with a love for paint and canvas. Encouraged by her father to accompany him on his painting trips, she learned her trade from a master painter and plies it well. Now an up and coming artist in her own right, everything seems to have come together, until Tom is tragically involved in a crippling accident and she spends the final year of her seven-year marriage nursing her paralysed and dying husband.

After his death, devastated by her traumatic loss, Clarrie is grateful for her mother's suggestion so Sarah gives up her original plans to buy an apartment and, instead, moves into Clarrie's home.

Being able to immerse herself in her art proves therapeutic, but the immersion is so complete that Clarrie barely notices the changes in her perception of the world around her, often blurring the reality of the present with the realities of the past and that proves dangerous... Having two psychics in the house is a recipe for trouble, even if one is trying for the "quiet life" and the other is in denial...

The Ghostly Echoes Series by Mai Griffin

The horrific prologue to Ghostly Echoes, launches Mai Griffin's dramatic psychic mystery series. Reflecting the darkside of the mysteries that plague the day to day life of unwilling psychic Sarah Grey and her artist daughter Clarrie Hunter, the plots twist and spiral around the edge of the reader's vision. How do they face the dilemma of trying to live normally, when everything around them isn't.

Overcoming the temptation to live in denial of their unwanted psychic abilities, Clarrie and Sarah are gradually drawn in to help solve strange problems and to resolve issues surrounding unexpected deaths

No matter where she goes, danger keeps intruding into Clarrie's life and painting is not keeping it at bay...

Reviews for 'Ghostly Echoes' (then Deadly Shades of Grey)

Publisher's Note: We sent out several review copies prior to publication. These are a few of the comments on 'Deadly Shades of Grey' that we received from our first three reviewers:-

1 - I received the book at 5pm and started reading it that evening, I couldn't put it down and I certainly couldn't sleep, until I finished it at three in the morning!

2 - I usually read a book for five or ten minutes, last thing at night, before I go to sleep - I never have time to read in the day, but night after night, until I finished it, I found an hour had gone by, I was so absorbed.

3 - I thoroughly enjoyed this book, it kept me gripped til the end. I cannot wait until Book Two.

As publishers, we feel that this book never loses momentum, every page is a cliff-hanger and everyone who has read it has thoroughly enjoyed it. Available by order from all mainstream UK Book retailers.

"Deadly Shades of Grey" A gripping page-turner writes Barbara Power, (Spain). The creativity of some artists, it seems, just cannot be contained or constrained within the limits of one particular medium, and so it is with the internationally-acclaimed painter, Mai Griffin. In the first of her series which introduces the Grey family, she has turned her artistic talent to the written word and proves as adept with her pen as she is with a paint brush.

For widow Sarah Grey, who only wants to live a quiet life, being psychic is a cause of much anxiety and discomfort. However, she knows that to maintain her peace of mind and sanity she must force herself to respond to the messages that haunt her. Adding to Sarah's anxiety is the fact that her daughter, Clarrie, seems to have inherited the same psychic ability, a situation which could lead her into terrible danger

Deadly Shades of Grey is a well-crafted mystery/murder novel with a gripping and taut plot that has intriguing twists and turns. It is a good and thoroughly satisfying read. Although Book 1 is a stand-alone novel, I cannot wait to get hold of Book 2 to learn more about this interesting family and what happens to them.

About Mai Griffin

During her successful career as an artist (www.maigriffin.com), travelling the world and painting portraits of Royalty and other prominent figures, Mai has never stopped writing. The Echoes series may be built around purely fictional characters, but Sarah Grey and her late husband Stephen were inspired by Mai's parents. Mai now lives in Spain. Dividing her time between painting and writing is a challenge, but helps to still her own ghosts...

by Mai Griffin

Renaming an already published book series was a heart-wrenching decision – the contents of the books and the stories have not changed, however, so for your convenience the new and the old titles are below

Deadly Shades of Grey is now 'Ghostly Echoes'
A Poisonous Shade of Grey is now 'A Poisonous Echo'
Grey Masque of Death is now 'Dangerous Echoes'
Haunting Shades of Grey is now 'Haunting Echoes'
'Restless Echoes' is the last in the series

Somebody Came (Stand-alone)

Follow Mai on **www.maiwriting.com & maigriffin.com**